I0772150

The Miss Without a Mister

Katherine Grant

This is a work of fiction. Names, characters, places, and incidents either are the product of the author's imagination or are used fictitiously. Any resemblance to actual persons, living or dead, events, or locales is entirely coincidental.

Copyright © 2024 by Katie Flanagan

All rights reserved. No part of this book may be reproduced or used in any manner without written permission of the copyright owner except for the use of quotations in a book review. For more information, address: katherine@katherinegrantromance.com

Cover design by Julia Gerbach

ISBN 9798990252226 (ebook)

ISBN 9798990252233 (paperback)

www.katherinegrantromance.com

WHAT TO EXPECT FROM THE MISS WITHOUT A MISTER

Two hearts, one vow, and a world built to keep them apart. Can true love conquer all, or is this romance destined for heartbreak?

AT AGE ELEVEN, CAROLINE Preston and Eddie Chow vowed to marry.

At sixteen, they renewed their pact with a kiss under a starry sky.

Now, at last, Eddie is done with his apprenticeship. Caroline assumes they can finally begin planning their wedding. Even though she is a baron's daughter and he is a tradesman, she knows her open-minded father won't object - not when love is involved.

But when they are finally reunited, they discover that Lord Preston has very different plans in mind. Plans to keep Eddie away from Northfield Hall. **Plans to separate Caroline and Eddie forever.**

Threatened with never seeing each other again, **Caroline and Eddie are forced to break free from their families in hopes of finding a happily ever after.** As they come face-to-face with the challenges Lord Preston predicted, they must answer the ultimate question: **is their love strong enough to survive the real world?**

For content advisories, please visit www.katherinegra ntromance.com/contentadvisories.

CONTENTS

ALSO BY KATHERINE GRANT

The Countess Chronicles:

The Ideal Countess
New Year's Masquerade
The Duchess Wager
The Husband Plot

The Prestons:

The Baron Without Blame

The Viscount Without Virtue
The Governess Without Guilt
The Charmer Without a Cause
The Sailor Without a Sweetheart
The Countess Without Conviction
The Miss Without a Mister

Northfield Hall Novellas

(an unordered series for the mood reader)
The Hellion of Drury Lane
It's In Her Kiss
Three Nights With Her Husband
Letters to Her Love

Plus, a free short story, The Spinster, available exclusively at www.katherinegrantromance.com

Prologue

Summer 1816

Caroline Preston never felt more alive than on the summer night of a Northfield Hall festival. The air as warm as an embrace; the fields wafting a sweet, heady perfume; the sun clinging in tendrils to the horizon, refusing to submit to the dark's demands. All around Caroline, people celebrated: dancing around the great bonfire, jumping into the cold pond with shrieks, sitting under the lilac bushes for talks that lasted as long as the evening.

Caroline could burst for how happy she was—and for this whole festival to be celebrating *her* sixteenth birthday—and to be in a new linen summer dress with embroidery to make a princess jealous—and most of all, for Eddie Chow, who had returned from London for two whole weeks to celebrate with her.

Of course, his visit was not *entirely* about Caroline. It was one of his few holidays from his apprenticeship with a London glazier, and so he had spent most of it with his parents and two older brothers who lived in the family cottage at Northfield Hall.

Still, Eddie—her best friend since before she could remember—was there for her birthday.

Caroline really could burst with joy.

She had lost track of him as the sun sank lower in the sky, distracted by a toast in her honor, followed by a folk dance performed by some of the maids from the North, and then there had been honey cakes and sweet wine to drink.

Now Caroline spotted Eddie by the bonfire, on a boulder a little way from the logs. Gangly and tall—he had grown so much in London, yet boasted barely any flesh on his bones—he sat with his long legs stretched ahead of him, his dark hair and eyes looking black as ink in the firelight. Even with his lips drawn down, his expression slack, the mere sight of him made Caroline's heart drum in triple. On either side of him, fellow Northfield Hall laborers were engaged in animated conversations, but Eddie was still, silent, and staring into the fire.

Caroline could almost believe he was morose. Except this was her birthday, and they were in the same place again at last, and he had no reason to be sad.

Skipping over to him, she held out her hand. "Come with me."

He smiled immediately, which had been the whole point. When he asked, "Where?" Caroline invented an excuse:

"I have something to show you."

He took her hand long enough to stand. Long enough for her whole body to leap like a flame in reaction to his touch. Then he dropped it. They were too old to run around the estate hand in hand like eight-year-olds anymore, a bittersweet truth. Bitter because Caroline wanted the freedom to touch Eddie whenever and however she wanted; sweet because their age brought them closer and closer to the day when she could, as his wife, do just that.

She led him away from the bonfire and the pond and the friends laughing under trees. There was a path into the woods that he might not know about, as it had been years since he had spent more than a week or two at Northfield Hall at a time. And he most likely wouldn't know the circular grove, as it had been newly created when the laborers had cleared a few trees for timber.

And even Caroline didn't know what the night sky looked like from the ground there.

They moved in silence. Caroline found herself holding her breath, the way she had done as a child to avoid detection when she and Eddie tried to sneak away from their minders. She glanced over her shoulder as they entered the woods, but Eddie's expression was lost to the gray night.

Out of sight of the rest of the festival, Caroline reached back and grabbed his hand. This time, his fingers intertwined with hers, and neither of them let go.

There was much Caroline didn't know about Eddie these days. What it was to be an apprentice, beyond the platitudes Eddie recited when she asked; what food he ate in London; whether he went to

Covent Garden for the theater or the Five Dials for card games or even to a church for Sunday sermons.

She pushed the questions out of her mind. Knowing the small details didn't matter, especially when Eddie never offered them. Caroline knew Eddie at his core, and she knew his core hadn't changed. He would always be sweet, thoughtful, and steady.

"Is this what you wanted to show me?" Eddie asked when they reached the grove. "Trees?"

"Actually, I wanted to show you the *absence* of trees." Spreading out her arms, Caroline twirled with her head tossed back, excitement propelling her every movement. And there they were: stars, twinkling in the sky above the oval clearing. Tugging Eddie's hand, Caroline dropped to the ground and laid her body flat.

They had lain side by side like this dozens of times. In summers past, they had whiled away afternoons counting clouds in the sky; they had named the constellations at night with their siblings; they had shared a mattress at naptime and kept each other entertained with fairy tales when they were meant to be sleeping.

But then, they had been children. Now, Caroline's mouth went dry from noticing Eddie's muscular arm against hers. She could measure the distance between their hips in yearning inches. She could smell his warm skin and the soft scent of ginger beer on his breath.

She could hardly see the stars in the sky anymore.

A question leapt from her heart: "Have you fallen in love with anyone in London?"

Eddie turned onto his side. Suddenly, he loomed over her, his nose only a breath or two away from hers.

His lips were close enough, too, that even in the dark she could see them clearly.

"What kind of question is that?" he asked.

"An interrogatory one. Not rhetorical. I should like an answer, please. Have you fallen in love with anyone in London, and if so, with whom and is she prettier than me?"

"No, I have not fallen in love with anyone in London." Tentatively, Eddie reached out and removed a curl of hair from Caroline's forehead. She hadn't noticed it until he touched her; now even her hair felt alive with desire.

Eddie looked at her with soft, mysterious eyes.

"No, there is no one prettier than you."

Caroline found she could reply with nothing more than "Good."

"And you?" His voice was gentle, as opposed to her playful brusqueness. "Have you fallen in love with anyone while I've been in London?"

"No." He didn't have a curl of hair on his face, but she reached out anyway and cupped his cheek. "And there is none prettier than you, either."

Neither of them smiled at her joke. To tell the truth, Caroline had never felt so overwhelmed by her own body; her breath and heart were out of her control, and instead of rational thoughts, she seemed able to comprehend only the feel of Eddie's warm cheek beneath her fingertips.

"Well," she said, because she knew she had something clever to say somewhere in her mind. "Then our agreement still stands?"

"Agreement?" Eddie's thumb brushed down the sweep of her jaw.

She hoped he asked because he was in a daze, like she was, and not because he had forgotten.

"To marry." They had first made the pact at the age of eleven, after her sister Ellen's wedding, when they both supposed they would have to marry at some point and as they wouldn't like it to be to anyone, it might as well be to each other.

A year later, on the morning that Eddie was sent to his first apprenticeship in Reading, they had sealed the agreement with a kiss. A tentative kiss that hadn't felt like much of anything.

A kiss that, nevertheless, Caroline had never forgotten.

"To marry each other," Eddie said slowly. On her skin, his fingers stilled. "Yes."

There was probably more to say. Caroline didn't have the patience for it anymore. She had wanted only to hear that Eddie remained hers.

She plunged forward. A little too eagerly; their lips mashed together, and their front teeth clanged. She would have been embarrassed, except it was Eddie, and her body was on fire, and all they had to do was adjust their necks and their hold on each other and then the kiss was perfect. Eddie was perfect. The night was perfect.

Later, Caroline would wonder why they had not pushed further. She would wonder why they had not taken advantage of being alone on the ground to explore each other fully and to claim their love entirely. But that was when she was lonesome, when she was no longer anchored by Eddie's lips on her mouth and his ankles locking against hers. For now, she was sixteen, and love did not need to be proved, and she had Eddie all to herself.

They kissed until they might not be able to do anything for the rest of their lives *but* kiss. Then, somehow, they extricated themselves. Eddie, always the one to save them from the worst trouble, removed himself first, though he clung to her hand as if she alone could pull him from dangerous waters. They lay panting at the stars for a while longer. At last, they returned to the festival, hand in hand, and when no one said anything, Caroline decided their love was preordained.

It wasn't until much later that she realized Eddie's early return to London the very next morning had nothing to do with a letter from his master and everything to do with that perfect kiss.

And only much, much later did she understand that if anything was preordained, it was not her marriage to Eddie Chow.

Chapter One

Late Autumn 1820

A LADY DREAMED OF her first London Season from her earliest days. She practiced mincing her steps in delicate slippers; she drew sketches of fabulous gowns that would steal a gentleman's breath; she batted her eyelashes at the mirror and sometimes kissed her dear friends on the lips to prepare for the dizzying months that would define the rest of her life.

Even Caroline Preston, daughter of the eccentric baron who refused his family anything more luxurious than fine-spun linen, had dreamed of a London Season. Neither of her elder sisters had done one properly, so Caroline had never supposed she would, yet she collected the newspaper articles about so-and-so who danced with such-and-such. She studied descriptions of silk gowns and ostrich-feather hats so that she could judge good style against bad. She subscribed to a ladies' magazine that provided steps for the fashionable dances as well as instructions for handling a gentleman's flirtations—particularly if one wanted to encourage him.

Caroline had no ambition to ensnare some hapless heir from across a garden party with the perfect smile. She'd wanted only to be prepared, should she ever visit London, to hold her own among the rest of her family's society.

Yet despite her interest in London, she had still been surprised when Papa wrote that she should join him there for the final weeks of the year. Even more shocking, his letter had added, *Now that you are almost of your majority, I should like to take advantage of the Little Season to introduce you to more of society*—and most earth-shaking of all was his instruction to have a few new gowns made before she arrived.

Caroline had hardly known what to think, except that she wasn't going to second-guess her luck. In a single letter, Papa had delivered so many of her greatest dreams: to experience the Season, to order new dresses like a proper lady, and—best of all—to visit London.

The last dream was the most important to Caroline because it was in London that she could find Eddie Chow.

She had thought of him as she visited the seamstress. She'd pictured him as she packed her luggage. She'd remembered him as she said her goodbyes to everyone at Northfield Hall. Eddie had been in London for five years now; he hadn't visited since this past Christmas; yet soon, Caroline could see him again.

Because, after all, Caroline Preston's first London Season wasn't going to be at all like any other debutante's. Yes, she had already attended a ball or two in her rich new gowns, and yes, she'd even fluttered her fan a few times when a gentleman said something rather forward. But her father had not invited her to the Little Season to find her a husband. He had invited her to find her an organization she could join, whether it be The Ladies' Society to Protect Chimney Sweeps or The Ladies' Coalition Against Sugar, Tea, and Other Evil Imports.

Caroline did not need to ensnare a husband at a regatta, a breakfast, or even a ball. She had known since she was eleven that she would marry Eddie, and all she had been doing since then was waiting.

And now, at last, her wait would end. On this, her eighth day in London, Eddie was officially finished with his apprenticeship and coming to stay at the Preston townhouse. Caroline spent the afternoon with Aunt Charlotte at a meeting of the Society for the Widows of Sailors and Soldiers, which had been two hours of gossiping over tea and one hour of arguing over the hundred words they would include in their annual call for donations in the newspaper.

On the carriage ride back to Soho from Mayfair, Caroline couldn't help pressing her face to the glass window to see if Eddie happened to be walking past that very moment. Last time she had seen him—almost a year ago—he had grown a whole foot, so she reminded herself to watch for a taller boy than she expected. Then she reminded herself to look for a man, one whose shoulders were probably broader than before and whose walk was that of a confident twenty-one-year-old who had finished his apprenticeship.

She knew she would recognize Eddie even if he didn't look a thing like his old self. That was how it was with her and Eddie. From infancy, they had been drawn to each other. It didn't matter if they were one or twenty-one or one hundred and one: they would know each other.

"What are you looking for?" Aunt Charlotte asked. "You'll hardly see the latest fashions on display with weather like this."

Indeed, the day was wreathed with cold rain that made one long to be inside near a fire. "I'm not looking for anything," Caroline lied. "I'm taking it all in."

Aunt Charlotte clicked her tongue against her teeth, a sound of mild disapproval that immediately reminded Caroline of her mother. Even though she hadn't met Aunt Charlotte until Mama was on her deathbed, and even though Aunt Charlotte was different from Mama in a hundred ways, and even though Caroline had only been seven years old when Mama died of her wasting disease, sometimes Aunt Charlotte's presence felt like Mama resurrected.

Except Mama would never have admonished Caroline for curiosity, as Aunt Charlotte did when she said, "Sit back, child, or someone will get the wrong idea about you."

Caroline sat back enough to obey the order while still maintaining a view of the street. She was sure Eddie wouldn't walk through Mayfair, yet one could never know, and now that she was only a few hours from seeing him, she couldn't bear not to spot him that very second.

Aunt Charlotte, meanwhile, began cataloging their plans for the rest of the week. "We have breakfast tomorrow with Lady Gresham to discuss her school for the deaf, then we shall take a tour of the Tower with a nice party of young ladies. The following day, of course, is the Ladies' Society Against Slavery luncheon, which I know your father is eager for you to enjoy."

"I am eager to enjoy it, too," Caroline defended herself. "I am trying to enjoy all of these engagements, Aunt. Only I didn't expect that these organizations would be so busy with rules and tea. There is so much to be done that I don't see how we can waste forty-five minutes on motions congratulating each other on accomplishments since the last meeting."

"Structure is as important in directing a group of people as it is in keeping a gown erect on your body."

Which was all Aunt Charlotte ever had to say when Caroline burst with impatience in the various meetings they had attended.

Caroline very much wanted to take her place as an active participant in the *ton*'s rabbit warren of charitable organizations, but the more tea and cake she was offered, the less she could envision herself actually joining their ranks.

"I wish I could write articles to the papers instead, like Papa does."

"Your papa does much more than simply write articles to the papers."

Yet it was what had consumed his energy these past few weeks. As soon as Caroline had arrived at their Soho townhouse, Papa had presented her with a draft of an essay on what the experiment of

Northfield Hall could teach the rest of Britain about reform for agricultural laborers. It was long and technical, and in Caroline's opinion harped too much on the noble nature of the political class. She was proud that Papa had accepted her suggestions to remove a few sentences. He had even added in one of her own lines:

Until every Briton can afford his daily bread, none of us are worth ours.

Aunt Charlotte added, "Besides, a lady expresses her views as part of a group instead of on her own, if she must express them publicly at all."

Caroline, at least, did not express her views on this sentiment to her conservative aunt. She changed the subject. "I should like to invite the Chow family on our tour of the Tower tomorrow."

To her credit, Aunt Charlotte limited her reaction to a few fast blinks. "It is not done to take in the sights with family retainers."

A polite word for servants. Caroline knew it was true—after all, Mrs. Chow was housekeeper at Northfield Hall, and Mr. Chow oversaw the carpentry workshop—yet the idea that the Chow family was anything less than dearest friends to the Prestons made her want to laugh. "All the same, I should like to invite them."

"We shall ask your father to settle the matter." This, too, Aunt Charlotte had already said more than once during Caroline's first week in London.

Caroline was quite sure Papa would agree with *her* on this question. As a peace offering, she said, "Are you sure you won't stay for supper to meet them? You would quite like the Chows. Oliver is very funny, and Mrs. Chow could advise us on how to do more practically for the poor widows at this time of year." She stopped herself from mentioning Eddie. She preferred to keep him to herself, too.

"No, thank you." Then, as the carriage swayed on a rather dramatic turn, Aunt Charlotte added, "I have met them previously, a very long time ago."

At first, Caroline thought Aunt Charlotte referred to her visit to Northfield Hall to say farewell to Mama. Then, she realized her aunt meant even longer ago than that: she had been present when Mr. and Mrs. Chow first applied for help from Papa at Northfield Hall, which was also when Mama's father had disowned her for choosing to marry Papa after he welcomed the Chows.

"Then you know they are very dear to us." Again, Caroline couldn't bring herself to say anything about Eddie. She was quite sure that Aunt Charlotte knew about him, since all of Northfield Hall knew Caroline and Eddie were thick as thieves.

In fact, Caroline hadn't been able to mention Eddie to Papa of late, either. She knew *he* knew that she planned to marry Eddie, and so in some ways, it seemed unnecessary to say it aloud.

But sometimes, Caroline felt *unable* to say it aloud. Recently, whenever Eddie came up as a subject, Papa had a way of twisting his lips into something that was not a smile and redirecting the conversation. It was easier not to say anything at all so that she did not need to wonder at Papa's reaction.

The carriage pulled to a stop in front of the Soho townhouse. Aunt Charlotte reached forward to pat Caroline's hand. "Enjoy your supper, dear. We shall see what tomorrow brings."

Stepping down to the pavement, Caroline had to shake her shoulders to keep the parting from sounding too ominous.

EDDIE CHOW WAS SUPPOSED to be in Soho already.

He had promised his parents he would be there when they arrived from Northfield Hall that afternoon. Yet he had also promised Master Trowbridge that he would finish cleaning the workshop before he left, a task which, at the last minute, Master Trowbridge decided should include dismantling, cleaning, and re-assembling the entire toolkit.

He was supposed to be finished as an apprentice. He was supposed to be a man in his own right. He was supposed to be free to do what he wanted to do.

Instead, he was three hours late.

When at last Master Trowbridge declared Eddie finished, he held out a meaty palm to shake Eddie's. "Good luck, then, lad."

Eddie accepted the well wishes in silence. Master Trowbridge had been neither stingy nor cruel; he had treated Eddie as fairly as an apprentice could expect. His wife came to stand beside him in the threshold, an apron pinned over her housedress as always and flour coating her hands. "We won't forget you, and don't you forget us."

Kind words. She had never been unkind to Eddie. But he knew this was not an expression of their deep familial fondness for him, even though he had lived in their house and worked for their business and spent nearly every hour with them for five years.

Eddie was about to go back to Northfield Hall, where the working man earned the same money as the noble family, and where they fancied he had the ear of Lord Preston, Baron Ashforth. Now, at last, he might be of use to them.

"I won't," he replied.

Who could forget the soupy porridge served for supper every night except Sundays? Who could forget being tasked with scouring the wood floor while the older apprentices did the proper glazing work? Who could forget sleeping on a pallet by the fire with Mrs. Trowbridge's ne'er-do-well brother?

Like it or not, Eddie wasn't going to forget his time at the Trowbridges' any time soon.

At least he'd gotten Linnie out of the deal.

He heaved his leather sack onto his shoulder and called out, "Ready, Linnie?"

Mrs. Trowbridge winced—but she stepped aside, allowing Linnie to emerge from where she had been hiding in the kitchen.

Poor Linnie had her ears back, her black eyes darting this way and that. She could sense a monumental change, only she couldn't tell that, for once in her life, it was a good one.

Eddie crouched and held his palms out to the terrier mutt. She rushed across the workshop floor to sniff his fingers. Then, finally, she ducked between his ankles.

"We'll be off, then," Eddie said to the Trowbridges.

"That dog will be the death of you," Mrs. Trowbridge said for the hundredth time. Remembering herself, she added, "Send word of how you are doing when you can."

Eddie nodded, opened the door, and stepped onto the street.

Free, at last.

Free of obligation. Free of youth. Free of a deal brokered by his parents without any regard for what Eddie wanted. He was not free of everything—not the profession of glazing nor the body that marked him as not properly British—but soon, at least, he could be free of London and of being apart from everyone whom he loved.

Eddie tipped his face up into the cold rain spitting from the sky. Despite the terrible rush of people around him on the street, he stood still. From the fields of Northfield Hall years ago, he heard Caroline murmur, "You see it too, don't you?" And with all his heart, Eddie pretended that he could see the great cloud ship *Jolly Molly* sailing above the steeples of London.

He had called it from his imagination a hundred times these past eight years—always with Caroline's recitation of "white sails, white deck, and a bright red rose painted on its sails for good luck" humming in his ears—but this was the first time he envisioned himself leaping from the street onto its decks. Closing his eyes, he pictured the slate rooftops of Gray's Inn Lane beneath him like coral reefs under a schooner. And at the wheel, he conjured a golden-haired maiden in a yellow gown, swinging around with a smile to greet him.

Caroline.

Linnie returned Eddie to reality with a low, loud growl. Eddie opened his eyes just in time to jump out of the way of a hurdy-gurdy man's unwieldy instrument. "Good shout, Linnie," he praised, and hustled onward.

He may have been free from the Trowbridges, but he was still in London, still surrounded by strangers, and still late.

Better to hurry on to Soho than to finally allow himself to get lost in his daydreams.

Linnie stayed closer to him as they turned off the paths she was familiar with and onto the cobbled streets of Soho. Here, there were fewer people, and they were snobbish. The pedestrians were servants in good clothing—not all liveried, for this was still not Mayfair, where most of the nobility lived—and they were anxious to prove their superiority by sneering down their noses at Eddie and his black dog.

You're not supposed to be here, Eddie imagined one of the maids saying as she hugged the side of the curb in order to avoid getting too close to him.

I've been invited to dine with Lord Preston himself. What have you to say to that? He pictured her grim face opening with shock, and that was enough to keep his chin up while, in reality, a shining car-riage splashed a puddle onto his boots.

He wouldn't let that get him down. After a proper brushing, his boots would look good as new, and he could present himself at the front door of the townhouse like the successful young journeyman he was. Eddie pictured his parents in sturdy travel-ing costumes. He imagined Lord Preston in his usual woolen suit decorated with linen lace. And he tried to guess what Caroline would wear.

But when it came to imagining Caroline in the real world, Ed-die redirected his thoughts, as he always did. He didn't examine the impulse too closely; he only knew that if he attempted to guess the way she walked down a street or whether she wore her hair up in a coiffure, a sensation that was either great pain or great joy would overwhelm him.

Soon enough, he would see her in the flesh. And not long after that, he would return to Northfield Hall, where he could see her every day.

And perhaps, if she still meant what she had sworn long ago, before long they would be married, and Eddie would never have to wonder at all about what she looked like or where she was.

But Eddie didn't let himself linger on that possibility, either.

Linnie paused at the intersection of Peter Street, as if somehow, she knew where they were going. He let out a little whistle to make sure she followed, then turned onto the side street. From here, he had a full view of the Preston townhouse: red brick, with old broad sheet glass windows in leaded panes, a painted front door its only nod towards modernity.

For a moment, jealousy overtook him. What would life have been like had he been born into the Preston family instead of the Chows? What hopes or dreams would he harbor if he had spent the last eight years sleeping on a feather mattress instead of a lumpy straw tick? What would it feel like to eat a proper meal every day, instead of making do with the small portions offered at the mercy of one's master?

It only hurt to ask these questions. And yet they spun around him, like the inevitable ream spiraling through crown glass, with every step he took.

Until he looked up at the third story and spotted Caroline in her bedroom window. Blond and pale, like the sun emerging from behind the clouds. She swung the window open, stuck out her head, and waved.

At last, Eddie knew he was exactly where he was supposed to be.

CHAPTER TWO

CAROLINE AND EDDIE HAD been reunited a hundred times over their lifespans. When they were very little, every morning felt like they were discovering each other after an ocean's journey, and they had spilled into each other's arms and hurried off to play.

When Eddie was sent to his apprenticeship in Reading, it became a weekly ritual: Eddie arriving late Sunday morning, Caroline waiting impatiently for him to have private words with his parents, then finally sitting beside him at the midday meal to tell him everything that had happened since he last left.

Their reunions had been infrequent ever since, at the age of fifteen, he had been sent to London. He came back to Northfield Hall for a holiday or two, but never for long enough, and something always seemed to conspire to keep them from having private moments together.

Still, rushing down the townhouse stairs, Caroline felt as if she had done this every day of her life. Hurry, hurry, hurry to get to where Eddie had arrived, and then wait, telling herself that if she were still and silent, everyone else would finish their business with him and leave him to her.

In this case, "everyone else" was Papa, Mr. and Mrs. Chow, Oliver Chow and his wife Samantha, and Spencer Chow. Papa shook Eddie's hand and told him how proud he was that Eddie had dedicated himself to a worthy trade. Mrs. Chow hugged Eddie fiercely and started in on him about how thin he looked. Oliver made a joke, Spencer stood solemnly, and Mr. Chow intervened here and there among the family banter.

Caroline watched from the threshold of the drawing room. Mrs. Chow was right: Eddie was too skinny. He was tall, too, with the effect that he looked like he had been stretched up and down disproportionately. His clothes hung off him as if they had been tailored for a man one and a half times his girth, but they were too short, so that his waistcoat ended almost an inch above the waist of his trousers.

Despite all that, he was still Eddie. Handsome—those eyes, those lips, those shoulders looking so strong and brawny beneath his inadequate coat! And sweet. He ducked his head as his family spoke, but he watched them all with that steady gaze, as if he were saving each word like gold coins in a bank.

He probably was. Sometimes, Eddie brought up things a person had said two years before, when Caroline couldn't even remember conversations from the morning. He was that kind of man: one who paid attention to the details, who remembered everything, who tended to the people around him. The perfect balance for her, since

Caroline was impetuous and impatient and likely to forget how her actions impacted others.

Case in point, when Eddie had first returned on Sundays from Reading, Caroline had always rushed to greet him before anyone else—once even elbowing poor Oliver out of the way as she raced to meet Eddie's cart. Mrs. Chow had finally pulled Caroline aside for a stern lecture about how she was *not* Eddie's family and did *not* have the prerogative to welcome him before his own parents did.

Which was why now, Caroline waited. And waited. And did not clear her throat. And did not knock her fingers against the doorframe. And did not rustle her skirts.

She was not Eddie's family. Not yet, anyhow, and she would not spoil anything for him by letting her impetuous heart rule this afternoon.

At last, her patience was rewarded. The Chows had finished their greetings, and, when Spencer stepped aside, there was no one left standing between Eddie and Caroline.

He smiled at her. Caroline could see its restraint in the way his cheeks twitched a little, preventing it from overtaking his whole face. He took one step towards her and bowed from the neck. "Miss Caroline."

That was another rule enforced by Mrs. Chow, one that had arisen sometime during that Reading apprenticeship. All their lives, they had been Caroline and Eddie, until suddenly, he was Eddie the apprentice, and she was to be Miss Caroline, youngest daughter of Lord Preston.

Caroline didn't let him call her that in private. Those few, rare times when they managed to have privacy. This was not one of them. "Eddie." She allowed herself to rush a little now and took up his hands—same as if she were greeting her own brothers. It was not as if she kissed him, or even made to hug him!

Still, a tension whipped across the room, like cold air whistling on a draft.

Caroline ignored it. She focused on the feel of his fingers—firm, strong, and gloved—in her own. She basked in the fierce, steady look in his eyes. She let her heart trill at his nearness.

"It has been far too long," she said, as she always did.

"It has only been eleven months, twenty-nine days, and a few hours," he replied, as he always did.

Everyone laughed. Caroline, too, but not because it was a joke. She laughed because at last, she was with Eddie again.

Caroline looked stunningly like a lady. Eddie could barely keep his eyes on her because it was so shocking, yet neither could he look away. Her golden hair, which she usually kept in a braid or some loose arrangement that always came undone on their adventures, was twisted into a perfect coiffure. Her gown was fine Berkshire linen trimmed with lace and ribbon and tailored to look as delicate as the muslin gowns displayed on Bond Street. She even wore a necklace and matching amber earrings, when Eddie had never seen her in any jewelry before.

She was breathtaking. She was a diamond of the first water. She was not Monkey, his childhood friend, but Miss Caroline Preston.

He had no business being in the same room as her, much less holding her hands.

Mother suggested they move to the dining room, as the meal was ready. She had overseen its preparation herself: thick noodles, poached fish, a roast chicken, scallops, shrimp, turnips, cabbage, winter peas, and steamed sponge cake, all cooked the way her mother had taught her in Kwangchow.

Food Eddie hadn't had since his last visit to Northfield Hall at Christmastime. He tried to focus on its smell and on how it felt like a hug of its own, welcoming him home.

His heart was still on Caroline. Every particle of his being wanted to pull her into some other room and—what? Kiss her, like he had done under the summer sky on her sixteenth birthday? Talk, the way they always had, for the entirety of his life? Bask in her presence, soak up her cheer, worship at her feet?

Whatever it was, he couldn't do it yet. He must wait, as he had these last five years in London and, before that, three years in Reading, until they were at last alone together.

He forced his attention to his family. Mother, Father, and Spencer had all traveled from Northfield Hall just to celebrate with him.

Oliver lived in London with his wife Samantha, but here they both were, in their finest clothes, to dine and toast Eddie.

He should be basking in their love. He tried very hard not to look at Caroline in her seat at the far end of the table. Not to notice her nimble fingers lifting the silverware to her lips. Not to admire the elegant line of her wrist to her elbow. Not to glance up, hoping to catch her eye.

She was looking right back at him. Her cheeks burned pink for a moment. Eddie told himself to turn away. It was not polite to stare. Especially not at such a beautiful lady, even if she was his friend from childhood.

Even though Oliver was entertaining the group with a story from Drury Lane Theatre, Caroline addressed Eddie across the table. "After all these years, have you seen any of the sights of London?"

When he had first headed for London, Caroline had tried to cheer him up by promising him he would see wonderful things—even though she, herself, had never been. The Tower and its menagerie, the architecture of St. Paul's Cathedral, the excitements in Vauxhall Garden, the clothes on Bond Street, and the dandies in the windows of St. James's Street. Eddie had returned a year later for his annual visit to Northfield Hall without having seen any of them, and Caroline had been shocked into an angry tirade on how apprentices should be required to tour their environments.

That was Caroline: getting into angry tirades without meaning them, because one could only mean it if there was an actual injustice at the root of it.

He shook his head no now in reply.

"Well, we must go touring, then." Still, Caroline seemed to have no concept of Oliver and his story about a set piece that had nearly killed an actor. "Tomorrow, Aunt Charlotte is taking me to the Tower. You must come along."

"If there is time." Eddie looked meaningfully at Oliver, trying to cue her in. But even as he did so, he knew it would be useless. This was what meals with his family were always like: too many people talking, and most often Caroline interjecting over, under, and through all so that she could talk to Eddie.

Eddie knew he wasn't supposed to like it. His mother complained it was obnoxious. His father said it was disrespectful. His brothers laughed it off as Caroline.

It made Eddie feel like the center of the world. And he couldn't help liking that.

Caroline grinned at him. "We'll make time. One cannot leave London without having seen *one* of its famous sights."

Mother heaped more noodles onto Eddie's plate. "Keep eating. You haven't had enough." To Caroline, she added, "You, too. Fill your mouth with food instead of talk."

Caroline giggled at this, and then everyone laughed. It was exactly the kind of admonishment she had earned all her life, and it never worked. Caroline Preston did what she wanted, when she wanted.

It was one of the things that had always pulled Eddie towards her. Or perhaps she had pulled Eddie, physically, because even as a toddler, she had wanted him.

"You'll be happy to know Caroline displays much better manners when in company," Lord Preston said, a loving smile on his lips to soften his words. "She only interrupts when she truly feels as if she is with family."

Caroline grinned at the whole table. "Well, what are we if not family?"

No one reacted the way they should have, if they really had been a family. There was no echoing back of the sentiment, nor recollections of days gone by, nor even ribbing. There was only an awkward look exchanged around the table.

Caroline sent a glance Eddie's way. He didn't know why he could read it, since she hardly widened her eyes at all and didn't make any expression. Yet he knew what she was saying as clearly as if she said it aloud: *Why is everyone acting so strangely?*

Lord Preston broke the awkward silence by lifting his crystal glass in the air. "A toast to Eddie. You have displayed great dedication, perseverance, and patience in finishing this apprenticeship, and we are all very proud to call you our friend, brother, and son."

Father put his hand on Eddie's shoulder and cheered. "Hear, hear!"

The attention embarrassed Eddie. He lifted his glass in the air because everyone else was doing so and because he knew he was supposed to and because he hoped that would end the moment.

"Say a few words, Eddie," Oliver prompted.

"Don't make him," Spencer said swiftly—one of the few things he had said all night.

"He won't die if he says a few words. Will you, Eddie?"

"Stop pestering him," Mother cautioned.

All of which conspired to make Eddie stand. Arm in the air, like one of the fellows at a pub constantly giving toasts to excuse more drinking, he said, "Thank you. I am glad to have made you proud. I have learned much, not only about glazing but also about responsibility. I look forward to bringing everything I have learned home to Northfield Hall and contributing to the great experiment."

"Hear, hear!" Caroline, beaming, raised her glass in reply.

Beside him, however, Father grew stiff, and Mother looked away.

Lord Preston cleared his throat. "Ah, Eddie. I have some wonderful news for you. I took the liberty of asking around for a position for you. The regiments are in need of talented glaziers to assist in building fortifications in Lower Canada, and the pay is three times what you would earn here in London. Once the paperwork is sorted, you sail on January eighth."

The words washed over Eddie. At first, all he could do was stare at Lord Preston. This man whom he had known his whole life, who, while never a relative, had been a benefactor, an interested party, and the father of Caroline. Suddenly, the silver of his hair felt foreign, the creases of his face seemed sinister, and the smooth cadence of his words tasted like too-sweet syrup.

All this time, Eddie had told himself he could survive the apprenticeship because at its end, he would go home to Northfield Hall. His parents and Lord Preston had deemed it best for him to learn to be a glazier and to learn it far from home, but he had gone along with it because at some point, he would be allowed home. Welcomed back into the arms of his family and returned to the only place in the world where he could feel happy.

Now Lord Preston made it clear: Eddie was not welcome back at Northfield Hall. Not now, and if he wasn't welcome now, he never would be.

"Thank you, sir," Eddie heard himself say when Lord Preston's speech finally waned. "You are very generous to me."

Caroline hardly let Eddie finish the sentence. "The *regiments*? Surely you can't mean the army, Papa."

Lord Preston looked squarely at his plate of food. "I do."

"In Lower Canada? A colony?"

Eddie sank into his chair as Caroline's voice hiked higher and higher in register.

"A wonderful opportunity," Father said. "We thank you very much, sir."

As if it were his parents who would sign the paperwork. As if this were another decision in which Eddie could have no input.

Caroline asked, "How can you propose to send Eddie to the colonies as a part of His Majesty's army when our whole estate objects to the colonial economy?"

"It is only for a few years," Lord Preston said, "and it is good money. It will prepare Eddie for a prosperous life."

"They keep slaves in the colonies." The anger that usually filled Caroline's voice was absent, replaced by bewilderment. Her finger tapped in threes against the tabletop.

Lord Preston rebutted with a surprising amount of annoyance: "He is going to be building fortifications along the border with the United States, not leading a plantation."

"It must be at least two months' sailing to get there!" Caroline cried.

"Eddie will be a rich man by the time it is over," Oliver interrupted. "Don't go looking a gift horse in the mouth, Miss Caroline."

It occurred to Eddie that he might appreciate a gift horse instead. A horse had a personality and a heart; he could earn a horse's love as he had earned Linnie's, by feeding it and brushing it and seeing that it got its exercise; and besides, a horse could help him go more places faster.

"Is that what you want, Eddie? To be rich?" asked Caroline.

When he looked up, he got caught in her brown eyes and the worried frown above them. She wanted an honest reply; she deserved an honest reply. Yet Eddie had long ago grown accustomed to not giving Caroline the full truth. Not when it came to his life. There was too much she didn't understand about being a commoner—or about being a Chow.

He tried his best to be honest when he answered, "I wish to make my family proud."

At which Caroline shrank in her chair, looking more bewildered than ever, and made no reply.

CHAPTER THREE

CAROLINE LOST TRACK OF the rest of supper as she tried to make sense of Papa's news.

When he had invited her to London, she had thought it was to introduce her to worthy organizations. Yet he must already have been investigating positions for Eddie. Why, then, would he want her to waste her mornings drinking tea in the name of deaf orphans when he knew that in a matter of weeks she would sail to Lower Canada?

Unless Papa did not intend for her to join Eddie on this expedition. Yet Caroline was twenty years old, an appropriate age for marriage. While she had never said it aloud to Papa, she was certain he knew she intended to marry Eddie. Surely, he understood that she would want to join Eddie wherever he went, even if it was one of the colonies.

But why had Papa found Eddie a position so very far away? Caroline had always imagined marrying Eddie at Northfield Hall and establishing a household in one of the estate's cottages. If Papa wanted Eddie to stand on his own two feet, why wouldn't he find a position in London or Reading or somewhere else from which Caroline could visit easily?

Caroline couldn't imagine not marrying Eddie—not now that he was right in front of her, close enough to hold in her own arms—yet the thought of removing to Lower Canada was making her cold with anxiety. Especially if she had to leave in six weeks, without a chance to say goodbye to Ellen at Montchampion Manor or Sophia on the Continent or Benny in Ireland.

She drummed her fingers against the table in a triplet tattoo to try to make sense of the situation. What she needed was a plan—and to make one, she needed to speak to Eddie in private. Yet when everyone finished eating, Papa did not suggest they retire to the drawing room. He said to Oliver, "I suppose we had better call for a hack so you do not stay out too late."

Oliver turned to Eddie. "Have you got everything?"

The question was posed as if Oliver thought Eddie was going home with him to Covent Garden. Even though the rest of the Chow family was staying right there in the townhouse.

Caroline expected Mrs. Chow to set Oliver straight, or Eddie to look pained as he prepared to reject his brother, yet everyone reacted as if Oliver had made a reasonable assumption.

Leaving Caroline no option except to object: "Oh, but Eddie is staying here!"

Every single face in the dining room—even the footmen who were clearing away the plates—turned to look at her, as if she had proclaimed something as absurd as that the sky was green.

"There is not enough room," Mrs. Chow replied. "Where would we put him?"

There were plenty of rooms. Caroline had reviewed them with Mrs. Leeson that morning: Mr. and Mrs. Chow were in Benjamin and Lydia's suite, Spencer was in Max's apartment, and that left Sophia and John's set of third story rooms available for Eddie. Rooms that were conveniently across the corridor from Caroline's apartment.

Before Caroline could even answer, Papa added, "Oliver wants to steal his brother away. Who are we to stop him?"

Mrs. Chow and Papa were trying to act as if it were rational and obvious that Eddie wouldn't stay at the townhouse. Perhaps it was. Perhaps Caroline was the one being unreasonable when she expected that Eddie could stay in the luxury of Soho while celebrating the end of his apprenticeship.

She didn't think that was the case, though. The room was full of that strange undercurrent Caroline was all too familiar with, the same one that arose whenever she asked after Eddie or mentioned how excited she was to see him. When she had wanted to invite Eddie to her brother Nate's wedding that past summer and Mrs. Chow had replied, "He is an apprentice. He cannot leave for a wedding." When she had tried to send him a letter after he was sent to London and Papa had removed it from the mail, saying, "You know very well that it is not done to write to a young man, no matter how long-standing your acquaintance."

But he was no longer an apprentice. They were no longer too young. And now Eddie had employment, even if it *was* in Lower Canada! If Papa and the Chows allowed Eddie and Caroline alone in a room together, it was no longer a case of two youths getting each other into trouble.

It was a case of two lovers finally being able to plan their future.

Caroline looked at Eddie. He was stiff as a corpse, staring down at the table in front of him. Caroline willed him to return her gaze—to give her some sort of indication of his preferences—but he didn't, almost as if he thought that by refusing to look at the people around him, he could disappear.

She didn't blame him. The unspoken undercurrent was strong. Caroline almost didn't have the courage to reply to Papa's rhetorical question.

Almost—but she found it somewhere in the depths of her chest, mingling with all the frustration she had felt for eight years at being separated from Eddie.

"I had Sophia's room made up for him," she answered the table.

Eddie shook his head. "Caroline…" It came out as more of a growl than a word.

He hated it when she made a fuss. And when they were younger, she always made a fuss, especially if things weren't going her way.

That wasn't what she was doing now. This wasn't about getting *her* way. This was about calling Papa's bluff. This was about making sure Eddie was given every kindness—because he deserved that and more—and not shortchanged because of whatever it was that made Papa and Mrs. Chow so uncomfortable.

But she did not want to upset Eddie. Not now, on the first night, when they hadn't even had a chance to speak alone. "You choose, then. There is a room here ready for you, if you should like to stay, or you may go home with Oliver and Samantha. What would you like to do?"

For the briefest moment, Eddie glanced up at her. His eyes were full of fire—the strongest emotion he had exhibited all night. Then, before her breath ended, he was looking back down at the table. He tilted his head to the right, towards his mother. And he said in words that could hardly be understood: "I suppose I'll go with Oliver, then."

Caroline couldn't help but feel left behind.

E DDIE HAD NEVER ASSUMED he would be allowed to stay at the townhouse. All these years he had lived in London, he had hardly even been invited over for a meal. Father and Mother might be Lord Preston's most trusted servants, but Eddie had learned early on that he was not their trusted son. He was their expendable son. Martin, his eldest brother, had left Northfield Hall of his own accord. His parents had kept Spencer and Oliver at home at the carpentry workshop. Eddie had been surplus, like the extra honey that Northfield Hall sold at local markets. He had been too much, and so they had sent him away.

He didn't need Caroline to fight with anyone about it. He didn't want to hear anyone say it aloud explicitly, nor did he want to see Mother turn away with that severe face she always pulled before proclaiming something nonsensical like, "It is best for everyone if Eddie goes with Oliver tonight."

Eddie never quite knew why the things they chose were the best options for him. He trusted that they knew. Otherwise, it would feel too much like they didn't love him at all.

The party broke up. Eddie said to Oliver: "I have my pack, and I have to fetch my dog from the kitchen."

"Dog?" Oliver laughed. "I agreed to take in a stray brother, not a stray dog."

Eddie wasn't in a joking mood. Linnie didn't understand words, didn't know what Northfield Hall was, wouldn't care where they ended up so long as she had food to eat and somewhere warm to sleep, but he had been telling her all these months that soon they would be in the country where she could run free.

And now, if Lord Preston had his way, Eddie had only a transatlantic sail to offer her.

"I won't be long," he promised, and headed for the kitchen.

It was in the back and down the stairs. Eddie had gone there first upon arriving at the townhouse and asked the scullery maid—Virginia—to look after Linnie before circling back and knocking at the front door. Eddie forged onward in a haze. He just needed to get out of the house. He just needed to get somewhere he could be alone with Linnie. Then he could sort out everything that had happened tonight.

He could make a decision about what he was going to do.

He was halfway down the stairs when Caroline caught up with him. "How long have you had a dog?"

She was at the top of the steps, pulling the door shut behind her. Again, Eddie felt blinded when he tried to look at her. She was too brilliant, too forceful, too much.

He turned away and focused on getting down the stairs. "A while now."

"The Trowbridges didn't mind you keeping it?"

"If they minded, they didn't say." Eddie landed at last in the kitchen. It was huge, at least compared to the London establishments he was used to, and it took him a moment to spot Linnie curled up on the far side by the door.

Virginia looked up from where she was washing pots. "She hasn't been any trouble. She has just been sitting there waiting for you to come back."

"Thank you." Eddie whistled through his teeth to catch Linnie's attention. In a half-second, she was on her feet and bounding across the kitchen to him.

He wasn't expendable to *her*.

"What's her name?" Caroline asked.

Crouching, Eddie ran his fingers through the dog's fur and let her lick his wrist in greeting.

Virginia answered for him: "Linnie."

Eddie blushed. Linnie was such an obvious nickname for Caroline. He hadn't thought too hard about it when he named the dog: she simply made him smile the same way Caroline did.

It was a little humiliating to reveal that to Caroline, though.

She didn't react to the name. "How sweet Linnie is." She bent low enough to offer her fingers to Linnie, who sniffed them suspiciously before darting into the safety of Eddie's squat. "Perhaps a little shy. I'm sure we shall soon be fast friends, though."

"You probably won't see each other again."

Eddie hadn't meant to say that aloud. When the words came out, he couldn't look at Caroline. He held onto Linnie a little more tightly.

"What do you mean? Is she dying?"

The problem—the thing that was making Eddie so angry—was that Caroline was acting so ignorant. She was a smart woman. Even as an eight-year-old, she was always the one reading the room to come up with the harebrained schemes that got them into trouble.

Now, when the room was so easy to read, she acted as if she were completely illiterate.

"No, Caroline." He stood; his knees were growing tired. "You and I probably won't see each other again after this, either."

At the sink, Virginia banged pots together extra loudly.

Caroline rose. "What on earth are you talking about?"

"Don't be obtuse, Monkey."

She crossed her arms. "Obtuse? Were you not at the same dinner that I was?"

"The one where your father announced I am to exile myself to Lower Canada?" The words escaped Eddie before he could measure them. "It will be difficult for you to drop in for tea to visit."

Assuming he took the post. Eddie always did as he was told; everyone assumed he was going to take the post. Even himself.

"*Us.*" Caroline swallowed. "He exiled *us* to Lower Canada."

Virginia clanged her pots together again. Eddie barely heard it this time because his ears were already ringing. "You can't come with me."

"Why not? Even if the army won't pay for it, I will. My dowry is not large, but it should be ample to pay for my transportation."

"The regiment sails January eighth. Six weeks from now. There isn't time."

"We'll marry by special license. Papa will sort it all out."

Marry. The word almost stopped Eddie's tongue. It was so wonderful; it was so impossible.

It made him bitter as he tried to make her see: "Monkey, don't you understand? He's sending me to Lower Canada so that I'll be nowhere near you. He doesn't want us to marry."

Her mouth formed around words that didn't emerge from her lips. She looked away. "That's not true."

"You're to marry a gentleman."

"John is an accoucheur, but Papa was all too pleased when Sophia married him."

"An accoucheur is a gentleman. Or close to it. I'm a glazier."

"Papa isn't like that." Then, glaring, Caroline said, "And it doesn't matter anyhow. I'll marry who I want."

Her determination was too sweet and too strong for Eddie to manage. He turned back to the stairs. "I have to go, Caroline. Oliver is waiting."

Caroline grabbed his hand. Her fingers were so soft and delicate. "You're not an apprentice anymore. You don't have to do as anyone says. You can stay, and we can tell Papa what we want."

No, he was *supposed* to be an obedient son. He was supposed to be grateful for the opportunity to earn money. He was supposed to comply when they told him to know his place.

Eddie wanted to spread her palm across his whole body, but he pulled away from it instead. "It's not that simple."

"It can be." Caroline followed him up the stairs, pressing so close that they both almost tripped over Linnie. "Eddie, please, wait. Go away tonight if you want to keep the peace. But don't you..." Her voice wavered a little and finally got quiet enough that Virginia wouldn't overhear it. "Do you not love me like that anymore?"

They had never actually declared themselves to each other. They had agreed at some young age that they would marry because they were best friends and it seemed like an obvious solution to the problem of having to marry someone of the opposite sex. When he had gone off to his first apprenticeship, they had agreed that at the end of it, they would be old enough that they could go ahead and get married. And when they were sixteen and he had been home for her birthday, they had shared a magical quarter hour of kisses.

Never had they told each other they loved each other, not in any form of the word.

But Eddie supposed they had known it.

He looked back at Caroline. Even in the dark stairwell, she shone bright. That was his heart talking, probably. She was only a human, a very flawed one at that, not a candle or an angel or a source of light.

He didn't know when he had started loving her the way adults loved one another, but he knew he had been lost to her for years. His body wanted hers on a deep, terrible, essential level, and his soul yearned to expose itself to her with every beat of his heart. He was so used to denying it that he had almost forgotten what it was like to give his desire room to breathe.

It felt good to have her waiting for him like that. It felt good to have her asking him that question. It cut through all the terribleness of the day and got him to speak honestly. "Of course I still do."

She grinned. Her shoulders fell back into their natural, commanding position. "Then go stay with Oliver. We shall find a way to marry, whether they like it or not. After all, in June, I'll be twenty-one and won't need anyone's permission."

And though he hated to deceive her, his Caroline, he let her believe that.

EVERYONE RETIRED FOR THE night after Eddie disappeared into the carriage with Oliver and Samantha. Caroline followed their lead at first, but only long enough that the Chows could settle in their rooms before she tiptoed down the corridor and knocked on Papa's door.

He was, as she expected, sitting by the fire in his robe, reading some papers. He offered her a seat and a sip of his warm milk. "It has been an exciting day."

Caroline accepted the chair but not the milk. "Yes."

"You have had a busy week, taking the ladies of London by storm with your quick ideas. Aunt Charlotte said everyone is eager to have you join their societies." Papa smiled at her, as if this was supposed to be the best news she had heard in months.

Caroline knew she couldn't respond to that, or else she would end up wasting the conversation on the wrong topic. She took a fortifying breath. "I was excited to see Eddie today."

Papa's smile disappeared. "Yes, you two have always been so fond of each other."

Fond wasn't a strong enough word. One of Caroline's earliest memories was of racing down a path as a three- or four-year-old because she knew Eddie was at the end of it. Eddie was as much a part of her as her own lungs.

But again, Caroline would not let herself get distracted arguing that point with Papa. Not yet. Right now, all she wanted was to hear from him directly what his reasons were for not bringing Eddie back to Northfield Hall. "Eddie thought that he would be setting up a workshop at home next, not sailing away."

"Hmm." Papa watched her from behind the rim of his mug as he took a long, measured sip of milk.

Caroline held herself still. She knew this tactic of Papa's. He was waiting for her to say something else because he did not yet want to reply.

She would wait longer than him.

Except it proved excruciating to sit there, pinned under Papa's gaze. They were staring at each other like seven-year-olds in a contest, and Caroline couldn't help feeling like a terrible, insolent, disrespectful child.

She blinked. "I have been looking forward to Eddie returning to Northfield Hall. I miss him."

"The Chows are family to us. It is only natural you would miss him, as you miss Benny and Nate." Setting down his milk, Papa continued, "Your life so far has unfortunately been marked by so many departures of people you love. Your mother, of course, whom you barely got a chance to know. Your siblings, as they have each grown up and embarked upon their lives. I know even Miss Hoggart's departure last summer was difficult for you. The solace—or hope—I can offer you is that now as you become an adult in your own right, you shall soon be able to find a man to marry and begin a family of your own. Then I shall be the only one left behind at Northfield Hall holding onto memories of when we were all together."

Picturing her father alone at Northfield Hall brought hot tears to Caroline's eyes. "I do not want to be so very far away from you, Papa."

They were not a family to shy away from emotions, but neither did they frequently cry in front of each other. Papa froze at Caroline's reaction. "Why, you didn't imagine you would remain at Northfield Hall for the rest of your life, did you?"

"Yes, I did." It was exactly what she had pictured: a nice little life on the same five hundred acres on which she had always lived. "Why shouldn't I have?"

"You are destined for much more than organizing my papers for me. You are more forward-thinking and energetic than the majority of parliament. In this past week alone, you have taken London by storm. You, Caroline, are going to be a force of good in your generation."

"And I can't do that from Northfield Hall?"

"You can, if that is what you choose," Papa said, "only I suspect that within a few months, you'll decide you want to make a life of your own somewhere."

Within a few months, Eddie would be sailing for Lower Canada. Which meant there was no misunderstanding at all. Papa *did* intend for Caroline to go with Eddie. Enthusiasm replaced Caroline's fears:

Papa planned on sending her to the colony to do some good there. He wanted her to meet with all the societies in London so she would know how to establish her own in the fort towns bordering the United States. Perhaps he even wanted her to bring some education to the regiments to help them advocate for their rights when they returned to Britain.

Caroline fished a handkerchief from her pocket and dabbed at her nose, which had gone wet with dramatics. "Even so, I shall miss you, Papa."

He touched her shoulder in comfort.

That was more tenderness than Caroline could tolerate. "We have many plans to make, then, but tonight it is late, and you have your papers to finish with."

"And you have another exciting day tomorrow," Papa agreed, "with Aunt Charlotte taking you to both a meeting and to the Tower."

"Oh, yes, and I wanted to ask—may I invite Eddie to the Tower? Aunt Charlotte said I must secure your permission."

To her surprise, Papa hesitated, that strange look on his face that had appeared at supper, too. "Don't you think Eddie would be uncomfortable in Aunt Charlotte's company?"

"I don't see why he should. Besides, the Tower isn't Almack's. No one will be standing in judgment of him. He has been here five years, Papa, and he hasn't even seen the Tower! Don't you think he had better come along before he leaves for Lower Canada?"

"Fine, of course, you should bring him along. Only if he wants, mind you. Don't go bullying poor Eddie into doing things *your* way."

"I never bully him!" But Caroline didn't want to argue with Papa about that. She hugged him in thanks. "I shall leave you to your hard work, then, and we can discuss our plans more tomorrow. Don't forget that even the greatest of men must slumber occasionally."

"Yes, ma'am." Papa kissed her cheek. "I love you with all my heart, Caroline. I hope you know that."

She did. That was why it didn't need to be said.

Chapter Four

Eddie knew he should be comfortable at Oliver and Samantha's. They lived in a collection of rooms above their carpentry workshop and had cleared out one of them for his use. They had even found a stuffed mattress and bed for him to sleep on. Compared to the Trowbridges' kitchen floor, the room was the lap of luxury. And in the morning, Oliver went out and purchased hot sausage-stuffed pasties, so that even with a foggy chill in the air, Eddie was warm and well fed.

Despite all of that, it was an awkward morning. Eddie woke at five to the sound of bed creaks and muffled cries from his brother's room. Over the sausage pasties, Eddie had to force himself to look Oliver and Samantha in the eye without blushing. Linnie wouldn't settle, either, and barked each time Samantha moved from one part of the common room to another. "Is she always this loud?" Samantha asked, and Eddie heard the warning in her tone: if he didn't find a way to quiet Linnie, she wouldn't be welcome in the house for much longer.

Which meant Eddie wouldn't be welcome in the house for much longer. Not a problem, if he were to join Lord Preston's regiment.

It made things complicated, however, if he decided to make his own plan.

"She just needs to get used to things," he promised.

As did Eddie. Get used to the idea that he was no longer legally bound to anyone—not the Trowbridges, not his parents, and certainly not Lord Preston. An idea that, from the very first mention of the regiment, had whispered to him: *You don't have to do it.*

Eddie wasn't sure what he would do instead. He had expected to free himself of the Trowbridges and return to Northfield Hall. If that wasn't an option—and it clearly wasn't an option—then Eddie would have to make a life for himself.

He knew that wouldn't be in the colonies. He hoped it wouldn't be in London. He longed for the countryside with an ache almost as deep as his longing to be near Caroline. No matter what he decided, however, he would need to save up far more than the nine shillings currently secreted away in his spare stockings. That would get him to the countryside; he needed at least a pound for room and board as he established himself, and another to purchase the cutting diamonds necessary to do proper glazing work.

It was a welcome interruption when a footman knocked on the shop door at midmorning. He was all done up in green velvet livery and looked down his nose a little as he said, "Lady Pemberly awaits Mr. Eddie Chow in her carriage."

"Lady Pemberly?" Oliver asked, raising an eyebrow at Eddie.

"That's Aunt Charlotte, I think." Eddie knew the title because Caroline had always been so excited to receive her letters.

"Ah. Is Miss Caroline Preston in the carriage as well, by any chance?" Oliver asked the footman.

The man was clearly too superior to entertain such a question. "Will Mr. Eddie Chow please respond to the lady's request?"

"I am coming presently."

As soon as he fetched his coat and hat, Linnie skipped to his heels. Eddie looked from her to Oliver and then Samantha. His brother, as always, looked amused; Samantha managed to look stormy without even frowning.

Eddie decided it was better not to risk leaving Linnie behind to get up to mischief on her first day. With a whistle, he invited her to follow him onto the street.

The carriage waited at the end of the lane, for it was too broad to fit on the shop's narrow street. Almost as soon as Eddie spotted it, Caroline swung open the door and leapt to the pavement, grinning.

"Are you prepared to see all the sights of London?"

She was so vibrant, a great swirl of color on the gray street, that Eddie couldn't help but smile back at her.

Whatever plan he concocted, he hoped it would include her. Even if he could only see her in small snatches of time. "And here I thought you had come to kidnap me."

Caroline swooped down to extend her fingers towards Linnie. "Oh, and you shall come with us too, yes you shall, you sweet little thing!"

From within the carriage, a firm voice called, "Let us not tarry. The Tower awaits."

"Aunt Charlotte," Caroline murmured to Eddie. For a moment, Eddie was dropped back into Northfield Hall, with her whispering to him in conspiracy and his heart lifting, waiting to see what she had chosen for them to do next. He held out his hand; she placed her palm in his and leaned her weight on him as she climbed the tall step into the carriage. Then, not breaking their touch, she twisted her fingers to lock against his, and she tugged him close.

Eddie climbed into the carriage in a daze. A wonderful, golden, Caroline daze.

"You may take the seat opposite me," intoned Aunt Charlotte, shattering the mood. "Your dog may ride up front with John Coachman."

Linnie was on her hind legs, whining, trying to judge if she could jump into the carriage. The snobby footman scooped her up.

Eddie could just imagine what the man would do to her. Kick her with his heels if she made a sound. Eject her from the box if she bared her teeth. Lose her in London so that Eddie might never see her again.

Faster than a breath, Eddie leapt from the coach. He had a hand on Linnie's coat before the footman could disappear. "Then I shall walk with Linnie."

"Don't be ridiculous," Caroline said at the same time as Aunt Charlotte sniffed, "As you choose."

"Really, Aunt, then Eddie would be hours behind us." Caroline turned on her aunt, her voice tightening and chin stiffening into that of Determined Caroline, who never could be denied. "He is my guest today."

"I do not permit mongrels in my carriage."

She meant the dog, yet the word was so icy it made Eddie's skin prickle. He took Linnie, one-handed, from the footman and nestled her against his chest.

"In that case, I shall walk with Eddie," Caroline declared, rising off the carriage bench.

Aunt Charlotte stuck out a rigid arm, blocking Caroline's movement. She exhaled, a little huff that contained all the frustration in the world. Then, she said, "You will both ride. The mutt will remain on your lap, Chow, and will not touch a single fiber of my carriage."

Caroline grinned. For his part, Eddie wished he had refused the outing altogether. He made himself as small as possible as he took the seat indicated by Aunt Charlotte and gripped Linnie so that she couldn't make a move of her own.

The carriage began to drive with a great rattle against the cobblestone.

"So." Aunt Charlotte folded her hands in her lap and, without smiling, said, "*You* are Eddie Chow."

Measuring him with her eyes from the opposite bench, she was a formidable woman. Although she was Lady Preston's sister, she did not follow any of the strictures that the Prestons did; she wore a rich silk gown, a pearl necklace, and several colored jewels on her fingers. Stout, with good posture keeping her back and shoulders in a perfect line, she did not frown at Eddie so much as she directed a strong, disapproving energy towards him.

Eddie didn't know she had heard of him.

"Yes, ma'am." Then, unsure of the etiquette, he added, "My lady."

"You shall be on your best behavior today, I am sure."

Caroline huffed. "Aunt Charlotte, *really*."

"I would not like any misunderstandings. Good behavior depends so much upon what one considers good manners. For example, Eddie, could you tell me how close you should stand beside Caroline while touring the Tower?"

The question was insulting as well as infantilizing, but Eddie did not plan to begin another battle with Linnie in his lap. "I should not stand close to her at all."

"Indeed, you should always remain two steps behind her."

"Aunt Charlotte, *really*! Eddie is not a retainer. He is my guest."

Something soft and kind leaked into the woman's face as she turned to Caroline. "I know that, dear, but the rest of the world does not. They shall make wrong assumptions if they see Eddie presuming to behave a certain way when he should be behaving another. In their eyes." She glanced at Eddie. "It would do as much harm to your reputation as a glazier as to Caroline's."

Caroline was not satisfied. "How could anyone make assumptions when they don't even know who we are?"

That feeling that had filled Eddie the night before—the one suspiciously like anger—crept back at how Caroline kept herself so willfully ignorant. "Look at my clothes." Eddie gestured to his suit. Rough wool, wooden ornamental buttons, and leather boots that would have to last a decade.

A tradesman's suit. One that he would wear day after day until no amount of patching could salvage it.

"Look at yours." Even though Caroline didn't wear fine silks and cottons like most ladies of society, her outfit was expertly constructed to display that she was a young woman of quality. Her spencer jacket and gown were of fashionable designs; she boasted bright white lace as decoration; her half boots were new that season and still shone with polish because she traveled by carriage instead of by foot.

"They don't need to know us to tell at a glance that you are a baron's daughter and I have no claim to gentility at all. That is all they need to draw conclusions."

Caroline crossed her arms. She did not like to be wrong, and she especially hated when Eddie took someone else's side instead of hers. He could see a hundred arguments forming behind her frown.

She glared out the window. "People should not waste their time drawing conclusions about perfect strangers."

"Yet, they do." Aunt Charlotte withdrew a handkerchief, blew her nose, and returned it to its home in her sleeve. "In any case, not everyone at the Tower will be perfect strangers to us. My dear friend

Mrs. Spurrier is joining us with her nieces and a few other people she invited."

As if she could hear this news, Linnie growled. Eddie rubbed between her ears to calm her—and to hide his own reaction to spending the day playing servant to a genteel outing of debutantes.

He couldn't help glancing at Caroline. She looked a little green at this idea, too, but she caught his gaze and blinked back three times slowly.

Their old signal that somehow, sometime, they would find a way to sneak away from the group.

"Mrs. Spurrier, you know, is Max's relation," Aunt Charlotte continued. "She is eager to meet you, Caroline."

Eddie didn't know how they would get away with Aunt Charlotte watching. And they definitely shouldn't—not if they wanted to remain in her good graces.

It made him feel better, despite all that, to know that Caroline wanted to steal a private moment with him.

T HE DAY WAS NOT going at all as Caroline had envisioned, but she was trying hard not to feel frustrated. She could not stop Aunt Charlotte from being snobbish, and so she must let it wash over her. She focused on the good: Eddie, so close that she could see the muscles of his jaw clenching when he buried his feelings.

When they arrived at the Tower, Caroline made a point of walking in line with him, no matter that Aunt Charlotte wanted him to remain two steps behind. "How do you think Linnie will fare at the menagerie?"

Eddie looked down at the dog. She was a handsome mutt: black fur, black eyes, black nose, all sleek as midnight. One could tell at a glance that this was a beloved dog, one who was fed and sheltered and brushed clean every day. Caroline would guess that Eddie let Linnie sleep beside him in bed, and she was ashamed of the embers of jealousy that flamed in her own heart.

"She might be a little afraid of the lions," Eddie answered.

"I might be, too."

Now Eddie's smile was for Caroline and Caroline alone. "You're not afraid of anything."

Not true. Caroline merely refused to consider that the things she feared might one day come crashing down upon her. "Will you stand close anyhow, just in case?"

Aunt Charlotte called from where she walked three paces ahead, "There is Mrs. Spurrier. Come meet her, Caroline."

Caroline played along. It turned out that Mrs. Spurrier had brought along half a dozen people: her two nieces, their friend Miss Smith, and three gentlemen by the names of Colquhoun, Horlock, and Popham, whom Caroline immediately couldn't keep straight. All she knew was that they were dandies with forgettable faces, their complexions on a spectrum of lily white, sunburned red, and nutty tan.

Caroline made a point of introducing Eddie, particularly because it seemed as if Aunt Charlotte was about to turn away without doing so. "This is Mr. Eddie Chow. The Chow family are dear friends of mine and most instrumental at Northfield Hall."

The Misses Spurrier nodded their heads politely. The sunburned man—Popham?—held out his hand to shake Eddie's. "A friend of Miss Preston's must be a friend of mine."

No one acknowledged Linnie.

They moved as a clump through their tour of the Tower. Caroline found herself filing along the first walkway beside Mr. Popham and glanced backward to see that Eddie trailed with Linnie behind everyone. The casual observer might not even realize he was with their group.

Exactly as Aunt Charlotte wanted, and the opposite of what Caroline had intended by inviting him along.

As she looked at him—only for a second or two, since she had to watch where she was going—Eddie looked up, met her gaze, and offered a smile.

How she wanted to be at his side. She didn't even care about the tour; she had planned this outing so that she and Eddie would have another excuse to see each other.

She turned away. That night, she would sit Papa down to discuss his plans for their marriage, and then she and Eddie wouldn't need excuses to be beside each other.

"Is this your first visit to London, Miss Preston?" asked Mr. Popham.

"It is."

"Your father, I imagine, has been keeping you tucked away at Northfield Hall for as long as possible to keep us rogues from setting our caps at you."

Caroline wasn't sure how to respond to that. "I'm sure you are no rogue, Mr. Popham."

"Not such a rogue that I am immune to a pretty young lady who might be suitable as a wife, but enough of a rogue to say something so forward." He winked at her.

She suddenly felt that they were standing far too close together. They were in the Jewel Office where Charles II's Imperial Crown gleamed, and Mr. Popham was half an arm's reach from her. A few steps behind, Aunt Charlotte was not close enough to hear what the man said. Eddie hadn't yet even crossed into the room.

Pretending to sneeze into her handkerchief, Caroline edged away from Mr. Popham.

"I've embarrassed you," Mr. Popham said, and his friend, Mr. Horlock, suddenly turned towards the conversation to say, "Popham has embarrassed a young lady? I am shocked! I am stunned! I am appalled!"

"You are an—" Mr. Popham held a finger to his lips to suggest the sentence should end rudely.

Caroline wished herself about fifty feet behind them, where Eddie and Linnie had finally crossed into the room. Instead, the group kept moving, some invisible momentum pulling them along and somehow always keeping her from reaching Eddie's side. When she tried to drop back, Aunt Charlotte called her to look at something; when she tried to linger in the Small Armoury, one of the Misses Spurrier crowded in to look at the broadswords with her; and always, it seemed, Mr. Popham or Horlock or Colquhoun lay in wait to annoy her with some joke or another.

The only person, in fact, who wasn't vying for her attention was Eddie. He remained at the back of the group, as instructed. Each time Caroline glanced at him, he was absorbed in the displays, as if he were there to see the sights and he weren't a member of their party at all.

Caroline hated that Aunt Charlotte made him feel that was the part he had to play. She hated even more that she couldn't seem to break either of them free from the farce.

It didn't even make sense to her. Eddie had made a point: they didn't look like they were of the same background. Even as he stood peering at the brass cannons with his hands clasped behind his back, he was clearly a tradesman. It was in the broad strength of his shoulders, the sturdy construction of his clothes, the deferential way he had when others passed him.

Caroline didn't see why that mattered. Everyone knew she was a Preston, and everyone knew the Prestons lived by different rules at Northfield Hall. If they drew the conclusion that she was lowering herself by the company she kept, then they could stay away from her. Caroline didn't care if she lost that type of connection.

Especially not if she was about to disappear into the wilds of Lower Canada.

She didn't know why Eddie cared. Yet in the carriage, he had been fierce and clear: he agreed with Aunt Charlotte. So Caroline followed his lead, even if it meant they spent the whole outing apart.

At last, when they reached the menagerie at the end of the tour, the whole stupid party was disrupted enough for Caroline to steal her moment. It started with the lion, who roared so loudly that one of the Miss Spurriers cried out she was going to swoon. When Mr. Horlock rushed forward to catch her, the commotion startled poor Linnie, who took off running back towards the armories they had just left.

"Linnie!" Eddie sprinted after her, but the dog was fast.

Caroline didn't hesitate even half a second before chasing after them both. By the time her legs had run out of speed and her lungs began to complain, they had crossed a bridge and turned down three unrecognizable corridors and she didn't even know how to get back to the menagerie if she wanted to.

She didn't want to.

Trapping Linnie in a corner, Eddie knelt and scooped the dog into his arms. "Why did you run, you silly goose?" he crooned. His cheek landed on silky black fur. "I wouldn't have let that lion hurt you."

Jealousy seized Caroline that he could care for a dog so deeply yet leave her at the mercy of Mr. Popham's whims all day.

"What are we going to do?" Her words came out in huffs. She hadn't run like that in eons, and her lungs couldn't take it.

Eddie peered at her. "About what? Linnie?"

"No." Caroline dug her hands into her hips to keep from doubling over from exertion—and to keep her frustration from boiling over. "About us!"

None of this was going at all how she had envisioned. When she had come to London, she had thought she and Eddie would be planning their wedding. After Papa announced Eddie's new employment, she had thought today would at least be spent catching up on everything they had missed in each other's lives since they last saw each other.

Even in Aunt Charlotte's carriage on her way to fetch Eddie, Caroline had expected the day to go differently. Last night, Eddie had promised her he still wanted to marry her. She had expected that Aunt Charlotte might be a little stiff towards him, and she had known they couldn't run off and start kissing each other senseless—but had it been so ridiculous of her to think Eddie might *try* to run off with her for a kiss?

If he loved her the way she loved him, he would be cradling *her*, not Linnie.

"Aunt Charlotte is practically forcing Mr. Popham upon me." An exaggeration, but it felt true enough. "How can you just stand there and watch it happen?"

Eddie bent down and set Linnie back on the ground. He didn't look up at Caroline when he replied. "What did you expect? We are not of the same breed, Monkey. You didn't really think we could mingle in society together, did you?"

"Yes, I did." She didn't care for his tone, as if she were the stupidest person in the country. "What else are we going to do when we are married?"

"That's why no one wants us to get married."

She wished he would look at her. She had already forced him to say it aloud once. The next time Eddie Chow declared he wanted to marry her, Caroline wanted it to spring voluntarily from his heart, not be coerced from her in the middle of an argument. "Papa wants us to marry. I'm going to arrange everything with him tonight. Hang Aunt Charlotte. I want you to walk beside me. I want to *talk* to you, Eddie. I want to hear what *you* think about the Spanish Armada, not listen to endless prattle from Mr. Popham."

Still crouching, Eddie lifted his chin—that sharp, wonderful chin—a brief glance connecting his eyes to hers. "You don't find him charming?"

"I find him inane." Caroline crossed to his corner and joined him in a squat, reaching out to pet Linnie as a pretense. "How many jokes can one dandy make about the length of a man's lance?"

"Apparently a dozen." Eddie's fingers slid through Linnie's fur to thread between Caroline's. Her breath tripped over itself, and this time, it wasn't because she had been running so fast.

"Eddie..." She didn't know what sentence she was trying to begin.

"It would be more days like this." His thumb caressed the top of her hand. "If we were to marry. Our whole life would be awkward like this."

That wasn't true: it wouldn't be awkward at Northfield Hall. It might not even be awkward in the colonies. Yet Caroline didn't care to argue. She barely even heard his words, in fact.

She was lost in the way he was looking at her. Linnie was there, yes, but Caroline felt like she was alone in the room with Eddie. And that it was exactly what he wanted.

Her mind quieted for once. She hooked her fingers onto his. In the next instant, he pulled her out of her squat and onto her knees, cocooned in his arms and thighs and chest.

She didn't have to wait much longer for him to kiss her. Only a breath or so, as he stared at her, as if she were something precious he had never seen before. Then, running his finger along the rim of her jaw, he led their lips together.

Tears pricked Caroline's eyes. How long she had been waiting for this. How many nights she had been dreaming of this. How many heartbeats she had been counting until Eddie could kiss her again.

She would not ruin the moment by crying. She pushed her body against his: hands in his hair, elbows on his shoulders, breasts against his chest, and hips—oh, she tried not to be too eager in pressing her hips against his. Tried not to wonder too hard about whether the mass she felt was muscle, bone, or something else—something mysterious and compelling and so very forbidden.

Eddie was surprisingly demanding in the kiss. His lips were firm, his tempo urgent, and his breath furious through his nose and against her cheek. It was as if now that he had her, he was going to consume every ounce of their passion in one go.

She wanted to tell him they could take their time. She wanted to assure him they would spend the rest of their lives kissing. She also didn't want him to stop, not even a little: he was lighting her whole body on fire and she loved it.

His hand was just spreading across her ribs when Linnie growled. And then, a second later: "Oh dear, I am interrupting."

Eddie separated from Caroline so fast that she tumbled backward. The heels of her hands scraped against the stone floor as she caught herself.

Mr. Popham offered her a sad smile. "Your aunt sent me to return you to the group. I shall see you safely back to the menagerie, if you would be so kind as to accompany me."

The code behind his words was threatening—or would be, if Caroline were afraid of being ruined.

Delight ran through her instead. Let Mr. Popham think she was compromised. Let him declare to Mrs. Spurrier and the whole party that he had caught Caroline Preston being ravished by Eddie Chow.

The faster they married, the better.

Chapter Five

Early in Eddie's time in London, a man had grabbed him by the collar in the middle of the green market, claiming Eddie couldn't have come by his shopping money honestly. The man—tall, genteel, yet utterly ruthless in his grip around Eddie's neck—had marched him the full half mile back to Mrs. Trowbridge. He had been certain she would thank him for catching a thief; Eddie had been certain he would be turned out for having put suspicious thoughts in a stranger's head.

It had all worked out, but Eddie had never forgotten the terrible sound of fear pulsing through his ears, nor how time had stretched into long, eternal footsteps as they got nearer to the workshop on Gray's Inn Lane.

It all came rushing back to him now as Mr. Popham led them through the twisted corridors back to the group.

He had caught them kissing. He had caught Eddie kissing Caroline. He had caught Eddie ravishing Caroline's mouth and roving his hands over her body.

He had caught Eddie in the act of thievery, and this time, Eddie had neither innocence nor Mrs. Trowbridge on his side.

Eddie tried to push away the feeling that something terrible was about to happen. It made his hands shake and his mouth dry up and his mind race. He thought about Linnie, who trotted silently at his feet, as if even she could sense the gravity of the situation. He thought about Caroline, who walked in front of him, the tips of her ears still pink from excitement. He thought about what realistically might happen when Mr. Popham informed Aunt Charlotte that her niece had been in the arms of the glazier: he would be scolded, he would be barred from any good jobs, he would be forbidden from ever seeing Caroline again.

He could survive all of that, except for the last part.

Seeing Caroline—even if he couldn't talk to her—was the only good thing that ever happened to Eddie these days.

Then again, the outcome could be even worse. Mr. Popham and his friends could decide the offense was too gross to be ignored and take Eddie onto some side street for a beating. Or they could accuse him of theft of something tangible—a necklace or ring—and have him hanged.

All Eddie knew was that each step he took brought him that much closer to the consequence of stealing Caroline's kiss.

The group was still by the menagerie, though now the space was crowded with more visitors peering at the lions, grizzly bear, and panther. Eddie's whole body tensed as Mr. Popham wound his way through the crowd to join Aunt Charlotte. Caroline was close behind, so Eddie walked faster to keep pace, but he couldn't hear what Popham said. He could only see the man murmur into Aunt Charlotte's ear. They both looked over at Caroline and Eddie. Aunt Charlotte was expressionless, while Mr. Popham's lips twisted into something that could equally have been either scorn or wit.

Caroline turned back towards Eddie. She raised her chin, shoulders straight, and looked almost like a lady.

Except for the hair that fuzzed out of its style to either side because Eddie had dragged his fingers through it.

"This shall work out for the best," she said, quietly enough that Eddie almost didn't hear her. "We will turn this to our advantage."

Eddie didn't know how. But he wanted what Caroline said to be true. So he believed her.

Aunt Charlotte nodded at Mr. Popham, then waved him onward to lead the group out of the menagerie. She held out a hand to Caroline. "Come along, my dear. You mustn't get lost again."

The crowd was large enough that it carried Caroline away from Eddie before he realized what was happening. Eddie waited, even once he saw he was separated, because he was sure there must be something else coming. A group of guards marching over to seize him or a matronly chaperone informing him he must never see Caroline again.

Eddie stood still. The lion roared again. Some visiting children screamed. Linnie ran circles around his unmoving feet.

And no one came after him.

No one even looked his way.

Linnie barked, one sharp yelp of warning. As if he had been dreaming, Eddie awoke to the reality around him. He didn't know how long he had been standing there, waiting for disaster, but it was time to start moving again.

"Come on, Linnie," he huffed, as if it were the dog's fault, and hurried out of the menagerie.

He finally caught up with Caroline and Aunt Charlotte in the courtyard at the end of the tour, where they waited for their carriage. Mrs. Spurrier and Aunt Charlotte were taking a long leave of each other; the young Misses Spurrier and Miss Smith waited patiently to the side, and Popham and his friends were nowhere to be seen.

Caroline brightened when she spotted Eddie. Bending, she stretched out her hand and called to Linnie, "Come here, sweet girl!" But her eyes remained on Eddie, so that the beckon felt like it was for him alone.

He answered it, one step at a time, until he was close enough that, if he had found the courage, he could have reached out and touched the gold of her hair.

Caroline ruffled Linnie's fur, then rose from her crouch. She wore that old expression of hers, the one that promised adventure with a heaping dose of mischief. "Come back to the townhouse with us," she murmured. "Ask to speak to Papa."

"Why?"

She blinked. There was no direct sunlight, yet she shielded her eyes with her hand as she peered up at him. "To ask for permission to marry me."

Eddie's heart thudded. He tried to remember what she had said just moments ago in the Tower—words he hadn't believed even when she said them. "I thought you and he were already making plans."

"This must be the start of it." Caroline looked briefly back at Aunt Charlotte. In a hurry, she whispered, "Mr. Popham may not have said anything yet, but he still found us in a compromising position. Papa will understand. We mustn't wait, not even for you to sign your regimental paperwork, or else my reputation will be at risk."

As far as plans went, it was relatively innocuous. It did not involve climbing trees or sneaking into rooms or leaving coded messages.

Eddie had a bad feeling about it anyhow.

There was no time for further discussion. No time for him to admit to Caroline he didn't plan to go to Lower Canada. Aunt Charlotte glided over and placed a hand on Caroline's shoulder. "Come along, then. You had better get some rest before the supper party tonight."

Caroline remained where she was. "Mr. Chow is going to ride back to the townhouse with us. He must discuss some urgent business with his parents, and there is no sense in making him walk when we are all going to the same address."

Aunt Charlotte hesitated. She looked Eddie over again, and he stood as straight as possible, as if somehow he could turn into the gentleman she wanted him to be.

He did not. On a sigh, Aunt Charlotte said, "Very well," and turned to the carriage.

She managed not to look at him again for the rest of the trip.

CHAPTER SIX

LORD PRESTON HAD JUST returned home a half hour ago, a housemaid informed them when Caroline inquired, and was shut up in his study. Eddie thought they had better wait until he emerged, in case he was in the middle of writing up a speech for parliament, but Caroline marched up the stairs to his second-floor office and knocked on the door before Eddie could object.

Or perhaps it would be better said that Eddie didn't find it within himself to object, though he had the time it took to follow her upstairs and even the space of a breath between her raising her fist and her knuckles rapping on the door.

"Be plain with him," Caroline whispered, turning away after they received an "Enter" in response. "Don't let him bluster around the topic."

The topic: permission to marry her. Permission to be husband to Caroline Preston. It didn't feel real. It didn't feel right. Eddie reached out to touch Caroline—even just a brush of her hand would have been enough—but she bent, murmuring, "Let me take Linnie so she does not distract you."

From beyond the door, Lord Preston said more loudly, "You may enter!"

Eddie gulped in the image of Caroline: gold hair, yellow gown, black dog in her arms, and her brown eyes wide. Trusting him to do right by her.

He loved her with all his heart.

He pushed open the door.

The study was not a large room. A window, a desk, and two bookshelves full of leather-spined books. Lord Preston wore both a coat and a blanket across his legs to keep off the November chill. He was, indeed, scribbling away at something, but when he saw it was Eddie entering the room, he set aside his pen.

"Eddie, I apologize, I thought it was Caroline knocking at the door."

Latching the door behind him, Eddie approached the desk, hat in hand.

"She told me you were joining them on the visit to the Tower. Did you enjoy it?"

"Yes, sir." Eddie's voice came out reedy, as if he didn't have any air to breathe. He forced himself the luxury of a deep inhale.

"I am glad to hear it. You deserve some leisure after working so hard all these years. London is an exciting place to live. Do you love it as much as Oliver does?"

The answer was categorically no. Oliver had visited London once and then moved there permanently with such enthusiasm that Eddie sometimes wondered whether he loved the city or Samantha more. Eddie, meanwhile, had been counting down from his first arrival to the day he could leave.

But Eddie wasn't there to discuss London with Lord Preston.

"I must ask you a question, sir."

"Ah?" Lord Preston picked up his pen and looked down at his paper. "Go ahead then."

Fear pumped through Eddie again. His voice sounded strange through the thud of blood rushing his ears—or perhaps it was because his mouth was so dry he could barely get his tongue to work.

He was doing this for Caroline. For the two of them. For their future, which she was so certain lay on the other end of this question.

"Sir, you see, well...I don't suppose it is any surprise to you that I admire Miss Caroline very much. We have been close all of our lives, and throughout the years, I have come to love her with all my heart. While I know I cannot offer her the wealth or status that she is accustomed to, I believe it to be her dearest wish to marry me—for which I consider myself the luckiest man—and so I beg your permission, sir, to marry her. Miss Caroline. I would like to marry Miss Caroline."

Saying the words made them actually feel possible. Eddie had never said it aloud before: he wanted to marry Caroline.

He wanted to see her every day. Hold her every day. Kiss her every day. He wanted to plan a life with her, even though he hadn't any clue what that might look like. Speaking it into existence there in Lord Preston's study, Eddie could feel the idea of marriage taking form, and it was a comfort like a shawl wrapped around his shoulders on a cold winter day.

Until, that is, Lord Preston responded. "Oh, Eddie." The older man stood. The blanket that had been spread across his lap fell to the ground. He walked around the desk and put a hand on Eddie's shoulder. "Eddie, I honor you for having so good a heart, but I am afraid a marriage between you and Caroline is impossible."

Eddie's imagination slammed shut.

"You are a very worthy man, but Caroline is my daughter. A baron's daughter. What she is accustomed to is very different from what you can provide. As you said. And while I know Caroline loves you dearly and she believes it doesn't matter, as her father, I must protect her. Marriage would make you two very happy for a short amount of time but miserable for much longer. I must think about the full span of your lives. And so I must refuse you."

Eddie should have known this would be the answer. He *had* known this would be the answer. It was why he had never said the idea aloud before.

He and Caroline were not meant to marry. He would love her all his life, but she would marry someone else, someone better, and she would love her husband instead.

Her words rang in his ears, though: *My reputation will be at risk.*

So he tried again: "Sir, I beg your pardon, but I'm afraid we must marry. You see, at the Tower..." Eddie didn't know if he could do it. Lord Preston was not just a baron: he was a friendly figure from Eddie's childhood, he was the man deciding Eddie's future, and he was Caroline's father.

Now, standing so close that Eddie could smell the peppermint tisane on his breath, Eddie was supposed to confess that he had put Caroline's reputation at risk?

"My dog ran away. Caroline and I ran after to fetch her, and we found ourselves alone. Then one of the...Lady Pemberly's friend Mr. Popham came looking for us. He...Caroline is afraid he will tell someone he came upon us alone and that he will ruin her reputation."

Lord Preston's hand fell away from Eddie's shoulder. "Did he discover you in a compromising position?"

Eddie stared at his boots. Mud had flecked from them onto the ornate carpet beneath. He should have known better than to enter the room.

"Were you in an embrace?" Lord Preston pressed.

"Yes."

On a sharp inhale, Lord Preston wheeled away. He ended back at his desk, sagging into his seat, holding that damn pen. "This does not change my answer, Eddie."

No, better to let Caroline's reputation be ruined than to allow her to marry a...but Eddie didn't know how to finish that thought. Was Lord Preston's objection based only on the narrow life he could imagine for Eddie? "I don't intend to go to Lower Canada, sir. If that is your concern. I plan to find a job for myself, and I would get a proper set of rooms for us. Caroline would never go cold or hungry. I can promise you that."

Lord Preston, staring at that pen, only shook his head.

Eddie couldn't force his feet to move. "Is it because..." He swallowed. He didn't want to finish the sentence. "Is it because of my parents—"

Lord Preston spoke over him. "It is not enough, Eddie. I wish I could promise you that love is stronger than the ugliness of the world, but I have lived too long to believe that. For a woman of your class, I'm sure the promise that you would not let her go cold or hungry would assure her father. But Caroline will marry a man who would never even put her at risk of going cold or hungry. Do you understand?"

Eddie remembered, suddenly, something his brother Martin had said—shouted—to their parents in an explosive argument before taking his leave of Northfield Hall over a decade before. *If Lord Preston values us so much, why aren't we sleeping on feather mattresses too?*

As a boy, it hadn't made any sense to him. He liked his bed and thought Caroline's feather mattress was far too soft for proper sleeping.

He saw things through Martin's eyes now. And he realized why Lord Preston's answer was as heavy as manacles on his wrists. No matter that Lord Preston had known Eddie since he was born. No matter that the man had ruffled Eddie's hair and given him sweets when he was a boy.

Eddie had always been, and always would be, unworthy.

Lord Preston cleared his throat. "I must ask that you leave now, and that you do not attempt to see Caroline again."

Fury surged up Eddie's throat, but he swallowed it down.

He knew better than to enter a fight he couldn't win. "Goodbye, then."

And, fists curling, Eddie left.

CAROLINE DIDN'T WANT TO go down to the drawing room with Linnie in her arms. Aunt Charlotte had retired there, and Caroline couldn't bear to make small talk, nor endure an unhappy glare in Linnie's direction. So she did the unladylike thing—the *un-adult* thing—and sat at the top of the stairs to wait for whatever would happen next.

"It will be well," she murmured to Linnie, trying to settle the dog in her lap. Linnie was small but strong in a wiry way, and she kept twisting out of Caroline's hands to try to get back to the study. "He will come back soon, and then we shall have reason to celebrate, and we shall find a nice bone from the kitchen for you to chew on. Would you like that?"

Linnie whined.

Caroline tapped her toes three times against the stair. After a pause, she did it again. It was a little ritual of hers, though she couldn't explain it. It made her feel slightly calmer, that was all. And right now, she needed to feel calm. She was hovering in a moment of in-between; soon, there would be an "after," and it would redefine all these past days as the "before."

It was like when her brother Nate left for the navy, and all of a sudden her childhood was divided into "before"—when he was there to join her on escapades and guide her away from her worst ideas—and "after"—when she was the only one of Papa's children to still be a child.

Or when Ellen and Max moved this past year to Montchampion Manor, and life at Northfield Hall was redefined as "before"—when Caroline had always had her sister nearby to absorb responsibilities—and "after"—when Caroline was suddenly the de facto mistress of the estate.

Or the day that Mama died, when Caroline was seven, and she went from being a child who kissed her mother every day to a child without a mother at all.

This would be a good before and after, though. The "before" would be young Caroline with all her hopes and dreams; the "after" would be life with Eddie. Hopes and dreams that were transformed into reality.

Caroline was sure the twisting of her stomach was excitement, not nerves.

Linnie let out another whine, which brought Caroline's attention back to the study. The door opened, and Eddie stepped out.

Papa didn't follow him.

Like a bullet released from its chamber, Linnie raced to Eddie's feet. Annoyance spiked through Caroline because she knew how Eddie would react to that: he would let himself get distracted by the dog instead of telling Caroline what had happened.

Except he didn't kneel down to comfort Linnie. He bent down enough to touch her head. But his eyes were on Caroline the whole time.

They were not happy.

Caroline decided not to leave the step just yet. If she remained there—and, for good measure, if she tapped her foot three times again—then when Eddie joined her, he would explain why he looked so sad. And whatever it was, she would make it right. So long as she didn't leave her seat, she could make everything better.

Slowly, Eddie walked toward her. He did not sit down on the step beside her. He reached out his hand, like he had just done with Linnie, and rested his palm gently on the side of her head. "He said no."

Caroline's stomach flipped. "How could he say no?"

"He wants you to marry someone more worthy of you. Someone who can provide you the life you are accustomed to."

Eddie's fingers started to drop away. She grabbed them to keep them there, soft against her hair. "I don't care about that."

"He says we would be unhappy in the long term. He says he must make the decision thinking about the future, not just the present."

Caroline wished it were harder to believe. But there had been a part of her that had expected this. That had twisted her stomach in knots; that had made her think she needed to come up with her own plan, or else never marry Eddie.

Which reminded her of the plan. "Didn't you explain to him about what happened today? About my reputation?"

Eddie looked away. He was so tall, standing over her, and his face felt so far away from her. She wanted to pull him to sit beside her. She wanted him to wrap his arms around her.

"I told him. It did not change his answer." Eddie swallowed, and Caroline watched his Adam's apple track up and down his throat. "He told me I need to leave now and that I mustn't try to see you again."

"Never see me again?" The words propelled Caroline onto her feet. She knew Papa was reluctant about the match—and she could admit to herself now that she had avoided addressing it directly the night before because she did not want to hear his hesitation—but to forbid them from seeing each other was beyond the pale. It was stupid. It was cruel.

"I have to go, Caroline." Eddie caught her from barging towards the study. "I have to leave now before he calls a footman to throw me out."

"But I can fix this. I should have spoken to him first. I should have made things clear."

He held her as if she were a sheep trying to escape its fence, in a grip so strong that Caroline didn't recognize it. She could not break free of his hands just above her elbows. She stared at him, at that face she had known for all her life. Dark eyes, sweet lips, the only version of handsome she had ever cared for.

Panic set in. Could Papa really expect them to part now?

"I am going to fix this," she vowed.

Eddie's lips twitched into a small, sad smile. "There's no changing his mind."

"Go, if you have to." She knew he thought he had to. "I'll see you in a day or two, once I've set Papa straight."

His hands loosened and fell down to rest against her palms. "I'm going to come up with a plan, Caroline. I'm going to find a way for us to be together. But if it doesn't work—if something happens to me—I want you to be happy."

"I told you, I'll see you in a day or two. Before that, even. All I need to do is talk to him. I shall fix it."

"And if you don't, I want you to be happy."

"In half a year I'll be of age, and then Papa won't be able to stop us."

Eddie leaned forward. Caroline thought he was going to kiss her, but he only rested his forehead against hers. It lasted a mere second; she felt it for eternity. "No matter what, be happy."

Then, before she could even breathe, he let her go.

Chapter Seven

C AROLINE MARCHED INTO PAPA'S study without knocking. He couldn't possibly be expecting peace, anyhow, not if he had really said those things to Eddie. Caroline couldn't imagine a world in which Papa thought she would accept his edict without a fight.

He stood by the window, looking down at the street. Almost as if he were watching to make sure Eddie really had left.

"He's gone." Caroline shut the study door but didn't bother trying to keep her voice quiet. "He did not want to disobey your orders."

"They were not orders." Papa turned and held out a hand to her. "Caro, I know this makes you unhappy."

She did not move an inch closer to him. "I did not think I needed to make myself clear, but apparently I do. I want to marry Eddie. He is the only man I will ever want to marry. I intend to marry him, and all I need is your permission."

So much energy rattled through her body that she could have kept going—could have spewed a thousand more arguments. She bit off her words to wait for her father's reaction.

Papa didn't move a muscle. "I cannot give it. I know you love Eddie now, Caroline, but you are young. You have not even had a Season. You do not know yet what life can be like."

"If I do a Season, then? If I wait until Eddie goes to Lower Canada and back? Is that when you would give us your permission?"

"Caroline..." On an exhale, Papa moved to lean against his desk, as if she were the most wearisome creature ever to curse him. "At Northfield Hall, our lives might not feel so different, but the truth is that Eddie is a tradesman. If you were to marry him, you would be a tradesman's wife. You would live in cramped quarters. You would worry about money. You most likely wouldn't be able to afford servants—maybe a maid of all work, at most—which means you would spend your days cooking and cleaning. Your life would have room for nothing beyond *surviving*. How can I wish that for you?"

"We would live at Northfield Hall, in one of the cottages. We would live the same kind of life as Mr. and Mrs. Chow and Spencer and Harriet and everyone else."

"That is not the life I want for you."

"Why not?"

"How could you be happy like that?"

Caroline was almost sure she must have misheard her father. Her whole life, he had raised her to know that everyone at Northfield Hall shared the same human condition. "Are the Chows not happy?

Are the laborers living at Northfield Hall not happy? Then why could I not, too, be happy?"

"Of course they are happy. They are in their natural class." The words—words that Caroline had read in his writing for years as part of his persuasive arguments for empowering laborers—twisted in the air as they leapt from his tongue. "Eddie was born into a family that has always been in service; they know how to be happy with that life. You were born into a family that has always had the luxury of improving our minds and our hearts. If you were to give all that up—if your life were to become a litany of chores and worries—you could not be happy."

"My life would be days with Eddie and with whatever children we were blessed with. That would make me happy."

Papa shook his head. Anger edged into his voice. "I'm sorry, Caroline, but my answer is no, and you will not change my mind on this."

She enlisted every debating skill he had ever taught her. "Is slavery not evil and worthy of ending, even though there are some who call it a *natural* product of human behavior?"

"That is neither here nor there—"

"Is the Irishman not equal to the Briton, even though there are some who call them our *natural* inferiors?"

Papa replied calmly, "Just because other men use the word *natural* improperly does not mean I cannot use it in its correct context."

"No, instead you join those men in hiding behind the 'natural order' of things to justify your..." The trouble was, Caroline didn't know what exactly was making Papa so unreasonable. Was it really a blanket judgment he cast upon the entire laboring class? "Your prejudices. Are you not the man who has spent his life empowering laborers? How can you not see that permitting me and Eddie to marry is the most *natural* thing in the world?"

"I empower laborers economically, as well I should. I do not empower them to threaten the happiness of my family."

Desperation seared through Caroline. Desperation—and horror. "I cannot believe this is truly how you feel. What would Mama say, if she heard you speaking now?"

Caroline had never used Mama's death as an excuse for her bad behavior, nor had she held the specter of her mother over Papa's head before to win an argument.

Even now, she wasn't asking the question to try to change his mind.

She was asking the question because nothing Papa said made any sense to her.

He drew into himself, like a penknife folding shut. "I have discussed this at length with your Aunt Charlotte as well as Mr. and Mrs. Chow. We are all in agreement. You and Eddie do not have our permission. You will never have our blessing."

Caroline felt sick all over. It was one thing for Papa to object—that was bad enough, even though Caroline had suspected it.

It was another thing entirely for Mr. and Mrs. Chow to deny the match. Especially Mrs. Chow, who had always been so kind to Caroline, who had felt almost like a second mother.

Caroline's heart pounded. "I'll tell all of London I've been ruined. No respectable man will get within ten feet of me."

"Be reasonable, Caroline. I am not requiring you to marry *anyone*. I am offering you the society of London as you have always dreamed. I am setting you up for a future that you can determine by your own talents. I'm trying to do right by you, Caro."

As if any of that mattered when he obstructed the one thing she wanted most. "You can't stand in my way, Papa. I love Eddie, don't you understand that? Just like Mama loved you, against *her* father's wishes. I'll marry him no matter what."

As sharp as a sword, Papa snapped, "Do not compare yourself to your mother. This is nothing like that. I offered her a future that was worthy of her."

"It is *exactly* like that, only it is worse, because Mama's father never stopped you from marrying her, but you are sending Eddie away. To a colony, of all places! Tell me, Papa, if my mother were here to see what you are doing, would she call you a hypocrite or a monster? Because it seems to me that shipping Eddie away from all his friends and family to be a stranger in a colony is the most monstrous thing I've ever heard."

Papa grew redder and redder in the face as Caroline spewed her vitriol until finally he cut her off: "Do not say such ugly things!"

He stalked to the window, his shoulders heaving a little, but Caroline could hardly see him for the fury filling every inch of her.

"You may be angry with me, Caroline, but you may not disrespect me."

"Or what? You shall turn me onto the street, where I will meet an even worse fate than becoming a tradesman's wife?"

Whirling around, he advanced towards her with such ferocity that for a moment, Caroline thought Papa—her gentle, kind father—was going to strike her. Yet he passed her entirely, barging all the way to the study door, which he yanked open. "You shall remove yourself to your quarters, where you shall remain quietly until we both have a chance to calm down and apologize to each other."

"Unless your apology includes your permission to marry Eddie, I shall never apologize and I shall never calm down."

Caroline did obey him, though, and carried herself from the room with the best posture she could muster. Perhaps he didn't believe her. Perhaps he thought she was arguing because she was used to getting her way.

Perhaps he didn't understand that Caroline would choose Eddie over him.

Caroline didn't know why her father was suddenly this unrecognizable man. She only knew that there was no point in fighting with him anymore.

It was time to come up with another plan.

Chapter Eight

E DDIE WAS NOT USUALLY the one to make the plan.

The plans for his life had always been organized by his parents—with heavy assistance from Lord Preston.

The plans for his days—the ones free to him, anyhow—had been organized by Caroline. Eddie was the one who played along, not the one who suggested jumping on the *Jolly Molly* or raiding the kitchen for sweet honey cakes.

His plan now left many details undecided. Where he would go, once he saved up enough money. How he would get in touch with Caroline, when he was ready. How they would earn forgiveness from their families, once they ran away.

He wasn't even entirely sure that Caroline would run away with him, if and when he was ready. He didn't doubt her kiss, nor her determination that day on the stairs that she wanted to marry him, but after her father explained to her about the reality of being a tradesman's wife? After he forced her to contemplate living without money or servants? After Aunt Charlotte pulled out all the gowns Caroline couldn't wear and left her with only a basic wardrobe, on account of not going to any parties or balls while they eked out an existence as glazier and wife?

By the time Eddie got to Caroline, he wouldn't be surprised if she had changed her mind.

In the meantime, he clung to the only part of the plan he could formulate: to earn as much money as possible, as fast as he could.

He took any odd job available: fixing the window frames of Oliver's neighbor's house, running errands for the corner pub, even walking down to Gray's Inn Lane to see if the Trowbridges could use an extra hand.

It was lunchtime on the third day that his parents came to call. Spencer had already returned to his family at Northfield Hall, but their parents planned to remain in London until Lord Preston departed for Christmas.

Eddie gave up a job cleaning windows at an assembly hall in order to have luncheon with them, steeling himself to announce that he would not be joining the regiment at all.

Mother brought a hamper full of food: whitefish, steamed oysters, and vegetable soup with clear noodles. She came with her own tablecloth, too, which she spread out across the cherry wood table in Samantha and Oliver's common room. Eddie watched her smooth its corners; everything Mother did was so precise, as if she had practiced it a hundred times just to perform it this very minute.

Eddie used to think he would feel that confident at something one day. First, he assumed it would be carpentry, later he figured on glazing.

Now, he realized confidence didn't come from practice. It came from some deeper well, some inner resource he didn't have.

He would imitate it today, anyhow, in order to make his announcement.

Oliver filled the room with chatter as they settled around the meal. He was so much more familiar with their parents than Eddie was; even as he told them stories about his London shop, he linked it back to this anecdote or that from the carpentry workshop at Northfield Hall. As Mother set out the soup, he laughed, "Remember when you tried to make this with leaves from the oak tree, and Spencer ended up retching for three days?"

Eddie didn't have memories like that with his family. He had vague recollections, like tableaux on a stage, from before he was sent away, but nothing adult. Nothing he could use to ease the awkwardness of the room.

"The next time we see you," Father said to Eddie as they finished eating, "you will be so rich from your work in Lower Canada that you will own a house yourself."

Eddie wasn't ready yet to make his announcement. He found some other way to reply. "Why should I want a house?"

"What else would you do with your wealth?"

Mother added, "You will want a house for a family. When you are ready for a family."

The oysters turned sour in his stomach.

"A job like that will set you up for a family," Father said. "You will make good connections. You will be able to come back and set up your own shop, and then you will want a wife to help run it, and children will follow."

"*Sometimes*, children follow." This from Samantha—with an edge to her voice—because of course, she and Oliver had been married three years already and there was no sign of a child.

"Either way, you will want to live in your own lodgings."

Eddie wished his parents would address the issue directly instead of talking around it like this. They were staying at the townhouse; they would have heard in a matter of hours all about how Eddie had been ejected from the presence of the Preston family.

It was bad enough that it had happened. Eddie didn't want to participate in a charade about some false future just to reassure them that he was not heartbroken.

He *was* heartbroken, whether they wanted him to be or not.

"I don't think I shall get married."

"Even Spencer got married," Mother retorted. As if with a little cajoling, she could persuade him to forget Caroline the same as she could convince him to have another helping of fish.

"Spencer was allowed to marry the woman he loves."

Oliver's hand landed on Samantha's. Eddie didn't look up from the table to see the expressions on his parents' faces.

He had seen their dismay before, every time he had argued against leaving for his apprenticeships.

He would see even more dismay soon, when he told them he was not taking Lord Preston's position.

Mother wiped her fingertips clean. "You should have known better than to ask. We told you a long time ago not to set your cap at Miss Caroline."

"Enough," Father said, as if they had actually gotten into an argument. He set a gentle hand on Eddie's shoulder. "A man can love more than one woman in his life. Most do. You will find someone else when you are ready."

"It isn't easy to be in the trades," Samantha said. "It would be hard for Miss Caroline. It's hard for me sometimes, and I grew up in this life."

Oliver didn't say anything at all.

If this was their idea of comfort, Eddie didn't want it. He mustered all his willpower to remain at the table instead of calling for Linnie and running off.

"I don't think I am going to take the position with the regiment." Even now, with the decision already behind him, Eddie could not bring himself to say it outright. He forced himself to rephrase it: "I am not going to go to Lower Canada."

"You won't find a better job on your own," Father exclaimed.

"Where will you go?" asked Mother in the same breath. "Not Northfield Hall."

"No. Not Northfield Hall. I know there is no home for me at Northfield Hall." How he had come to deserve that, Eddie wasn't sure. He hadn't so much as kissed Caroline before he was packed off to Reading. "I haven't decided yet. I'll stay in London until I have saved enough money to establish myself somewhere in the countryside." Then, buoyed by being honest at last, he expressed an idea that crossed his mind that very moment: "Perhaps I'll board an East Indiaman and see if I can find Martin in China."

Mother went white. Eddie's eldest brother, Martin, had left England for China nearly ten years ago, and they hadn't had so much as a letter from him since.

If his parents ever discussed their concern for him, Eddie hadn't heard them.

Father's reassuring hand landed on Mother now. "Don't be cruel."

"I'm not being cruel. If Martin can go there, why can't I?"

Oliver replied in Cantonese, with a speed and vocabulary Eddie didn't quite have. He understood the gist of the barb, though: *Because you hardly even speak the language.*

It didn't matter. Eddie wouldn't go to China if he could run away with Caroline. And if she didn't want to marry him after all, then Eddie would go anywhere, whether he spoke the language or not. If he could guarantee he would never accidentally see Caroline Preston happily married to someone else—then he could figure out the language and the money and the work.

"There is no reason to rush," Samantha interjected. "You can stay here as you decide what you want to do next."

His parents still objected. Oliver still stared at him, concern and anger mixing in his eyes.

Eddie didn't need time. From now on, whether he eloped with Caroline or not, he was going to live on his own terms and no one else's.

T HE EVENING CAROLINE SAID goodbye to Eddie, Papa had her things moved to a bedroom in Aunt Charlotte's Hanover Square house instead of apologizing. "I understand you do not want to see me right now," he explained, as if their brutal argument were just a family spat.

When Caroline begged off from the next day's engagements on account of a headache, Aunt Charlotte introduced her to two maids—Webb and Fielder—who were both middle-aged and wore buns so severe that their foreheads lifted. As Caroline moved through her aunt's cavernous rooms, one of the maids followed, so that she could not so much as use the privy without a neighbor.

The next day, when Caroline cried off with the excuse of terrible cramps, she discovered that if she wanted to take a walk around Hanover Square, a footman in Aunt Charlotte's green livery stayed within twenty paces of her at all times. When she turned towards Bond Street, two more materialized, so she was flanked by three men and two maids.

She returned to her rooms in a barely suppressed fury. Climbing into the silk-and-feather bed, she ordered Webb to bring her the previous week's paper, and she tore through its ironed folds until she found Papa's article. The one she had helped write. The one about the nobility of the laboring classes.

For thirty years, I have hosted a grand experiment at my home, one that has been much discussed, and I wish now to share its results with those members of society who are motivated to make reforms to bolster our agricultural laborers. I have seen for myself how, once the labels of religion, nationality, and even crime are lifted, the heart of one man is much the same as another. I have watched education bring higher levels of thinking and living to child and adult alike. I have reaped the profits thereof with a happy laboring class that produces more from my land than any of my forefathers ever achieved.

When Caroline had approved this paragraph for publication, she had thought Papa meant it with the best intention. His point, she had believed, was to advocate for removing the label of class, too.

Now all she saw was how he excluded it. How, throughout the article, while he advocated for laborers to be given more economic support and even more political rights, he never stated the obvious: that class was just another division erected by those with power.

Without the laborers, we cannot thrive, and so we owe it to ourselves as much as we owe it to them to provide proper care.

"We." Caroline had assumed that pronoun included everyone, the same as she trusted his definition of "man" included her.

She realized now that Papa's "we" was exclusive. It included only select people and excluded everyone else—most especially Eddie.

Rereading the article only made Papa's decree feel more real. It made Aunt Charlotte's confinement feel more damning. Caroline hadn't been sent away because she was being obstinate; she had been locked up because Papa really feared a marriage between her and Eddie.

She crumpled the newspaper in her hands. But when she went to throw it in the fire, Webb intervened. "That is Lady Pemberly's paper," she admonished, and retrieved it from Caroline with equal parts care and censure.

Aunt Charlotte commanded her presence at breakfast the following morning. A footman—different from the ones who had followed Caroline on her walk—served her a plate of eggs, toast, cake, sausage, and bacon, none of which she wanted.

"There are facts you must face," Aunt Charlotte intoned. "Your father has forbidden the match you prefer. You are a baron's daughter. You must set your sights at least as high as a second son, no matter how much tenderness you might feel for young Eddie. And, in the meantime, you must eat."

It was not that Caroline had been making a conscious effort *not* to eat. The food at Partridge House was too rich: it was all sugared and fried in butter and seasoned with spices she was unaccustomed to. And besides, she was too angry to have an appetite.

"I disagree with the premise of your argument. Just because I am a baron's daughter does not mean I *must* set my sights in any direction whatsoever."

With a great sigh, Aunt Charlotte made a long pour of tea from her gilded china pot. "I understand young love, Caroline, I really do. Each and every one of us has lost our heart to some person or another. Most of us have also had to say goodbye to that person instead of joining our lives with theirs. I understand how you feel, yet now you must understand that you are part of a long tradition of broken hearts that eventually heal."

Caroline's heart wasn't broken—at least, not by Eddie. She knew she had his love, and he had hers, and somehow, they would find their way to each other.

No, if there was any heartbreak simmering beneath her fury, it was from Papa.

And she couldn't imagine that Aunt Charlotte would understand that at all.

"Your father has entrusted me with the rest of your stay here in London. I do not expect you to find a new love these next few months. However, I do expect you to act in a way that makes me proud. You shall present yourself promptly looking like an attractive young lady whenever I arrange an engagement for you, you shall be pleasant and charming to my friends, and you shall make every effort to find the good in your situation instead of dwelling on the bad."

Caroline stared at the food in front of her. "And if I fail to behave in such a way?"

"You won't be sent back to Northfield Hall, if that's what you're angling for. Perhaps your father will banish you to Benny's estate in Ireland. I leave the consequences to him." Aunt Charlotte took a prim sip of tea. "However, if you should impress me with your behavior—if you prove to me that I can trust you—then I shall no longer worry you need the services of both Webb and Fielder."

"You lock me up like a prisoner when I have done nothing wrong. I have been unwell."

"Headaches and cramps—after running off with Eddie at the Tower and making a disgrace of yourself in front of Mr. Popham? Do not think me a fool, Caroline. I was young once, too."

Caroline could make no reply to that.

"This afternoon, I am at home to callers, and you shall join me in the parlor unless a physician declares you too ill. From there, we shall resume our schedule as previously planned."

The truth was that after three days of stewing, Caroline agreed with her aunt that enough was enough. She needed to put aside all her fury and instead come up with a plan—one she could enact before Eddie sailed. Taking an obedient sip of tea, she asked as innocently as possible, "If I behave myself, would you permit me to take a walk with only a maid and not also an entourage of footmen?"

Aunt Charlotte's lips twitched in a hint of a smile. "We can discuss it when your behavior proves to me you are making the best of this situation."

And so, eight days after saying goodbye to Eddie, Caroline found herself touring the hothouse of Lord Haldimand. They were with

Mrs. and the elder Miss Spurrier again, although this time the gentlemen accompanying them were an earl, his brother, and his cousin. Caroline walked with the cousin through the aisles of orange trees, listening to his stories of traveling to Brazil to try to bring back a particular type of flower.

"The plants in the wild there are beyond your imagination, Miss Preston," he explained. "My heart raced just from the sight of them. It is my dream to open an exhibition for all of England to see. And their perfumes!" Blushing, he said, "A woman wearing the sweet smell of those flowers would be absolutely irresistible."

Caroline understood that he was flirting with her. He seemed a nice enough fellow, and he was objectively handsome, with sandy hair that fell expressively across his brow and muddy eyes peering earnestly through fans of blond lashes.

His brown eyes only reminded her of Eddie, whose irises were darker and so eternally endless.

She was hoping that if at the end of this week Aunt Charlotte was still happy with her behavior, she could rid herself of the footmen. Then—and Caroline wasn't exactly sure how yet—she would have a chance of getting a message to Eddie, if not visiting him herself.

"Do you have a favorite perfume?" the earl's cousin asked Caroline, the blush still staining his face pink.

"I don't make a habit of wearing it. I sneeze at everything, you see." She felt a little bad for taking this man's attention when she had no designs on it.

Then, behind him, she spotted a dark mass. It was on the other side of the glass ceiling, suspended above the ground. For a moment, Caroline's brain couldn't process it; an instant later, she realized she was looking at a person, cleaning the outside of the hothouse.

And an instant after that, she recognized Eddie.

He saw her at the same time. Their eyes connected through the glass—and even though he was yards above her, Caroline could see the anguish in his.

Her heart reacted instinctively by galloping away. Half of her consciousness was already running towards Eddie to call him down from his post and pull him into her arms. She would kiss him—no, she would ask him why he was working at the hothouse of all places—no, she would tell him she had a plan—she didn't know what she would do, other than cling to him and make everything right again.

The other half of her remained very still in place beside the earl's cousin.

If she ran to Eddie now, in plain sight of Aunt Charlotte, it would make all her good behavior worth nothing. She might steal an embrace with him. Perhaps even a conversation.

But then she would be locked into Partridge House for even longer. Instead of freeing herself from the footmen, she would be flanked by a whole army.

Caroline had only a breath to choose between instinct and reason. She lifted her chin and twitched her lips into something that was not quite a smile, but that she hoped Eddie would recognize as one.

Then, tearing her heart in two, she returned her gaze to the earl's cousin and made a polite reply to his inquiry about her allergies.

Chapter Nine

EDDIE ALMOST FELL OFF the narrow wooden platform between him and the ten-foot drop to the ground.

He wasn't sure which was more shocking: spotting Caroline at the odd job he had agreed to just that morning, or spotting Caroline walking with a toff in a silk waistcoat.

For a moment, she looked straight at Eddie. He thought she would smile; he waited, forgetting to breathe, to watch the sun come out from behind the clouds again.

But she looked away. Almost as if she hadn't seen him at all.

Eddie placed a sweaty palm on the hothouse to brace himself, never mind that he had just cleaned that section of the glass.

If Caroline wasn't smiling at him, it wasn't because she suddenly hated him—nor that she hadn't seen him. Even if she had decided she didn't want to marry him, she wouldn't suddenly ignore him.

The only reason she would pretend not to see him was if their parents had conspired so that now Eddie's love was being used to punish her.

Damn Lord Preston, and damn Mother and Father, too.

No matter that they had practical reasons to say no.

No matter that Eddie himself didn't know if Caroline could be satisfied living in a tradesman's home on a tradesman's budget.

Everyone else at Northfield Hall was given to believe that they deserved to be happy in life. And now, when Caroline and Eddie declared what would make them happy, the very people who should celebrate with them made them feel as if they should be ashamed.

"Damn all of that to the devil," Eddie whispered to himself—and earned a wonderful jolt of freedom as he did.

Beneath him, Caroline meandered onward with the toff. He saw now that they were not alone: ahead of them, Miss Spurrier walked with two other gentlemen, and behind them strolled Aunt Charlotte and Mrs. Spurrier. Trailing Aunt Charlotte, Eddie spied the snooty footman who had fetched him to the carriage on the day they visited the Tower, along with another man in matching livery.

Eddie returned his attention to Caroline—remembering, as he did, to continue cleaning the glass. Her gown was a beautiful yellow, which would make her golden hair all the sunnier and her brown eyes all the doe-ier. She wore a large bonnet that was overly decorated with lace. Jewels sparkled on her wrist as she moved it to point at a plant.

She didn't look much like herself. Eddie's heart tugged towards her anyway. He found himself stilling again, staring, as if one glance from her would soothe the ache in his body.

He knew she wouldn't look again. If she couldn't even smile at him at first glance, she wouldn't allow herself to turn back to him. Eddie shouldn't want her to put herself in jeopardy. He should let her be, as Lord Preston had ordered him, until he had saved up money to pay room and board for the both of them.

Except Caroline couldn't free herself from her father as easily as Eddie could. While he took these odd jobs to save up money, she was at the mercy of Lord Preston and his plans—which, it seemed, had far more to do with finding her a proper husband than permitting her to do as she pleased.

If Eddie waited until he could afford to support Caroline, she might end up forced into marriage to someone else. Or sent away on a tour of the Continent. Or locked away in some country house where he never could find her again.

The moment he formed the fear, her head turned his way, almost as if she heard him. She had walked far enough ahead that she had to twist her shoulder back a little, like a ballet dancer, to raise her eyes to him. A big enough gesture that Aunt Charlotte might catch on.

A big enough gesture for Eddie to feel it in his heart. Even though she didn't smile. Even though she was too far away for him to tell if she blinked a special message.

It was big enough for Eddie to make a change to his plans.

IT WAS A STRANGE sensation to have Eddie hovering above her for all the rest of the tour. One part of Caroline felt safe, as if he had reached out and taken her hand, to know that they could see each other for these passing minutes.

The other part of her felt on display. She could hardly reply to the poor earl's cousin because she was so distracted by worrying what Eddie would think if she tilted her head a certain way, or how he might take it if she reached up to pick an orange from the tree.

She wanted desperately to pass along a secret message to him, yet she didn't have anything to say, much less a code of flowers and arm gestures to communicate it, so she feared Eddie was reading the wrong thing into her every movement.

The tour lasted another quarter hour. They ended where they began, near Lord Haldimand's collection of blooming hibiscus shrubs. The flowers were beautiful: pink and violet and orange petals with long yellow noses stretching out from their centers. The earl's cousin pulled an extended branch outward for Caroline to smell. "I mean to make this a perfume that every lady in London will wear."

On the other side of the glass—only a few yards away—Eddie jumped from his platform to the ground. To keep Aunt Charlotte from noticing him, Caroline bent her head obligingly to the hibiscus and conjured up one of the legendary Preston sneezes.

Actually, they were Turner sneezes, since Caroline came by hers through Mama. She had once witnessed one from Aunt Charlotte: a terrible racking of the body, accompanied by something of a shriek as the sneeze traveled through the vocal cords to the nasal cavity and finally ejected all offending particles in a great ooze of mucus.

Caroline caught most of the sneeze in her gloved palm. The earl's cousin still took a gigantic step backward from her. "Are you ill?"

"As I said"—Caroline rummaged for a handkerchief to wipe her nose—"I am allergic to every flower I have ever met."

It was all she could do not to look out the glass wall again to see if Eddie had disappeared. She wanted him to be gone so that no one would recognize him, but at the same time, she could hardly breathe at the idea that she had stolen her last glimpse of him.

Aunt Charlotte bustled forward and looped an arm through Caroline's. "Oh dear, not those pesky allergies again. Come along, let us find a retiring room where you may collect yourself."

Caroline forced herself not to glance backward in search of Eddie. At least she knew where she might find him, when she did rid herself of Aunt Charlotte's footmen.

Aunt Charlotte hurried Caroline down the pea gravel path back towards Lord Haldimand's main house. It, too, was lined with flowers—rose bushes, this time, and despite the December chill there were still pink buds on a few of them—so that Caroline had to hold her breath or else sneeze again. Behind them, the footmen clipped along as guards, while she heard Mrs. and Miss Spurrier laughing with the earl and his guests still in the hothouse.

She and Aunt Charlotte were halfway to the main house when Linnie came shooting out from the rose bushes. She launched at Caroline with a fierce growl and locked her little jaw on the hem of Caroline's yellow wool skirt.

Aunt Charlotte screamed in horror.

Caroline let out a shriek, too, even though she recognized Linnie almost immediately. She playacted at pulling her skirts, crying, "Shoo! Shoo!"

Then, before the footmen could come kick Linnie, she crouched and grabbed the dog by the collar. A fat piece of paper was tucked between it and Linnie's fur; Caroline slipped the note into her bodice in the commotion of freeing her hem from Linnie's mouth. "There's a good dog," she said, turning Linnie by the collar and pointing her back towards the bushes. "Off with you, you little terror."

"Whose dog is that?" Aunt Charlotte blustered, one hand on a footman's shoulder as if she was so startled she couldn't even stand on her own. "Whoever let it run around like that should be arrested."

"I think it was a stray," Caroline said, for she didn't want Lord Haldimand to start an investigation among his household. "Got in chasing rats, probably."

"It has no business attacking innocent young ladies like that!"

Caroline had no choice except to agree. She took her aunt's arm and ushered her along the path again. "Let us sit down for a cup of tea inside to calm down."

The rest of their party was coming, too, a huddle of concern and alarm. Caroline looked back once, to see if Linnie had made it back to Eddie safely: she spotted them in the shadows of a tree by the garden wall. Eddie tipped his hat to her. Then, while the commotion was still alive and well, he slipped away.

Caroline dedicated her concentration to playing along with the group. She pretended her heart thumped because she was afraid. She imitated their outrage and agreed that dogs were worse than mice. She even accepted a cup of Chinese tea, since no one remembered that her family did not imbibe imports.

All the while, Eddie's note sat like a hot ember between her bodice and her breast.

At last, she slipped away to the privy. Aunt Charlotte asked a maid to accompany her—"so poor Caro doesn't lose her way in this large house"—but inside the room, Caroline was alone with the chamber pot. Hands shaking, she pulled the note free and held it up to the candle:

Come to Scotland with me?

Caroline grinned.

Only one thing ever happened in Scotland.

Chapter Ten

ENACTING A PLAN WAS as heady as a rich pint of ale. Eddie returned to Oliver's with a buzz of hope in his veins. Samantha asked, "What put you in such a good mood?" and Eddie realized it was because for once—for the first time in his life—he felt as if he held his future firmly in his own two hands.

"I'll be leaving soon," he replied to Samantha.

"Did you decide where you're going, then?"

"I'll write to you once I get there."

Oliver, returning from the shop, started pestering Eddie with questions, but Eddie found ways not to answer. He didn't technically have a reply from Caroline; he certainly wasn't going to ruin everything by confiding in Oliver.

Instead, Eddie focused on executing the newest portion of his plan. He counted the money stuffed in his spare set of stockings: fifteen shillings, five pence. If he were traveling alone, it would probably cover the cost of a seat on a stagecoach and a couple of nights at inns. With Caroline, it might only get them halfway through England.

No matter. They would sort out money once they were together.

Eddie packed his satchel. He didn't have much—an extra suit of clothes, his set of tools, a winter cloak, and a brush for Linnie—but the pack was soon so full it threatened to overspill.

He hoped Caroline didn't have too many bags.

The buzz of his plan kept his spirits high. However much luggage Caroline wanted to bring and whatever kind of travel she wanted to do would sort itself out. Once they were together.

He supped with Oliver and Samantha—a simple stew and bread—and then waited a little longer, until a distant church chimed ten and the streets of Covent Garden were starting to hum with late-night activity.

Then, hugging Oliver, Eddie got on his way.

He knew from his parents that Caroline had been sent to stay with Aunt Charlotte, and he knew from Caroline's stories that Aunt Charlotte lived in one of the fancy buildings of Mayfair called Partridge House. It took only a penny to a street urchin to find out where that was, and then Eddie found himself in front of a great white marble façade with more windows than he cared to count.

He couldn't knock at the door and ask for Caroline, nor could he bribe one of the servants into delivering a message. He had no earthly idea how to tell her he was there. And yet, Eddie still felt afloat on a river of hope. This was Caroline.

Somehow, he would find her.

Eddie turned down the lane that led to Partridge House's stables, then took the alleyway off that snaking towards the great house's outer buildings. Linnie followed along at his heels, her nose alert in the air. When they reached a wrought-iron gate—locked, to keep riffraff like him from slipping into the kitchen garden—she let out a low, frustrated growl.

Which gave Eddie the idea. He didn't know which window was Caroline's, and he didn't have the aim to throw stones at it anyhow. If Linnie barked, however, Caroline just might hear it.

And since Caroline had gotten his note, Eddie trusted she was waiting for a signal from him, wherever she was in the house.

Withdrawing from his pack the extra slice of bread he had brought, Eddie tore off a piece, squashed it into a ball, and tossed it through to the ground on the other side of the gate. Then, he gave Linnie a nudge. "Go get it, girl!"

She didn't need any further encouragement. Collapsing to her belly, she wriggled under the lowest bar of the gate and chased after the bread. Then, turning back to Eddie, she let out a happy bark.

"More!" Eddie had trained her to get quiet when he said *hush*, but he had never before anticipated a case when he would want her to bark. He remained where he was, unresponsive, until she started barking faster and louder.

Somewhere nearby, a door opened, and a coarse voice called out, "Oi, who goes there?"

Farther away, on the second story of Partridge House, a white curtain moved across a window.

"Come here, Linnie," Eddie hissed, offering more bread, and the dog slid under the gate again before the servants could find her. Eddie led her down the alleyway a bit to wait in the shadows.

Too soon, someone stomped from the house to the gate. A man in livery hesitated at the gate, holding a lantern high, and peered into the alley. Holding tight to Linnie's collar, Eddie shrank back so that they wouldn't be caught in the radius of light. He could only pray that Linnie remained quiet, because if he dared whisper *hush*, they would be caught.

Finally—after an eternity—the footman turned away. "Just a passing mutt," he called to someone in the house.

Eddie let out a breath. Now he had only to wait for Caroline to find them.

He hoped that had been her behind the curtains.

He hoped she knew where to look for him.

He hoped she was able to slip away. If she didn't come find him, Eddie wasn't sure what to do next.

But if there was one thing Eddie and Caroline excelled at, it was coming up with harebrained schemes like this. And so, even though his heart raced wildly with anticipation, Eddie wasn't surprised when someone finally approached the gate without a light, slipped it open, and entered the alleyway.

"There you are," she said, and Eddie felt drunker than he had ever been on ale or gin combined.

"Here I am," he replied, and he pulled her into his arms.

CAROLINE HADN'T KNOWN SHE desperately wanted to be ravished in the shadows of an alleyway until that moment, when Eddie grabbed hold of her elbows and yanked her into his body.

Their lips met before they could share any further words. Caroline knew it was Eddie not because she could see or hear him but because her heartbeat recognized his. Her skin knew his touch. Her mouth knew his taste.

She devoted herself to the kiss. She was hungry, desperate, and shameless in trying to keep his lips on hers for the rest of eternity. If they parted—even to take a breath—Caroline thought her heart would break. She growled, like Linnie, when he withdrew a little, and fastened him in place with two firm hands on either side of his neck.

He responded by turning them around and pinning her against the alley wall. All down her back, Caroline felt cold, hard stone; the rest of her body felt nothing but the fiery heat of Eddie. She wrapped an ankle around his calf, which lifted her hips enough that they collided against his. His long, hard rod edged against her eagerly sensitive area—and she let out a moan of excitement.

"You can take me right here," she said, forgetting that she wanted their mouths never to part because now his lips had moved to the sensitive line of her neck and her mind was spinning towards the heavens. "I'm yours."

"You have always been mine." He was the one growling this time, his words hardly forming properly because of the desire drowning them.

Caroline bucked her hips against his. "Always have been. Always will be."

His hands gripped her waist. Caroline's heart sped up. She didn't actually know the precise physics of the act, but she knew prostitutes could be had on the streets and so she assumed Eddie could take her against the alley wall if he wanted to.

And she wanted him to. Her body demanded he resolve the need building in her like steam in a teapot. Even more, Caroline wanted to prove to Eddie how much she loved him. She needed to erase whatever Papa had said to him and replace it with all the conviction in her heart that Eddie was the man she wanted to spend her life with.

Bracing against the alley wall, Caroline hooked her other ankle around his thigh, so that her whole body was suspended in the air. Eddie's palms caught her rear end, quilted by her traveling cloak, and now his rod lined up almost directly with her slit, barred only by their clothes.

"I'm yours." She could do no more than hiss this into his ear. Every other ounce of her energy was directed towards her desperate sexual organs.

Linnie let out a sharp bark—and just like that, Eddie dropped Caroline.

Drop was an exaggeration. His hands remained on her body long enough to make sure her feet landed on the ground. But his lips removed from her neck instantaneously, and as soon as she was standing on her own, he rushed to the other side of the alley entirely.

Linnie trotted to his heels, barking once more, and he crouched to pet her head. "No one is coming, then? You disapproved, is that all?"

Jealous of a dog—again. Caroline adjusted her clothes to get herself out of such a state of mind. Someone *could* have caught them, so it was better for everyone that Linnie had put a stop to things.

Still, she wished Eddie hadn't rushed away from her quite so quickly.

"I suppose we should get on our way." She noticed for the first time that he wore an overstuffed pack on his back. For her part, Caroline had tied a spare petticoat, a simple day gown, a hairbrush, and a few necessities into a bedsheet—the only makeshift bag she could filch under the watchful eyes of Webb and Fielder. In the pockets of her travel cloak, she had additionally stowed a small sewing kit, an amber necklace, and several handkerchiefs. "I don't have money," she confessed. "Aunt Charlotte said a young lady doesn't need any, and she had my maids search my things and locked it all in a safe box in her bedroom. She said she would give it back when Papa took me home."

Just saying it made Caroline feel helpless—and angry.

She had never thought her own family would reduce her to such a damsel in distress.

"We will sort it out." Eddie reached out and took her bedsheet bag. "I have enough to buy us passage on a coach, I think."

"A stagecoach?" Caroline tried to swallow back her objections. She knew that was how most people traveled through England. It was just that she had heard such horror stories: people freezing to death on the top, or falling to their death off the top, or having all their possessions stolen and starving to death.

Perhaps it was because it was the dark of night with London fog pressing close to them, but suddenly, a stagecoach seemed equivalent with death.

"I'll make sure you have a comfortable seat," Eddie said, slipping his free palm into hers. He had to give a little tug to get her to start walking.

"I don't want to sit apart from you. Whatever seats we get, they should be together." Even if they had to travel in the bitter wind on a roof. "Is there a stagecoach that goes directly to Scotland?"

"I'm not sure."

"Where do we catch it?"

"I'm not sure yet. We'll have to ask around."

"Will they let Linnie come along?"

The dog growled a little at the mention of her name.

"They'll have to," Eddie replied.

As a plan, it left much to be desired. Caroline didn't like to criticize, but she also knew this wasn't Eddie's strength. Growing up, she was always the one to come up with the schemes—and it was *her* quick thinking that kept them out of trouble, for the most part.

Eddie was an excellent second-in-command, but when she let him do the planning, they ended up doing dangerous things like wandering the streets of London in the dead of night asking strangers to point them in the right direction.

She took a deep breath as she evaluated her options. She did not want to insult Eddie by scrapping his plan. However, she also wanted to survive the night and keep whatever money they did have. Perhaps he wasn't frightened because he had lived in London so long—but evidently, he didn't know it so well that he knew which coaching inn to go to.

And here they were, passing Aunt Charlotte's mews.

The solution presented itself so neatly that Caroline couldn't resist it.

"I have an idea," she said, squeezing Eddie's hand. "We don't need a stagecoach at all."

"We don't?"

That was the type of question best left unanswered. Caroline led him to the mews. They were dimly lit by a set of lanterns, and she supposed there were some stable boys sleeping somewhere in the loft as guards.

She would deal with them if and when she had to.

"What are we doing?" Eddie whispered, but again, that was a question best left unanswered. He lifted Linnie into his arms to keep her from agitating the horses.

First things first, Caroline headed to the carriage room. There were three: a large traveling coach, the brougham for transportation around the city, and a two-person cabriolet to show off in Hyde Park.

It being December, Aunt Charlotte wouldn't even miss the cabriolet if it were misplaced for a few weeks.

Caroline took the bags from Eddie and stored them in the gap between the driver's bench and the floor. Then she got to work preparing the cabriolet for travel. "Will you get one of the horses to hitch to this?"

Eddie stood immobile. "Monkey, that's theft."

"She is my aunt. We are borrowing her things as family members. We will return both the carriage and the horse."

"We don't have her permission." Now Eddie grabbed Caroline's hand, stilling it from readying the reins. "This isn't skipping our supper to keep playing the *Jolly Molly*. I would hang for this."

For a horrible moment, Caroline almost believed him. Papa was so resolute in preventing their marriage—he would even prefer Caroline ruined instead of married to Eddie!—that she couldn't guarantee that her family wouldn't persecute Eddie to his death.

But marriage was different from the death penalty. However he felt about Eddie as a prospective husband to Caroline, Papa remained a reformer who regularly made speeches against the harsh consequences faced by Britain's criminals.

If they were caught, Papa would persuade Aunt Charlotte not to pursue a case against them.

And he certainly wouldn't let Eddie hang when anyone who knew her would see that this idea was Caroline's alone.

"They would have to hang me alongside you." She pressed a kiss to his knuckles. "And Papa would never let that happen."

I T WAS A TERRIBLE idea. It was exactly the kind of idea Caroline *would* have. Only they weren't at Northfield Hall anymore; they weren't surrounded by friendly adults who would laugh it off as Miss Caroline being peculiar.

If and when someone at Partridge House caught them, Eddie would be arrested, and he didn't have an ounce of faith that Lord Preston would stand between him and the noose.

But Caroline clearly did not want to take a stagecoach. If Eddie said no to her now, would she realize how desperate their circumstances were and decide her father had the right of it after all?

He set Linnie in the cabriolet and went to find a horse for hitching.

Somehow, miraculously, Eddie managed to coax a black mare from her stall, down the stable corridor, and into the confines of the cabriolet without waking a groom. He even scraped open the stable door and led the horse and carriage into the courtyard without attracting attention.

But of course, their luck ran out before they made it out of the mews. As Eddie put one foot on the carriage wheel to climb onto the bench, a gruff voice called out, "Where do you think you're going?"

A man stepped out from the stables wearing a heavy cloak over nightclothes. He pointed a carriage rifle directly at Eddie's chest.

"Ah, Phipps, there you are," Caroline said, as calmly and as coolly as if she had sent the fellow to fetch something for her. "I thought the whole place was abandoned, it was that hard to find one of your stable boys."

The man lowered his rifle—ever so slightly, so that now it pointed only at Eddie's feet. "Is that you, Miss Preston?"

"Quite. Now, I wanted to consult with you as to the best vehicle to take, but I'm afraid I am in a dreadful rush and cannot delay. It's my sister, you see. She has been taken with a terrible illness. If I don't get there in the next day or so, I might not have a chance to say goodbye."

Eddie swallowed to bring saliva back to his mouth. His heart thumped in his ears, and he couldn't say whether it was because of the gun trained on him or Caroline's brutal, callous lie.

"Your sister?" Phipps at last let the gun fall, its muzzle now pointing harmlessly at the courtyard cobblestones. "I haven't heard anything of this."

"Well, you wouldn't have, would you? I just received notice myself not half an hour ago."

"And who is he?" The man jerked his head to indicate Eddie.

"Our family's man, sent to escort me to Montchampion Manor. My sister is Lady Meretta, you know. Now, please, Phipps, I think I have explained myself beyond what is necessary." Caroline managed to sound both bored and insulted—like a true lady.

Which only underscored how believable it was that Eddie was as insignificant to her as any other servant.

"Begging your pardon, Miss, only it is Lady Pemberly's cabriolet, you see. I had better check with her before I let you go off."

"You are suggesting that I am stealing my own aunt's carriage?"

Eddie couldn't take much more of this. His body was coiled so tight he thought he would be sick.

"Your aunt might prefer that I escort you myself in the traveling carriage," Phipps said carefully. "The cabriolet isn't suitable for a trip to Norwich."

"Fine." Caroline leaned back, loosening her hold on the reins. "Go ask her, then. But be quick about it. If I miss my sister's last breath because of this delay, I shall hold you responsible."

Now Eddie felt cold—even colder than he should in the chill December night. With a brief nod, Phipps rested the rifle against the stable wall and hustled into the alley leading to Partridge House.

"What are we going to do?" Eddie's voice squeaked even though he tried to keep it at a whisper.

"Get in." Caroline brushed a hand over Linnie's head, murmuring, "Good dog, staying so quiet," as Eddie climbed into the cabriolet. Then, Caroline asked, "Do you hear his footsteps?"

They listened for a moment, but the only sounds in the courtyard were the gentle noises of horses sleeping in their stalls.

"I should go," Eddie whispered. "If I'm still here when he speaks to your aunt..."

"She will keep it in the family. I promise you, Eddie, you will not be pulled in front of any magistrate."

"I'm not family."

"By the time we return from Scotland, you will be." Caroline gripped his hand. Her fingers were as strong as an iron vise. "We are in this together, Eddie. From now until forever. Wherever you go, I go."

The words were a promise and a threat, like a delicious soup that would scorch his tongue if he dared taste it.

Eddie tried to focus on the here and now. "Then we should go. We can still find a stagecoach. If we make a run for it..."

But by then, Caroline had already released his fingers and raised the whip to the horse. In the next instant, the cabriolet lurched forward, and they raced into the London night.

CHAPTER ELEVEN

IT PROVED VERY EASY to flee London in the dead of night. The horse piloted naturally to Hyde Park, and from there, Caroline needed only prod her to go faster until they reached the turnpike leading north out of the city. Beside her, Eddie was pale and quiet, his hands gripping the side of the cabriolet as if he were about to be expelled from it at any second.

He was unhappy with her. Caroline couldn't blame him. She *had* stolen this horse and carriage, and he *was* the one who would pay the consequences, if there were any.

But there wouldn't be. Not for horse thieving, anyhow. When they returned to London, they would return Aunt Charlotte's property in perfectly good condition.

The consequences Caroline and Eddie would reap would be a result of eloping.

Aunt Charlotte would probably refuse to receive Caroline, same as how she and the rest of Mama's family had refused to receive Mama and Papa up until right before Mama died.

Mr. and Mrs. Chow would be furious, too. They didn't forgive as easily as Papa did, and Mrs. Chow in particular was talented at making one feel absolutely terrible just by withholding her words. Caroline didn't mind that so much—particularly since she and Eddie would leave for Lower Canada—but, for Eddie's sake, she hoped his parents came around quickly.

She didn't quite know how Papa would react. No one in the family had ever so flagrantly disobeyed him before. Ellen had fallen in love with the son of his political enemy, but as far as Caroline could tell, Papa had welcomed Max with open arms. Sophia had gone off to be a governess and come home married to a middle-class physician whose mother was from India; Papa had thrown them a spring festival to celebrate. Benjamin, as far as Caroline knew, had never rebelled against a single word Papa had said. And even though Papa hadn't wanted Nate to join the navy, he had finally given permission so that when Nate went off to Portsmouth to take his command, he did so with the blessing of the family.

None of her siblings had been forbidden from what their hearts desired, and so none of them had tested Papa by disobeying him.

Caroline hoped that, once Papa discovered she and Eddie had eloped, it wouldn't take him too long to realize the error of his ways.

They paid the turnpike toll from Eddie's wallet. Settling back in the cabriolet, Eddie took the reins from Caroline. He had found carriage gloves underneath the bench, but she still felt an irresistible tremor through her body at being touched by him.

"Try and get some sleep," he said to her, as he navigated the horse forward on the road north.

"I couldn't sleep if you paid me to." Though it *was* the dead of night, and she *should* be tired, energy bounded through Caroline instead.

After all, it wasn't every evening that a girl ran off to marry the man she loved.

Linnie jumped from the floor of the cabriolet onto the bench between Caroline and Eddie. Lifting the dog into her lap, Caroline slid closer to Eddie—for his warmth—and threaded her right arm through his left. "What do you think Scotland is like?"

"Cold. Rainy. Stern."

His list was so matter-of-fact that Caroline had to laugh. "Stern? The whole country? Do you imagine even the heather will glare at us?"

"At me, anyhow." Eddie didn't quite smile, but he was beginning to soften. Soon, Caroline would coax a grin from him, and then maybe a laugh—and then, she hoped, another kiss.

"I hardly think the country can be sterner than England if it is willing to marry us without parental consent."

"I imagine they have kept that law in place just to be a thorn in England's side. They've had to submit to our authority, but by God, they will facilitate as many illicit marriages as they can."

"They'll take English money as they do it, too. They can likely pay their taxes with the fees they charge for weddings." Caroline remembered, belatedly, that Eddie was worried about money. "We can afford it, of course. They are smart enough to keep their prices low enough for everyone who has had to run off without their parents' purses."

The truth was, she really had no idea how it worked. All she knew was people ran off to Gretna Green, and when they came back, their marriages were legal and binding.

"As long as we can afford to get there." The good cheer that had been warming Eddie's voice leaked away.

"Of course we can afford to get there. You've got money, and I've got a necklace we can sell off if we need to." Though it was true, Caroline's amber jewelry would hardly command the same price as sapphires or rubies or diamonds.

"I've got twelve shillings left after that toll. I've heard it takes five days or more to get to Gretna Green, and we'll need to pay more tolls. One for every three miles—isn't that what they say? We'll need to sleep, too, and change horses, and pay for meals." The worry was clear in Eddie's voice, though he looked straight ahead and—Caroline could tell—did his best to look stoic. "If we can afford to get there, we won't be able to afford to get back."

Which didn't suit Caroline's plan at all, since she intended to return Aunt Charlotte's cabriolet and horse before the family called a magistrate.

"And—" Eddie cut himself off. "Never mind."

"And what?" Caroline straightened so that her chin was almost level with his. "Say it. I am not afraid of difficult circumstances."

Eddie gulped. "And that is assuming we are not assaulted by high-waymen who are attracted to a lone couple traveling in a cabriolet without any protection whatsoever."

Highwaymen—the bane of Britain's roads. Caroline had heard terrible stories, and she knew they weren't exaggerations. If high-waymen stopped them and discovered they didn't have anything worth stealing, they would most likely murder them. Or murder Eddie and take Caroline for their pleasure, and then murder her.

"There haven't been highwaymen on the turnpikes in a decade." Caroline was quite sure she had heard Papa say something like that recently. Still, she asked, "Haven't we a gun?"

"I believe Phipps is in possession of your aunt's carriage gun. The one he was pointing at me, remember?"

The energy that had been lifting Caroline all evening disappeared, replaced by a terrible, foreboding knot in her stomach. "This isn't a very good plan at all, is it?"

Eddie didn't say anything. Which, Caroline knew, meant he both agreed with her *and* was unhappy with her.

"Why didn't you lay this all out for me in the stables before we left?"

"You were Determined Caroline. In all my life, I have never been able to dissuade Determined Caroline from even the worst of plans."

But that wasn't good at all. This was not a game to free them from chores for a beautiful afternoon in the spring sunshine. This was their future. It could even be the end of their lives, if the highway-men found them. "You mustn't let me lead you around like that.

You are not my servant. You are my husband—or you're about to be, anyhow. We must make these plans together."

Eddie stiffened at the word *servant*. "I did say that I could be hanged for horse thieving. If you weren't going to listen to that, I didn't see what reason you *would* listen to."

It was so rare for Eddie to be angry with her that Caroline didn't quite know what to do about it. She stared out at the road, which was lit only by the lantern hanging off the roof of their cabriolet. Cold fog circled around them; Aunt Charlotte's horse took slow, cautious steps, and Caroline couldn't blame it.

One could almost believe there was no road ahead at all.

"I'm sorry." At first, she said it because she knew that when one person was upset with another, an apology was owed. As she kept going, however, she warmed up to the sentiment. "I'm sorry I didn't listen to you. I was too excited to leave, but that is no excuse. Eddie, you and I must always listen to each other. I should have stopped and gotten on the stagecoach with you or found some other plan. It is my fault we are in this position now. If we die, you may blame me entirely."

Eddie laid a gloved hand over hers. "I don't care about blame. All that matters to me is that we get there safely." Then, finally smiling, he added, "All that matters to me is that we get married."

Damn the highwaymen and every other danger lying in wait. Caroline kissed him. It was brief—he had to mind the reins, after all—and not at all satisfying, lighting a fire on her lips that begged for more tending. Still, it was everything to Caroline.

She snuggled closer into the crook of his chest, her free hand draping across Linnie's warm body. "So then, let's make a new plan together. What shall we do?"

Eddie consolidated the reins into his right hand so he could keep his left palm draped over hers. "We could turn back."

It might solve the problem, but it was unthinkable. "We would never see each other again. Aunt Charlotte would lock me in her house."

"And have me arrested." Eddie squeezed her fingers. "We could stop at the next town we find, pay someone to take back the horse and the cabriolet, and make a life together until you turn twenty-one and we can be married in the church."

Caroline didn't mind the idea of being a common-law wife—she knew so many people at Northfield Hall who lived outside the norms of the church and law—but at the pace the horse was walking, they had hardly made it out of London proper. "Papa would come find me and lock me up and never let me see you again."

Whatever they did, they needed money, and there was no fast and easy way to get that.

It was strange, after reading so much about poverty in the papers and hearing so many stories from her friends at Northfield Hall, to suddenly be living without enough money.

"Why do you think the whole world is against us?" Eddie asked, his hand dropping away from hers.

Caroline pressed herself closer to him to refute the question. "Perhaps not the whole world. Perhaps just people too old to remember what it is like to be in love." As she said it, she thought of her sister Sophia, who would take up a gauntlet like this and find a way to set it on fire.

Sophia was off touring the continent, her husband John ensconced in the Welsh country estate of some great lady expecting to give birth. They could be of no help to Caroline and Eddie right then.

But perhaps Ellen and Max would.

"We should—" She almost said it as a dictum but caught herself in time. "What do you think about going to Montchampion Manor?"

Eddie looked at her sharply in surprise. "Why would they support us when your father won't?"

"They know we have hoped to marry." It was true: going to her sister's new home in Norfolk was a risk. Ellen might lock Caroline up, turn Eddie out, and send for Papa. But Caroline had never known Ellen to deal so harshly with anyone. Ellen always looked for the good in any situation.

Even if Ellen agreed with Papa, Caroline couldn't imagine her dealing so cruelly with Eddie.

"It might be just as bad an option as the others," Caroline agreed, "but don't you think Ellen would at least hear us out?"

For a moment, Eddie was silent, considering it. "We can get there sooner than Gretna Green, anyhow."

"Then you agree?"

He brought his hand back to hers. "I agree."

E VEN THOUGH THE DRIVE to Montchampion Manor was just as harrowing as if they had gone all the way to Scotland, Eddie felt at peace. He had Linnie at his feet, warming his boots; he had Caroline at his side, warming his heart; and they had a plan, flimsy though it might be.

They rode through the night on the northern road, then turned east for Norfolk at Chesterford just as dawn was breaking. It was another full day's ride, and Eddie's pockets were fast emptying as he paid the tolls, purchased feed for their horse, bought a hot meal for Caroline (which she insisted they share), and bribed an ostler who thought they looked suspicious and threatened to call the magistrate.

Still, the blade of panic that had been poised against Eddie's nerves ever since they left London didn't return. For once, this mess was of his making—and he couldn't consider it too much of a mess when he had Caroline by his side.

They passed the time talking. That had always been their way: when they could sneak off from the rest of Northfield Hall, they would lie side by side, staring at the sky, and talk about anything and everything. In the cabriolet, they were slightly more reserved. Neither of them, for example, brought up their families. They didn't talk much about the future, either, though they were running headlong into it. Caroline asked Eddie how being a glazier changed his outlook on the world, and he explained how he couldn't look at a single window now without seeing its flaws; that led to a debate about whether it was good to notice things that needed improvement (Caroline thought yes, Eddie said he would rather not know); from there, they wondered whose responsibility it was to make improvements.

"Surely if one can see a broken window and one has the funds to hire a glazier—or one *is* a glazier—then one should offer to fix the window, no matter whom it belongs to," Caroline argued.

"Perhaps one should *offer*, but doesn't the person who lives there have the right to decline?"

"Why should they want to decline having a window fixed?"

"Perhaps they like it broken." That was an indefensible position. Eddie cast about for another. "Or perhaps the person offering to fix it will hire a bad glazier—or even just a different glazier than the one the window's owner wants. Perhaps the offer is to replace the window, but with bad broad glass instead of crown glass, so that the whole house will be cast in a green hue."

"Surely a green window is better than no window." Caroline had that look on her face—where her chin jutted out and her eyes didn't quite meet his—that meant he had won the argument, yet she wasn't ready to admit it.

Eddie didn't mind letting her keep the upper hand. "*I* would certainly say so, but one never knows what a person who broke their window will prefer."

Grinning, Caroline agreed. "After all, they were already so negligent as to let their window be broken. There can be no excuse for them." Then she darted up to claim a kiss.

She had been doing that all day, and Eddie really couldn't bring himself to warn her off it. Even though it twisted him so that the reins and the horse started veering towards the left. Even though anyone else on the road might see. Even though it made him want to pull off into the nearby wheat field, throw her to the ground, and have his way with her.

He kissed her, and she kissed him, and at some point before the cabriolet drifted off the turnpike, they stopped.

Clearing his throat and adjusting his trousers—which suddenly felt very tight—Eddie realized they were within sight of a village. Not only that, but the poor horse was taking smaller and smaller steps. He could only imagine being a beast of burden, prodded onward with no more than a half hour break every few hours.

Eddie didn't want to be the kind of man who worked a horse to death.

"We should—" Eddie caught himself and rephrased his words, since he and Caroline had decided they would make their plans together. "I think we had better change horses now. We must be close enough that Max can send a groom to look after this one, once we get to Montchampion Manor. Would you agree?"

Caroline looked at the village a little nervously. "I wish we were there already."

Eddie did, too. Eddie wished they were already married and settled somewhere with a roof over their heads and a bed for the night.

Caroline leaned down to pet Linnie's head. "What do you think, Linnie? Had we better change horses now?" When Linnie licked her wrist—a very friendly overture for the dog—Caroline smiled again. "Yes, I think we had better take our chances here at this village."

It was small, no more than a pub and inn on one side of the road and a string of tradesmen's workshops on the other. As they approached, Eddie considered the best strategy to explain a young lady and a Chinese tradesman traveling alone together in a cabriolet.

"We shall tell them we are married," Caroline said, clearly worrying about the same thing.

"They wouldn't believe it." At the coaching inn where they had rested for luncheon, Eddie had been all too aware of everyone's eyes on him and more than a few whispers that he must be some kind of criminal.

"People will believe anything if you say it with enough authority."

Eddie didn't want to take the risk. "The quality of our clothes does not match. We had better tell them what they want to believe: that you are a young widow, and I am your manservant seeing you safely to your sister's."

"We won't be staying long, anyhow," Caroline said by way of acquiescence.

That proved to be incorrect. When Eddie inquired about a change of horses, he was informed their only spare horse had just been hired. "We've room for your mistress," the landlord said, "so you can rest as well and continue on in the morning."

Eddie didn't relish the idea of a night spent sleeping in the hayloft—or worse, if there was no space among the stable hands, twisting onto the bench of the cabriolet in hopes of a few hours of rest. Still, he didn't see that they had any other choice. They couldn't continue on with Aunt Charlotte's horse that night, nor did this village have any other horses for hire.

He returned to the cabriolet to deliver the news to Caroline.

"We could all use the rest, I suppose," she said at first. "Except Linnie, who has been napping ever since we left London."

"I'll pay for your room, then." It was almost the rest of their money; Eddie hoped there weren't too many tolls standing between them and Montchampion Manor.

"But where will you sleep?" Caroline asked, and before he could even answer, she descended from the cabriolet. "Let me speak to them. You'll have a bed, too."

"Don't make a fuss," Eddie begged, but the Caroline who had promised to collaborate on decisions had disappeared, replaced once more with Determined Caroline. Head high, she swanned into the tiny pub as if she were the queen.

Eddie considered his options. On the one hand, he should follow her in to make sure no one mistreated her. On the other, the cabriolet needed to be moved aside and the horse needed tending.

The latter option had the additional benefit of allowing him to miss out on Caroline's scheme. Eddie felt guilty that he was so relieved not to witness it. He would be there, waiting and ready, when she emerged to admit that she had been defeated, because after all, they were *not* at Northfield Hall, and they had no money, and no one knew who they were, and Eddie was just a Chinese servant who certainly didn't deserve to stay in an English bed designed for a good English commoner.

He wished Caroline had just accepted what was offered and let it be.

She took longer than he expected. He had already unhitched the horse and moved it into the stable when Caroline returned. Eddie picked up the currycomb rather than see disappointment on her face.

"I informed them I am uncomfortable sleeping alone in a pub full of strangers and need my man with me to fend off any drunkards who think they can take advantage of a vulnerable young widow. My concern grew doubly when I learned there is no lock on my door. The landlord's wife understood, and so you shall sleep on a pallet just inside my room as my protector."

She said it all in her playacting voice, undoubtedly because there was at least one stable boy who could overhear them. The words were so startling that Eddie couldn't help but look at her: triumph glowed from her eyes and gilded her lips and mantled her shoulders.

He was almost too astonished at her success to realize the implication of her announcement:

They would share a bedroom that night.

"As you like, madam," he replied, voice suddenly hoarse. "I shall finish here and then find you inside."

Regally, Caroline turned away.

Eddie forced himself to take his time with the horse. He brushed it down, made sure it had its oats and water, murmured some soothing words into its ear. It deserved all his care and attention—and besides, he didn't want anyone to deem him overeager to spend the night with his mistress.

The word clamored through Eddie's head. *Mistress.* Caroline was not his employer. *Mistress.* Neither was she his lover. He would sleep on the pallet, and they would wait until she was his wife.

Mistress.

Unless she wanted to be his mistress. Unless she wanted to undress him as eagerly as he wanted to unlace that gown from her body. Unless she, too, worried they would never find their way to Scotland and this might be their only chance to do what lovers did.

Mistress.

Eddie wouldn't hope for it. But he wouldn't turn Caroline down, either.

When he finished with the horse, he whistled to Linnie and entered the pub. It was more crowded than even a quarter hour earlier—as in, it had gone from three patrons to seven—and they were all men singing a bawdy drinking ditty. The landlord scowled at Eddie. "Your mistress is upstairs, in her private room, and it will be a shilling for the trouble."

That left them hardly any money for tolls the next day. Eddie pulled a sixpence from his purse. "Will this suffice, if I don't eat any meals?"

"What, Lady La-Di-Dah is traveling without funds?"

"Her sister sent for her in the middle of the night. She had no time to procure funds from the bank." Eddie wasn't sure what Caroline had told the landlord, but he took a chance and added: "They are close relatives of the Earl of Meretta. I am certain his lordship will be happy to pay you a bonus once she arrives safely at her destination."

"The Earl of Meretta, eh?" The landlord looked Eddie up and down. "A relative of the countess, I wager. One of them Prestons."

The name came out like a curse, but Eddie wasn't there to defend the family honor. "You wager correctly."

"Sixpence will do. His lordship can send full payment when you arrive."

And so all the details were sorted. Linnie at his feet—so close she was a shadow, which was good, since he wasn't sure the landlord would appreciate a dog inside the pub—Eddie climbed the crooked staircase to the little room where Caroline waited.

She stood by the window. Stooped, more like it, for the ceiling sloped so dramatically that not even Caroline could stand straight at its edge. The window was old broad glass and clearly hadn't been cleaned since it was installed a hundred years ago. "I thought I might find some scars in it, like you can," Caroline said, "but it looks like perfectly good glass to me."

She had removed her cloak and, surprisingly, her boots. Excitement surged through Eddie at the sight of wool stockings encasing her feet.

He focused on the rest of the room. In its tiny quarters, they had stuffed a small bed, a washstand, and a hideous watercolor of three cats. The door indeed had no lock, and in fact swung an inch or two inward even after Eddie latched it shut. In the corner behind it, he spied the straw-stuffed pallet intended as his bed.

He went to roll it out.

"Don't be silly," Caroline objected. "You'll share the bed with me."

"What if someone discovers us?"

"It's not as if they have maids bustling in and out of here."

Even as she said it, there was a knock on the door. Eddie inched it open to find the landlady waiting with a tray of hot stew, a chunk of bread, and ale.

Confused, Eddie said, "I told your husband I wouldn't eat."

"It's for your mistress." The landlady gave him such a look that he believed he wouldn't be allowed near that stew even if he could pay.

"I asked for it," Caroline said, coming to the door. "Thank you so very much, Mrs. Wallis. It smells delicious. Shall I leave the tray in the hall when I am done?"

"As you like, ma'am. It is our privilege to serve a relative of Lord Meretta." And the landlady curtsied before retreating back downstairs.

"I didn't mention Max," Caroline whispered.

Shutting the door, Eddie admitted, "I did." He took off his boots and set them on the ground beside the door to keep it from opening itself.

Caroline still stood with her tray of food. "Shouldn't you have discussed that with me first?"

Frustration flared—but Eddie didn't notice it too much, since lust and hunger were already devouring his body. "We don't have enough money to pay what the landlord wanted to charge, so I offered less money with the promise that Max will send more once you reach your destination safely."

"Oh." Sinking onto the bed, Caroline balanced the food across her lap. "Is that why you aren't eating? Because we haven't enough money?"

"Yes."

"Oh." That word felt even smaller this time. For a moment, Caroline stared at her stew, silent. Then, not quite looking at Eddie, she said lightly, "I shall get used to it soon. I've never had to worry about it before, but everyone else does, and soon it shall feel as natural as breathing to me."

Because she was choosing him. Because he could not even pay for supper. Because he was not, as Lord Preston said, worthy of her.

Eddie pushed the thoughts away. "Eat up. It might be your last meal before we make it to Montchampion Manor."

"*Our* last meal." She patted the mattress beside her. "If you don't help me eat this food, I won't eat it either, and then we'll both starve."

He didn't have it in him to refuse. Especially when it meant sitting beside her, the mattress sagging under their weight so that they fell into each other. The tray tilted, and Eddie had to catch the ale before it spilled.

"We are always just one step away from disaster, aren't we?" Caroline smiled. "At least we know how to make the best of it."

They ate quickly. Eddie sipped the ale while Caroline slurped half of the stew, and then they switched. Caroline tore the bread into three pieces and tossed a third to Linnie before handing Eddie his share. It was hardly the best meal Eddie had ever had, yet by the end of it, he almost didn't feel the shame of not being able to afford it.

"Well, then." Caroline rose, delivered the empty tray to the hallway, and shut the door again. She realigned Eddie's boots to make sure they were doing their job as doorstops. Then, fingers linking nervously at her waist, she regarded Eddie where he sat. "We shall share the bed."

Hunger satiated, lust lurched forward to overwhelm Eddie's brain. She was so unbelievably beautiful, and even after all their travel she smelled so appealing, and he had spent so many years dreaming of being shut in a room with her. He croaked out, "Yes."

"I'll need to undress. And so will you."

"Yes."

"And then we shall be two undressed people in a bed."

Eddie didn't have much breath left in his body.

Caroline licked her lips. "Perhaps we should do what two undressed people in bed do."

Somehow, Eddie's brain took over long enough to say: "Someone will overhear us."

She blinked. Her hands fell away, and suddenly she sat back down on the mattress beside him. "Is it impossible to do it quietly? Or is it inevitable that someone will overhear?"

Eddie gulped, trying very hard to think straight. He had witnessed it plenty of times: Mr. and Mrs. Trowbridge at least once a week, Oliver and Samantha rather loudly when they thought he was asleep, and then there were the whores he had heard pleasuring clients on the streets late at night.

"I don't know. I've only ever heard people doing it, which makes me think that whenever they do it, it can be heard."

Caroline's hand fluttered to her heart. "Haven't you done it before?"

"No." Heat rushed all over Eddie's body. "Who would I have done it with?"

"I don't know. A pretty girl or a courtesan…" Caroline licked her lips again, but this time, she didn't meet his eyes. "Hasn't every man done it? Before he marries, I mean?"

"I haven't. I love *you*." And it was all Eddie could do not to touch her right then. "Have you done it before?"

"No!" She glared at him. "I've been waiting for *you*, too."

"Good, then." Eddie had lost track of the discussion. She sat so close to him, and her legs kept swinging through the air.

He would die if her stockinged feet touched his. It would be too sweet an agony to survive.

"We have kissed. We know that can be quiet." Caroline set her big brown eyes on him, and Eddie knew he didn't have any resistance left. "If it gets too loud, we can stop."

"Yes," he agreed. "We can always stop."

The negotiations ended. Standing, Caroline began undoing the buttons along the side of her gown. Eddie followed her lead and removed his coat and waistcoat. His eyes, however, were on her, and he forgot what he was doing when she peeled off her outer layer to reveal her underclothes.

Stays over a long, white petticoat shift; those gray wool stockings; and her breasts, almost completely visible above the hem of her bodice.

"You don't wear your trousers to bed, do you?" Caroline prodded, but she sounded breathless, too.

"Do you wear your stays?" Eddie retorted.

And so they went further: he stepped out of his trousers and unrolled his stockings, and she removed her stays and stockings. Now he was in only his shirt, and she wore only her shift.

"On the count of three?" Caroline suggested.

Eddie could do nothing except nod.

"One, two, three."

Together, they lifted their final garments over their heads. Eddie kept his eyes shut until his shirt landed on the floor. Then, finally, he saw Caroline naked.

She looked cold and nervous. And beautiful. Her breasts were even more perfect than he had imagined: round and mysterious and prickled with desire. The lines of her waist were decorated by the soft curves of her belly, and her legs were thick and strong in a way that sent his cock jerking against his stomach.

"You're gorgeous, Eddie," Caroline said, inching towards him. "I hope you know that."

"You're divine, Monkey. But you already know that." He reached for her, daring only to touch her neck and chin—geography he already knew well—and drew her into a kiss.

This was a moment he had never dared dream would truly come. They landed on the mattress almost as soon as their lips touched, their bare legs tangling with each other. Eddie ran his hands across her arms, her ribs, her thighs, marveling at the smooth skin and soft hair that greeted his fingers. Caroline explored, too, her touch roaming from his shoulders to his back to his bum.

The sensations were so overwhelming that Eddie couldn't stand to keep his mouth on hers. He moved to her neck, teasing his tongue over that sensitive skin, eliciting a shiver from deep in her body. He closed his lips over the target and sucked, until her knees locked over his waist and her arms flailed in the air. "Oh, Eddie!" she cried—and it was loud enough that Linnie let out a growl.

Eddie remembered where they were. "Shh," he murmured, retreating from Caroline's neck.

"You're the one who stopped kissing me," she whispered back.

They linked mouths once again. Caroline was everything right in the world. Eddie was dizzy with the sensation of her skin on his. Bare. Soft, as if she bathed every morning in butter. Sensitive. As his fingers trailed along the side of her ribcage, she shivered, a coo of pleasure purring from her throat. Eddie muffled her with his lips even as his hand continued upward and cupped her breast in his palm. Caroline made another sound, her legs twining around his hips, her hands holding him fast.

Eddie had never known this feeling before, the one that made this moment perfect and also made it terrible because something even better was waiting for him, something that overwhelmed him if he tried even to think of it.

He squeezed her breast, opening his eyes to see it there in his hand, looking yellow in the candlelight. Her nipple was larger than he had expected, a tantalizing target at which he wanted to aim his whole being. He flicked it with his thumb, watching it rise taller in response. Her body rippled beneath him, and she sucked in a breath.

He flicked her nipple again.

"Don't ever stop!"

Her voice filled the room, light and airy but oh, so very loud. From the corner near the door, Linnie growled.

Caroline twisted around Eddie so that now he was on his back and she straddled him. Even as the bed ropes squeaked in response, Caroline whispered, "You haven't been keeping me quiet, Eddie. You must do better."

And now she was the one exploring. Her tongue to his. Her naked hips hovering above his—not joining them, not yet—but Eddie's thoughts centered on his cock straining into the warm, damp curls waiting just above it. Caroline's hands swept down his chest and under his buttocks, cupping his cheeks much the same way he was even now palming her breasts.

He moved one hand down to the juncture of her legs, as he had heard a man should do, and slipped a finger between her folds.

Wet. Hot. Strong. His finger barely touched her before she cried out—this time without words, only a scream of pleasure that could surely be heard all the way in Timbuktu.

Eddie grabbed her lower lip with his teeth to quiet her. He didn't mean it to hurt. He didn't mean *much*, since his mind was mostly liquid desire with only just enough fear left to protect them from the rest of the inn.

But Caroline yelped. As she pushed away from him, her hand flew to her mouth. And when Eddie scrambled to sit up, he saw blood dripping from her lip.

"I hurt you."

She dabbed at her mouth with the hem of her discarded petticoat. "Not really. Only a pinch." The blood came off in a smear, and none rushed to replace it.

Still, Eddie felt sick. "I hurt you."

"I liked it until the blood." Her head turned away, she glanced up at him, a shy smile on her lips. "I told you to keep me from being too loud."

"And so I *bit* you?" He had the odd sensation that he hadn't been present for the last few minutes. That whoever had been kissing her—touching her—had been some other man. Eddie propelled himself from the bed.

Caroline remained on the mattress, half-lying backward, like some sort of angel in a painting. "It was part of the game. You didn't mean to hurt me."

"No, I didn't mean to hurt you, but I *did*." He placed his palms on the wall to steady himself.

"Eddie, I'm better already. Come see."

He heard her patting the mattress in invitation. He didn't turn around. He was cold, his skin clammy, and he couldn't believe he had stolen her away from London only to make her bleed.

Lord Preston had been right: Caroline deserved a husband who would never worry about a roof over their heads or a meal for the night or hurting her like a brute.

"Eddie—" Her voice was gentle, coaxing, but he refused to listen to it.

There were some actions he couldn't take back. But at least he didn't have to add more irrevocable acts on top of them.

"We had better get some sleep."

CAROLINE HAD NEVER SEEN Eddie like this. At least, not since they were six and his older brothers told him he would be sent back to China for keeping a basket of plums under his bed just for himself.

He clung to the wall, not even looking at her. His whole body was tense, and all Caroline wanted to do was take him back into her arms.

But she was naked, too, and cold, and frankly didn't understand why he was making such a fuss. "Weren't you enjoying it?"

Eddie retrieved his shirt from the floor without replying.

"I think you are making this into a calamity when it is nothing more than a…" Caroline cast about for the proper description of lovemaking gone wrong. "A story we can laugh about later. We'll be old and gray and saying 'Remember when we were so green that we bit each other?'"

"Fine. We can laugh about it in the morning after we have had some sleep." Something hard lined his words. Eddie slipped the shirt over his shoulders, and soon it covered all the way down to his thighs. Caroline had only just discovered the gloriousness of his chest, the thrilling muscles of his legs, and the tantalizing throb of his cock. And now he had removed them again.

All because of one little mishap.

"I want you to kiss me again, Eddie."

He didn't look her in the eye. "We need to get some rest if we're to make it to Montchampion Manor tomorrow."

Did his body not tremble in need of hers? Did he not feel that the world might end if they didn't touch each other again, right now and all night long? Did he not look at her and see only desire that needed to be resolved?

It felt like scraping her heart against a rock, but she asked, "Did I do something wrong?"

"No." Eddie picked up her shift and handed it to her. "You didn't do anything wrong, Monkey."

But he wanted her to cover up. He had her naked and willing alone in a bedroom, and instead of ravishing her, he wanted her to put her clothes back on. That wasn't what Caroline had expected of physical love. She thought it was supposed to overpower a person so that they did stupid things like get discovered by the landlady.

She didn't mind doing something stupid like that with Eddie.

Eyes averted, he turned away again, as if to give her privacy. Caroline shimmied the shift over her shoulders, covering her breasts as he wanted.

Perhaps the problem was her body. Perhaps he had been expecting her to be one way—bigger breasts or more generous curves—and now, the discovery that under her gown she was just little old Caroline was too much for him to bear.

"It would be...That is, I suppose it might be natural..." Caroline tried to find the courage to say the words. "If I am not the kind of woman you lust after, then—"

Eddie grabbed her upper arm. "No, Monkey, it isn't that at all. You are divine, remember?"

At least he was touching her again. His grip was a little too tight, though, and none of this was at all what Caroline had pictured for the night.

"Yes, a perfect angel, but..." She tried to smile. She couldn't look him in the eyes. She couldn't even look at his face. "Am I appealing?"

Eddie's hand softened. It dropped from just above her elbow to her fingers, which were trembling. His other hand lifted her jaw, cradling her face as he forced her to look upward, towards him.

She latched her gaze to his mouth, which was pink and narrow and said, "You are everything I could want in a woman, Caroline. Your body is appealing. Your personality is appealing. Your heart is appealing."

That gave her the courage to look into his eyes. Meeting them—seeing their endless dark depth and the black eyebrows softening them from above—felt like going home.

His hand dropped from her jaw to her hip. "When we do this, let's do it properly. In a room with a door that latches. And when there is somewhere else we can put Linnie." Eddie laughed a little, so Caroline did too, and they both looked at where Linnie lay in her corner. The dog let out a happy growl at the attention.

"I want nothing more than to spend all night kissing you," Eddie whispered. "Please believe that."

"Yes." She reminded herself that mischief did not come easily to Eddie. It had been a trying day, anyhow, full of trouble that was worse than mischief, and it was all her fault for coming up with a wretched plan. Small wonder that Eddie did not have any nerves left for tonight.

Still, for all he said that Linnie was the problem, by the time Caroline had put on her shift and snuffed out the candle, the dog had leaped onto the bed and burrowed between Eddie and Caroline—and Eddie didn't object at all.

Chapter Twelve

They got on the road before dawn had completely given way to daybreak. Even though she wore the same warm travel cloak as before, Caroline was cold; she looped her arm through Eddie's again, but still she shivered.

"We'll be there soon," Eddie promised, though they had hours yet to go. He consolidated the reins into one hand and wrapped his free arm around her back so she could huddle against his chest.

Caroline accepted the gesture, even though it felt to her like he was being overly nice to make up for whatever had happened the night before. She was trying desperately not to think about it. She fixed her mind on the plan: get to Ellen and Max's, get to Scotland, get married.

So long as they could sort all that out, she had to believe that Eddie would want to make love to her properly. And if she believed that, then she could silence the doubt in her heart whispering that, in the end, he had discovered there was something dreadfully wrong with her.

She returned to some of her rituals to soothe herself. Together, they counted the number of cows in the fields they passed; when they stopped for a herd of sheep crossing the road, Caroline measured their delay by a time signature of the baa-ing; and every time they passed a graveyard, she made Eddie hold his breath.

"You don't really believe in bad spirits, do you?" he teased her.

Caroline wasn't in the mood to be teased. "Why not? We've had nothing but bad luck, haven't we? Well, maybe there are bad spirits following us."

"I'd say we've had good luck, considering we have made it this far without being robbed, murdered, or starved."

His last point made Caroline's stomach rumble loudly: they had skipped breakfast, and she did feel rather like she was being starved, though she knew there were people who went far longer with far less.

"I suppose it doesn't hurt to ward off bad spirits," Eddie amended, and he squeezed her a little tighter to his side. "Do you know any prayers for travelers?"

She did: one from the Church of England, an old Irish blessing, and a Romany prayer. She recited them all. "There's one your mother says, too, in Chinese, but of course, I don't know it."

Eddie murmured it. His voice sounded different when he spoke Chinese; it made her think of birds chirping at each other across tree branches. She had tried to learn some basic sentences through-out the years, but she couldn't get her voice to modulate properly around its tones, and Mrs. Chow always ended up shaking her head in discouragement.

"Will you speak to our children in Chinese?"

Perhaps it wasn't her question that prompted Eddie to withdraw his arm from around her shoulders. Perhaps it was the curve of the road, which was rather sharp and might well have justified holding one rein in each hand. Whatever the reason was, he ended up farther away from her, his elbow jarring her away from the comfort of his chest. "I don't speak it well enough to teach them."

Caroline thought that a stupid response. "You know enough. Besides, your parents will want to speak to them in Chinese, don't you think?"

She'd forgotten they had been avoiding the subject of their future. She remembered why now, as Eddie replied, "I don't think my parents will want to meet any children we have. They have told me not to marry you. They won't want to see us once we do."

"They'll forgive us once all is said and done." They had to. Caroline couldn't imagine life without Mrs. Chow scolding her and Mr. Chow doling out smiles when she pleased him, not any more than she could imagine never seeing Papa again. "It may take some time," she allowed, "but surely by the time we return with a child or two, they'll want to see us again."

"My parents haven't wanted much to do with me for a decade, and that was when I went along with their plans. Why would they want anything to do with me after I have explicitly disobeyed them?"

Something boiled beneath his words, as if they were the lid of an iron pot whose contents were steaming so hot that bubbles of froth began to escape.

Caroline wasn't ready to lift that lid from the pot entirely. "They'll forgive you," she insisted, and she lifted Linnie to sit in her lap for warmth in lieu of cuddling against Eddie again.

When they reached the village outside Montchampion Manor, Eddie asked, "Do you want to freshen up before we call on Max and Ellen?"

Obstinately, Caroline replied, "I haven't anything to freshen up *with*, and we can hardly pay for a maid to assist, can we?" She regretted being so spiteful immediately; it wasn't Eddie's fault they hadn't any luggage or money. "Let's just hurry on. I'm impatient to get there."

Eddie's reply was to tap the reins, spurring the horse on a little faster.

It was seven miles from the village to Montchampion Manor: two miles to the edge of the park, and then five miles to the great house. Having never been before, Caroline didn't expect the driveway to take so long. It was spacious, lined with great old lime trees, and on a constant curve so she kept anticipating it would end to reveal the house.

The horse—or Eddie—must have felt the same, because the longer the drive stretched, the faster the cabriolet went.

It was because they were so anxious to get help. Eager to get on with the plan. Excited to be one step closer to getting married.

It was not at all because they were running from all the things they could not say to each other.

Suddenly, the drive *did* end. Montchampion Manor unfurled before them: a monumental house with a marble façade gleaming in the sun, a matching fountain in the center of the carriage sweep, and a crowd as large as a village singing a hymn to Ellen and Max, who stood at the top of the house's stairs.

It hadn't occurred to Caroline that they might arrive at an inopportune time. But it was too late to turn back: as one, the crowd turned to stare at Eddie and Caroline, their hymn silenced in the middle of a chord.

There was nothing for it but to leap from the cabriolet, and, grabbing Eddie's hand, rush through the crowd to her eldest sister.

"I'm terribly sorry to interrupt your…" She didn't know what to make of the gathering, and her heart was pounding too fast to come up with an appropriate word. All she could say was, "I don't know what Papa has written you about Eddie and me, but whatever it is, I beg you will give us the benefit of the doubt. We are in desperate need of your help."

EDDIE KEPT THINKING ABOUT his brothers.

He had never quite gotten over being in awe of them. They were each so much older. Martin had been twelve years old at Eddie's birth, which had made him more of a god than a brother. Now he was only a legend, the one who had gone off on a ship, never to be heard from again. Spencer was six years older than Eddie and had never been interested in playing. Meanwhile, Oliver, three years older, had treated Eddie like his own personal doll, servant, or urchin, depending on what the game called for.

Eddie loved them all. He craved respect from each of them in a way he sometimes found humbling. But he hadn't any idea if, had he and Caroline turned up on *their* doorsteps, they would have helped.

When Eddie came back to the Covent Garden flat after being rejected by Lord Preston, Oliver had sympathized, offering to take him out to the pub and drink away the sting of it all. But he hadn't said "Don't listen to him" or "Whatever you want to do, I'll help." He hadn't even been surprised. And when Eddie had declared he was going to strike out on his own, Oliver had resisted, reminding Eddie how hard it was to find work. "You'll be rich if you only stay the course," he had advised.

Compare that to Ellen. Even though he and Caroline had arrived in the middle of a public display, she hugged them close to her—first Caroline, then Eddie—and said, "Of course we will help you." She had them both stand with the rest of the family as Max and the servants finished the ceremony of renaming Montchampion Manor to

Hope Hall by hanging a new sign. As she directed them to distribute jars of pickled vegetables to the crowd, she introduced Eddie to her housekeeper as "a dear friend of our family, Mr. Chow."

Eddie supposed she didn't yet have any idea what he and Caroline had done. Once she found out—once she realized he was there to threaten the virtue of her sister—she would send him into the wilderness of Norfolk to fend for himself.

First, however, she set them up in guest rooms, and Eddie was appointed an entire suite—as if he were a lord—that included a dressing chamber, a sitting room, and a bedroom with a silk-draped four-posted bed. Rich oil paintings of English hunters with red foxes decorated the walls. A servant in livery much finer than Eddie's own clothes appeared to inquire whether Eddie wanted a bath.

Even if any of Eddie's brothers had access to this kind of luxury, he couldn't picture them welcoming him without questions. They would put him in the kitchen, perhaps, to make sure he had food, and they would tell him he smelled, but if he had said, "I need your help no matter what our parents have told you," he suspected they would first ask, "What is it that you have done?"

It made Eddie wonder: was that because Ellen was exceptional, or because she loved Caroline more deeply than his brothers loved him?

He accepted the bath—for both himself and Linnie. It took a half hour and four maids to fill the tub with steaming water. Eddie passed the time at the wide plate glass window giving him a view of the ornamental gardens. It was so perfectly executed that he couldn't spot any flaws at all, except on the outside, where rain marks smudged its perfect surface. They could use a glazier to clean it properly.

He tried not to luxuriate in the bath. It would be the only one of its kind in his life, and he did not want to remember it too well. The soft cotton towels, the honey-scented soap, the water so hot and clear that he could see his skin turning red. These were elements of a dream, not his reality, and Eddie refused to spend the rest of his life yearning for them.

He tried, too, not to think about how Caroline wouldn't find a bath like this exceptional at all.

Dried off, he was just slipping into the robe left behind by the laundrymaid who had whisked away his clothes when someone knocked on the door.

Eddie's heart and stomach leapt with hope that it would be Caroline.

It was Max.

Max, otherwise known as the Earl of Meretta, otherwise known as an even more intimidating man than Lord Preston. Max was tall, broad, and blond, like a Norse god. Eddie remembered when he had first come to Northfield Hall—under an assumed name—and thundered around as if he owned the place. Then, once he married Ellen, he really did almost own the place.

He didn't abuse his privilege, but there was something in the way he moved and spoke that exuded the *right* to abuse it, if he so wished. Caroline thought of him as a brother, but Eddie never forgot he was a lord of the realm.

Max shut the door, leaned against it, and crossed his arms. "Miss Caroline tells Lady Meretta that you two have run off to elope without Lord Preston's permission."

He wielded the titles like broadswords, erecting a dangerous distance between Eddie and everyone else involved. Dutifully, Eddie ducked his chin. "Yes, my lord."

"She says he is withholding his permission unfairly and without reason."

Eddie could just imagine Caroline saying that, working herself into a dudgeon as she tried to justify why Ellen should help them.

He didn't dare try even the tiniest exaggeration with Max. "Lord Preston wants Miss Caroline to marry a man of her station who can provide an income similar to what she is accustomed to. It is a good reason."

"I'm glad to hear you think so." Max's voice got icier. "Do you have a good reason for eloping?"

The robe around him was embarrassingly thin. His legs were exposed from the calf downward, and Eddie felt a draft of cold air rushing up around his ankles to his knees and groin. He focused on the carpet beneath his bare feet, which had patterns of whirligigs and whorls. "No, sir."

"No?" The word boomed from Max. "You haven't anything to say for yourself?"

From where she lay by the fire, Linnie growled.

What could Max want him to say? The very room they stood in was designed to remind Eddie that he did not belong in this world—and that it was Caroline's birthright. Was Eddie supposed to object that he could fit into luxurious baths and picture windows if only given the chance? Was he supposed to defend the plight of the common man as righteous and good? Did Max want him to appeal to the family relationship between the Prestons and the Chows?

It was a losing argument all around. Eddie was nothing but a glazier—and an unemployed one at that. He had no savings, no leasehold, no plan except to arrive somewhere new and set himself up with work. Not even the father of a milkmaid would want his daughter to marry Eddie, much less Caroline's family.

Whatever Eddie said, he would likely end up tossed out of Hope Hall. So he almost didn't say anything at all.

Except he suspected this conversation would somehow make its way back to Caroline. He didn't want her to think he had surrendered without a fight.

"Love is not in the realm of reason. It is illogical and a poor justification for decisions that will change a person's life. Still, that is what I have to say for myself. I love Caroline." The admission loosened something in his chest. He felt his shoulders square. "I have loved her all my life, and these past years without her have convinced me I will continue to love her as long as I breathe." And Eddie paused, taking a sweet inhale as if that would bring Caroline to him. "If she agreed with Lord Preston and did not want to risk living as a poor woman with me, then I would leave her in peace. However, she loves me, too, and moreover, she says she wants to marry me. If you were in my place, sir, I think you would elope, too."

"I'm sure I would." Max's tone softened. "Yet a marriage needs more than love to survive. You cannot even afford to get to Scotland."

Eddie was a little shocked that speaking his mind had actually worked. "Not right now, no." He dared look up—not quite making eye contact with Max, but high enough to discover that Max now stood by the window, looking worried. "However, if you will permit me to say it, sir, the windows here are in a sorry state. Perhaps you are in need of a glazier to prepare them for your holiday guests?"

Max laughed. Crossing the room, he clapped a hand on Eddie's back. "You'll do just fine on your own, Eddie, and so long as you make Caro happy, you'll be welcome here."

As Eddie laughed in relief, he wondered if any of his brothers would ever say such a kind thing to him.

CAROLINE FELT MORE LIKE herself, even though she was wearing one of Ellen's gowns. Bathed, fed, warmed by the fire, she no longer felt as if anxiety were eating her from the inside out.

It helped that Ellen was being so understanding. After allowing Caroline time to bathe, Ellen joined Caroline in her private sitting room to ask what was going on.

Caroline had prepared in her head a certain version of the story. A version that made her and Eddie sound very adult, rational, and responsible. Yet as she opened her mouth, terrible details spilled out: how horrible it was to see Papa send Eddie away, kissing in the Tower of London, stealing Aunt Charlotte's carriage without the money to pay the tolls all the way to Gretna Green.

"I've made a terrible mess of things, Ellen, but please say you'll help. I love Eddie, and Eddie loves me, and I would be proud to be his wife, even if he is only a glazier. Please, you understand that, don't you?"

And Ellen did. "It has never been a secret that you loved Eddie."

"I thought..." Caroline almost choked on her words because tears surprised her. "I thought Papa would congratulate us and offer us a cottage at Northfield Hall."

"I always feared he might refuse permission at first, but only to make sure you knew your own mind. You *are* young, and it *is* a consequential decision. Still, once you made it clear..." Ellen trailed off, looking out the window instead of at Caroline.

"You don't think the same way as he does, do you? That Eddie and I are from different natural orders and could never be happy together?"

Ellen turned sharply. "Papa said that to you?"

"He kept using the word 'natural.'" In a gush of anxiety, Caroline added, "And I reread his most recent article, Ellen, and it sounds an awful lot like he believes we are born into classes by…I don't know, some law of God…and that the laboring class must only consort with other laborers and that they must never expect to be anything other than laborers. It's awful. Do you think Papa really thinks that?"

Ellen withdrew a little block of wood and a knife from her pocket and started whittling—her typical recourse when she needed to think. "You know, I saw Martin Chow a little before he left for China. He was so angry with us—our whole family—and Papa especially. It made *me* angry with Papa, too. Here I thought our father was a beacon of progress who could only ever do right, and yet it turns out, he was willing to muddy the waters when necessary."

Caroline wasn't sure what Ellen was trying to say. "There's a difference between not *always* doing the right thing and believing that there is a natural order that keeps one set of people in unfair circumstances."

"I don't think Papa would phrase it that way," Ellen rebutted gently.

"It doesn't matter how he phrases it. It matters what he does. And what he does is keep the common man under his thumb instead of trying to eradicate the classes that separate us."

"Papa has done so much work to eradicate so much of what separates one person from another. Perhaps it is not surprising that while he is looking at religion and economic prospects and nationality, he cannot see the social hierarchy that seems so obvious to you."

Caroline tensed. "You sound as if you would excuse him for this, as if it were so natural that our father is so prejudiced."

"I don't excuse his behavior." Ellen set aside her wood block and took Caroline's hands—rather forcibly, since Caroline didn't particularly feel like touching her sister in that moment. "Martin's words opened my eyes to the fact that not everyone at Northfield Hall feels our family's efforts result in the…well, utopia that I liked to believe it was. Perhaps we can understand, without condoning, that no one, not even Papa, is able to see the world without one or two remaining prejudices."

Which only made the cold chicken in Caroline's stomach turn sour. Somehow, she had hoped Ellen would make everything from the past few weeks make sense.

Instead, it seemed more necessary than ever that she and Eddie elope, or else Papa might never allow them to be on the same continent together again.

"Still, Papa has never been a man afraid to open his eyes once someone points out to him that he is walking around in the dark. I shall write to him and let him know you are safe and in earnest. By the time you return from Scotland, I am sure he will welcome you home."

"Thank you." Caroline tucked her hands under her skirts for her next revelation: "But we are not going home, you know. Eddie has a position lined up—so long as Papa hasn't gotten him removed already—to join the regiments going to Lower Canada as their glazier.

And since I'll be his wife, I can go with him." Swallowing, she added, "I *shall* go with him."

Ellen's hands stilled. "Lower Canada?"

Her face was as pale as Caroline imagined her own had been when Papa first made the announcement. "Papa arranged it, most likely to prevent us from marrying. But we shall make the most of it. Eddie will be earning excellent pay there, and we'll have shelter and food, so you see, we will come back in a few years with enough savings to establish ourselves somewhere." Caroline hadn't spent too much time imagining the future, and she didn't allow herself to now, other than to will it to be easy and blissful.

"Well, that is wonderful, then, though I shall miss you terribly when you are so far away."

Caroline forced a smile because she also didn't want to spend any time thinking about how homesick she would be.

Ellen peered at her, a blush rising in her cheeks. "I suppose you have already...anticipated the wedding night."

"Ellen!"

It was too raw a topic. Caroline pushed off the sofa, aware that her cheeks were flaming too, and tried to pretend her sister hadn't asked.

"You've run away together to elope. You have spent two nights alone in each other's presence. I must assume that you have already..." Again, Ellen lingered over what words to say. "...taken that step."

It was a horridly personal question. Worse, Caroline wanted to answer *yes*, but that would be a lie, and she still didn't understand why Eddie had not wanted her that night. She did not want to visit this topic with her sister.

"Which means you may, within the course of the next few months, become pregnant. Have you considered that? Are you aware of the precautions you can take to delay such an event?"

Caroline knew bits and pieces. Pennyroyal tea to bring down menses if one was worried they weren't coming, herb-soaked pessaries, and sheaths for the man's appendage. She had never paid much attention to the whispers she overheard because they had never applied to her.

Now it was strange to realize that she was becoming a woman who needed to worry about such things.

"I know the topic is uncomfortable, but if you are acting as a married woman does, Caroline, then it is not only appropriate for us to discuss it, but necessary. I won't let you leave this property until I am sure you know how to care for yourself in this regard."

Caroline obeyed the edge in her sister's voice and sat back down on the sofa. Then, even though she didn't want to admit it, she found herself confessing, "We have done nothing more than kiss. I thought we might do more, but even though we had the opportunity, Eddie didn't want to."

Ellen took Caroline's hand. "Is he protecting your virtue?"

"He..." But Caroline couldn't answer for Eddie. "I wanted to take that step. I thought *he* wanted to take that step. We were kissing and we had undressed. Then, he bit me—accidentally, and it didn't hurt at all—and he said we had better not continue. But I don't know. I think maybe he was displeased by me. Maybe I don't properly know how to kiss, or maybe my body isn't what he thought it would be."

She was aware of her voice getting small and her knees curling up into her chest, as if she were still a little girl.

Ellen scooted closer and wrapped an arm around Caroline's shoulders. "If there is one thing I know about this world, it is that Eddie Chow adores you. I'm sure it hasn't anything to do with you."

It was a gift to shut her eyes and lean her head into Ellen. "But when a man desires a woman, isn't he overcome? Isn't he unable to stop himself from taking her if she is naked on a bed before him?"

"Sometimes, lust will do that to a person. It overcomes you so that you make terrible decisions because your body wants to do that with the other person so badly." Ellen stroked her hair. "Other times, you can't forget about what else is happening around you. Your worries of the day don't fade away, or you hear the fire crackling and fear it is about to jump out of the hearth, or you worry about hurting the other person."

Yet Eddie's reaction hadn't been his usual trepidation in the face of one of her risky schemes. It had been extreme and sudden and it had made him feel as far away as if he had remained in London.

"Sometimes, holding your partner and talking to them is the best way to start things off, rather than going straight to kissing. After all, you and Eddie have been separated for a long time. As much as you love each other, perhaps you need time to get accustomed to each other again. You needn't be in a rush to have the experience. You're going to be married, aren't you? You'll have the rest of your life together to figure it out."

"Yes." Caroline felt buoyed again, reminded of that fact: she was going to marry Eddie. She was going to be his wife. It was all going to happen. "We will spend the rest of our lives together."

Smiling, Ellen kept hold of Caroline's hand. "That's sorted, then. Now, let me tell you about sponges…"

RESTORED TO HIS SUIT—WHICH was freshly cleaned, mended, and pressed—Eddie went in search of Caroline. They had only a quarter of an hour until supper would be served, which Max had informed him he *would* attend, along with the family and their guests who were visiting to celebrate the renaming of Hope Hall. But Eddie didn't want to see Caroline in the midst of people he didn't know.

He wanted to be alone with her.

Though they were both in the guest wing, Eddie had to follow the corridor around two westward twists before he reached Caroline's door. Even then, he was only half sure that he had the right room.

Luckily, it was her cool, confident voice that called out "Enter" in response to his knock.

She sat at a dressing table, watching herself in the looking glass as she pinned her hair up. When she saw it was Eddie, she rose, a quarter of her blond hair still spilling down her neck. "Oh, good, I was afraid Ellen had come back for another *talk.*"

"Is she very concerned for you?" Eddie left the door open as he stepped into the room; Caroline crossed behind him and shut it. Then, she took Eddie's hand and led him to the silk-upholstered sofa in front of a plate glass picture window.

"Oh no, she just wanted to make sure we had a proper plan."

Eddie was distracted by the feel of her fingers in his. It had only been a few hours, but it felt like weeks since they had last been alone together. "I don't suppose we can blame her, since we have arrived on her doorstep in need of help as a result of our poor planning."

"*My* poor planning." Caroline smiled at him, her brown eyes dancing around so fast that the conversation came to a halt. She inhaled, as if to say something, then stopped herself. Her fingers squeezed more tightly around his.

There was so much swirling between them; he wanted to reach out and pluck the right words from the air. He didn't know if he needed to reassure her or talk her down from a wild idea or confess his own feelings.

He wasn't quite sure what his own feelings were, for that matter, except that nothing made him happier than clutching her hand in the dusk and candlelight.

"Max came to lecture me." Without meaning to, he lowered his voice to a whisper. "He started off trying to intimidate me. You know, making it clear he could knock me around and also that he could have his entire household knock me around if he wanted to. I rather thought he was going to see me out."

Caroline's other hand landed on his knee. It felt intimate, not in the way of a mistress with her paramour but in the way of a wife with her husband. "But he didn't."

"He didn't." Eddie still couldn't quite believe it. "If we're serious about this, then he will put us on a boat tomorrow morning to sail to Scotland. He said it will be faster and safer than taking the roads."

Her eyes brightened. "Can the ship's captain marry us?"

Max had brought up that point before Eddie could even think to ask it. "Max isn't sure it would be legally binding, since it is a boat and not a proper ship and it won't leave English waters. It is better if we marry properly in Scotland, if we want this to last. Otherwise..." The end of that sentence was: otherwise, Lord Preston might get the marriage legally annulled before Caroline even turned twenty-one.

There was an expression on Caroline's face that stopped Eddie from saying it. Neither of them needed to hear it aloud, anyway. They knew the consequences they might face. Stating them didn't solve anything.

He focused on the more important question instead. "We could still change our plans, if you wanted. You could stay here, and I could go find a job somewhere in the countryside, and we could wait until your birthday. That way, I would already have a few months' savings for us." Eddie knew that was what most brides preferred, any-how. It was one of the reasons why apprentices couldn't marry by law: they couldn't even provide for a wife, if they had one.

Still, he hoped Caroline didn't want to wait.

"It would make your father happier," he added. "We might not get his blessing, but at least he might…"

Caroline tugged his hand so he leaned close. Close enough to kiss. Her other hand rose from his knee to thread through the hair just behind his ear. "I don't want to wait, Eddie. Whatever we have to face, we face together."

Relief made him giddy. He kissed her sloppily, almost missing the ridge of her lips because he was so busy grabbing her hips and pulling her onto his lap. She laughed in response, a throaty sound that tickled his skin. Eddie's cock was hard, his mind clouded with desire, and he believed again that he could do this. That he could be her husband and make her happy, despite all the odds stacked against them.

Then the supper gong rang.

Caroline lifted away. Her hands ran across her breasts, and she let out a long sigh. "We'll have to save the rest of that for later."

"For our wedding night." Eddie meant it as a promise.

"Yes, for our wedding night and every night after." Caroline turned to her mirror, gathering her hair up into its pins. "You had better go down first, or everyone will suspect we have been making mischief together."

Eddie stared at the ceiling and focused on the strange little cherubs carved into the plaster trim until his erection had calmed. Standing, he took one last look at Caroline.

She smiled at him in the mirror.

"We leave at dawn," he said, and before his desire could flood back, he fled for the dining room.

Chapter Thirteen

T HEY RODE IN A wagon an hour and a half to the sea, then Max saw them boarded onto a little sailboat that would take them north to Scotland. He himself handed Caroline onto the swaying deck, with the last words, "You can always come back to Hope Hall, married or not."

She thanked him because she knew he meant it kindly. But Scotland was only a day and a half's sail away. Caroline could count the time until she and Eddie married in hours. She was not worried about returning to Hope Hall unmarried. Especially not since Ellen had sent her off with a change of clothes, an extra pair of boots, a hairbrush and ribbons, and a pouch with nearly five pounds to get them back to London by January.

Settled onto the boat, she and Eddie waved goodbye to Max as the skipper navigated them off the shore. The vessel was no more than twenty feet long, with a compact deck full of winches and ropes and nowhere to sit. The boat transported wheat from Hope Hall to the north and coal back south to Hope Hall. The skipper and first mate were being paid ten pounds each to take Eddie and Caroline on this journey—and to say nothing about it to anyone.

Caroline settled with Eddie at the bow of the boat, where they seemed most out of the way. Linnie tucked in beneath Eddie's ankles, too. The sailboat clipped along faster than a carriage, buoyed by a cold wind that had Caroline shivering in minutes. Still, it was better to be cold while watching the shoreline than to be warm in the cramped, dark hold beneath the deck. Especially when Eddie wrapped his arm around her.

"After all our years on the *Jolly Molly*, we are finally actually sailing," he said.

Caroline remembered Mama encouraging her to play with Eddie. She even had a memory of Papa ruffling her hair and saying, "You are lucky to have a friend like Eddie. You must work hard to do right by him so he is a friend for all your life."

It had never occurred to her that Papa did not want *friend* to morph into *husband*.

She did not want to think about Papa and how he would react to their adventure. "What a story we shall have to tell our children," Caroline murmured, leaning into Eddie's heat. "We could write it into a novel and earn our living off the income."

Eddie stiffened—but was that just because of the cold water spraying into their faces with a change of direction? "I don't think novels earn enough money to keep a whole family."

Caroline had met a half dozen novelists among her set, yet she had no idea how the business worked. For all she knew, they were not paid at all.

She also didn't have any idea how much money she and Eddie would need in order to survive. Especially not if there were a baby added into the mix.

It was beginning to feel like she should pay attention to that kind of detail. "Do you think me very vapid for not knowing about money?"

"No." Eddie's arm tightened around her, his fingers digging softly into the flesh of her hips. "I think you're lucky."

Caroline knew she was. At the moment, however, it felt more like she was ignorant and ill-prepared. More like a child pretending to elope than a grown woman ready to become a wife.

It made her feel horribly like she was proving Papa right when all she wanted was to prove him wrong.

"I wish you didn't have to know about money," Eddie added. "I wish I were rich and titled so that you could live the rest of your life the same as you always have."

Some of his words were lost to the wind, but Caroline absorbed his sentiment from the way his body caved a little and from how his chin turned away from her.

She hated that everyone had made him feel as if he weren't good enough for her. "If you were rich and titled, I probably wouldn't like you at all, for you would be so worried about what to do with your money and title that you wouldn't have time to sit and talk with me."

Eddie's hand stroked her hip. "Rich and titled men have nothing *but* time. When I'm working, I'll have to rise early and go out to work, only to come home after sundown. I might not have time to do anything but sleep before I have to do it all over again."

Caroline couldn't quite wrap her imagination around a day like that. "At the very least, you shall have to sit down and eat supper with me. A supper that I shall learn to cook myself so that you needn't worry about affording a maid. I will learn how to keep house myself." She could see it now: a little house within the wooden fortifications of a Canadian town, with clean windows boasting gingham curtains.

"And you will be happy living like that?" Again, Eddie's chin turned away from her.

"Yes. I'm not a fool. I know it will be challenging, but it will be worth it. Besides…" She nuzzled his shoulder playfully. "You know I love a challenge."

Eddie responded as she wanted by returning his eyes to hers. He smiled, his gaze dancing down to her lips. "If we weren't in the company of others, I would kiss you right now."

"Oh, would you?" Heat rushed Caroline's body. "What else would you do?"

His grip on her hip now was motionless. "I would touch you."

"Where?"

"On your..." Eddie's eyes flicked away, as if checking to see if they had company. Then, patches of red arising on his cheeks, he whispered, "Your tits."

"I love that you call them tits." The word was so coarse. It made Caroline feel a part of the world. "And I would love for you to touch them. Would you leave my gown on?"

"Yes. But I would undo these buttons." His free fingers rose and touched the top button at her neck. "I would slide my hand underneath your clothes so I could get a proper grip on them." He licked his lips. "Your tits."

It was as if he were doing exactly as he said. Caroline was breathless, her innermost parts vibrating and wet.

She glanced down to check for a bulge in his trousers. It was there, so strong that she could almost see its full outline. She had to cling to her cloak to keep from groping him then and there.

"I would touch you too." Her voice surprised her by coming out raspy. "I would touch your..."

Eddie's hand on her hip tightened. "Pipe?"

That wasn't a word a lady should ever use, yet it wasn't coarse enough for Caroline. She wanted to use a term that the most experienced whore might employ. She only knew a few. "Prick."

"What would you do with my prick?"

"I would..." What did one do with pricks? Caroline looked at it again. She let her imagination roam. "I would open your trousers. So it could feel the sea air." Nervous, she joked, "It could do with some healthy sea air, after all."

Eddie touched his forehead to her hair. "What else?"

"I would..." Caroline wished she had paid more attention to all the naughty gossip at Northfield Hall. "I would move my hand over it. As if it were my body on top of it. I would..."

"Stroke it?" Eddie's suggestion was a bit of a groan.

Caroline grinned. "Yes, I would stroke it. I would stroke it as if it were the smoothest wood that I never wanted to stop touching. I would stroke it so fast and hard."

Eddie panted into her hair. It was the best feeling in the world to know she could make him so aroused, even just with her words. Caroline let her imagination go farther.

"I would kiss it, too. Gently, at first, to make sure you liked it. Then, I would kiss all along it. A trail of kisses." He moaned. Caroline kept going: "If you liked *that*, then I would stroke the length of it with my hand while I kissed its tip. And all this while, my dress would be open, and you could hold onto my tits. My mouth on your prick, your hands on my tits."

It sounded divine, actually. Caroline couldn't concentrate on what to say next because she got lost in fantasizing about how that might feel.

Eddie's hips jerked. "Stop, Monkey, you had better stop..."

"Oh, but I wouldn't, not until I had my fill. Not until I made you absolutely wild. Not until I had you screaming my name for the entire North Sea to hear."

"Monkey..." His head fell backward, and his whole body shuddered.

For a terrible moment, Caroline was afraid Eddie had been seized by some kind of fit. She clung to his torso in case he was about to fall into the sea. Then she looked down at his lap and saw a small damp spot emerging against the outline of his prick.

"Fuck. I'm sorry." Eddie's curse startled her. Caroline had never heard him say a word like that before. "You got me too excited."

"Is that...?" Once more, Caroline didn't have the words to describe the world—the very real world—around her, and this time, frustration made her a little angry. "Did you...?"

"I believe your set calls it *la petite mort*," Eddie answered. "That hasn't happened to me before, though." He tugged his cloak across his lap like a blanket. "I'm sorry."

"Don't be sorry." Whatever it was that had just happened, Caroline suspected it was a victory for her, not anything for him to be sorry about. Except he was stuck in wet trousers, and they still had at least a day and night left of sailing.

She glanced back. The skipper and his mate were busy sharing a flask, not even looking their way. "Would you like to clean yourself up? You could go down below."

"No. It will..." Eddie turned his chin away from her again. "It will be fine. Don't worry about me."

He didn't want her to fuss over him. Fine. Caroline could not fuss. She tried to resettle in the curve of his body. She tried to focus again on the shoreline off to the west.

She tried to pretend they were as comfortable as they had been only a few minutes before, but somehow, everything had changed.

EDDIE WAS AWARE HE was bollocksing everything up.

Even now, after Ellen and Max had intervened to make sure that Caroline could safely travel with him, Eddie couldn't manage to keep the sail pleasant and romantic. First, his body betrayed him because he was too weak to withstand the heat of her words whispered against his skin. Then his mood betrayed him: try as he might, for the rest of the afternoon, Eddie couldn't find any playful jokes, nor could he engage when Caroline switched to serious topics like what kind of god had created the world, nor could he even muster up anything more than monosyllabic grunts in response to her memories from Northfield Hall.

After a while, Caroline gave up. They sat in silence, touching but not interacting, and waited for the boat to make it to Scotland.

The problem, of course, wasn't that Eddie was bollocksing everything up. The problem was that *Eddie* was bollocks. He didn't have any money. He didn't have any connections in Scotland to find a job once they got there. He couldn't even flirt or kiss without hurting Caroline or coming too soon.

His mother sometimes told the story of how when he was a baby, he refused to suckle at her teat and she thought he would starve himself to death. From that moment, she must have known this child of hers was a bad egg. Small wonder his parents had sent him off from Northfield Hall at their first opportunity. Everyone—his brothers, Lord Preston, Mr. Trowbridge—must have known this whole time that Eddie didn't have it in him to be a proper human being.

Everyone except for Eddie and Caroline.

It was only a matter of time before Caroline realized it, too. Perhaps even now, as he failed to respond to her conversation, she was discovering that she had run off with the wrong fellow.

They were bad thoughts that stirred up bad feelings. If Eddie could have shaken them off, he would.

But of course he couldn't.

The boat made one stop, just as dusk was beginning to settle, to offload some wheat in one of the northern counties. The skipper directed Caroline and Eddie into the cabin below. "It would be a shame if anyone saw you, Miss Preston."

It was warm in the cabin. That was the only quality that Eddie could find to recommend it. It was cramped and dark, and it stank. He couldn't quite tell if the odors were shit, vomit, rodents, or the sea.

They were directed to take the two hammocks hanging from hooks on either side of the cabin. Eddie pulled himself together enough to help Caroline into hers: he held it steady as she climbed in. Then, Linnie in the crook of his arm, he scrambled into his own.

"This isn't so bad," Caroline said cheerfully. "I think I might be able to sleep through the night like this."

Linnie scratched Eddie as she crawled up and down his body in a panic, trying to find a purchase in the swaying hammock.

"You've been awfully quiet, you know."

He knew. He knew, too, she deserved more. Lifting Linnie, he settled her into the crook of his elbow against his waist. With his other hand, he petted her head in long, smooth strokes in hopes that it would calm her.

In hopes that it would calm *him*.

He needed to find something to say to Caroline. "I'm sorry. I don't mean to be."

"Is it because...should I have not said what I said?"

"No. It hasn't anything to do with you." Already, Eddie was sick of having to issue that reassurance. Other men never had to make apologies like this. Other men could pay for their own marriages and fuck their wives and not bollocks any of it up.

"Are you thinking too hard?" Caroline asked.

"Probably."

"Perhaps you had better tell me what is on your mind." Her voice edged towards Determined Caroline. "After all, remember how much better you felt after you told me you feared I would be strangled in the May Day ribbons."

That was when they were eight. Eddie's fear from watching the rehearsals of all the dancers running in opposite directions with their ribbons hanging taut from the maypole had consumed him, and he had been able to eat neither supper nor breakfast nor lunch until Caroline put her hands on her hips and forced him to confess why he was so upset.

It was hardly the same as trying to explain to her all the myriad ways he was unfit to be a husband.

Still, Eddie knew he owed her a reply. "How could you put up with me being so scared of such a stupid thing?"

"How is it stupid to be worried that your friend might *die*? We were very concerned about mortality that whole year, don't you remember? Mama had died and so did that baby in Thatcham. We kept worrying about who would be next."

"You're being generous. I believe it was *I* who was worried, and *you* who had to keep calming me down." He remembered vividly an afternoon when he had discovered the corpse of a bird in the woods and wept over it while Caroline waited with her arms crossed, begging him to please *get his grief over with* so they could continue on their planned adventure.

"You put words to what we were both feeling. When you said you were sad or scared or upset, I didn't have to admit that *I* was any of that. I could skip straight to calming us both down. Truly, I think about that sometimes. I don't know how I would have gotten through Mama's death without you."

When Eddie thought of Caroline's grief over her mother, he mostly remembered the day Lady Preston was buried. Per custom, the children remained in the Hall while Lord Preston and the men of the estate saw her buried in the family plot. Caroline had sat with her siblings, all of them holding desperately to each other. From his corner of the room, Eddie had watched her sob into Ellen's black skirts and ached to rush over and comfort her himself.

It seemed as if the very next day, she had returned to her normal self. Eddie considered now that perhaps he had been unable to comprehend all the ways Caroline weathered that storm of grief.

From the deck, the skipper let out a shout, and Eddie heard the thud of wood on wood. He hoped it was the tender boat come to relieve them of the wheat.

Instinctively, he reached across the space between their hammocks. After a moment, Caroline did the same, and their fingers intertwined in the dark.

The rough voices of the sailors drifted down from the deck. "Aye, we've got three more," someone called.

Another, gruffer voice said, "In the cabin?"

The skipper said sharply: "No, don't go in there."

For a moment, the voices all grew muffled. Eddie tried not to think about a gang of men on the deck. The skipper and his mate were well paid, thanks to Max. They wouldn't let any harm come to Caroline.

Then, clear as day, he heard the skipper say, "Letting her run off with some Lascar good-for-nothing. Might as well be sending her to a whorehouse, if you ask me."

Caroline's fingers tightened around Eddie's.

Rage made Eddie hot. He tried to let the emotion fuel him into action. A proper man didn't stop to think in moments like this.

A proper man would surge up, issue a biting remark, and take on a hundred men with his bare hands just for besmirching his lady's name.

Instead, Eddie was immobilized. The very rage that was supposed to propel him overwhelmed him. If he went up there, he could hold his own against one or two men, but he would more likely be thrown overboard than succeed in delivering a lesson. And if he *did* succeed, then he and Caroline would be stranded on the boat without any idea how to sail it to safety.

And the word *Lascar* rattled around his head.

"Let them talk," Caroline whispered. She was pulling so hard on him that their hammocks swayed towards each other. "I don't care about gossip. This time tomorrow, we'll be married in Scotland."

"Max paid them to stay quiet." But of course, that wasn't Eddie's money to protect. He and Caroline would be walking to Scotland if they had been forced to rely on his resources alone.

A raunchy laugh came from the deck, followed by something that sounded like, "Waste of English blood!"

Linnie growled.

"Let them have their fun," Caroline repeated.

Eddie's skin suddenly felt too tight. His breath felt unnatural. He pictured his reflection as he knew it and wondered what the skipper had been thinking all day, watching him and Caroline sit at the prow of the boat.

Apparently, Eddie wasn't worth Caroline, and not for any of the reasons he knew to be true. Apparently, it was that Eddie wasn't English.

"Do you think your father really objects because I am only a glazier? Or is it because my family is Chinese?"

Her fingers clung to his even as he tried to let go.

Eddie thought she wasn't going to reply. Or she was going to remind him of John, whose mother was from India and yet whom Lord Preston had welcomed as Sophia's husband.

When Caroline did respond, her voice was deathly quiet. "I don't pretend to know what my father thinks anymore. As for me, I love you entirely."

Eddie believed her. But he also didn't. He pulled his hand free. "I think we should try to sleep."

Chapter Fourteen

IT WAS A BAD night. Caroline didn't sleep much at all: the swaying of the boat made her nauseous, and each step the skipper and mate took above them resounded through the deck boards, waking her in a panic that they would do her bodily harm. She wanted to climb into Eddie's hammock and curl inside the safety of his arms, but he was snoring, and his hammock was full anyway with him and Linnie.

Caroline tried counting sheep in her head. She recited prayers—ones she had learned in church, ones she had learned from Uncle Maulvi, ones she had heard others at Northfield Hall murmur—and when she exhausted those, she moved on to all the poetry Miss Hoggart had forced her to memorize over the years.

None of it did much to quiet the clamor in her head. It was as if she were trapped in that moment of overhearing the skipper's offensive words. She knew time had passed; she knew she was no longer holding onto Eddie's fingers as if they alone would keep her from drowning; she knew Eddie was now snoring because he could brush off comments like that.

Yet Caroline felt frozen, like a fly caught in amber, unable to stop hearing the skipper say *Lascar* as if it were a curse and even more unable to prevent Eddie from asking if Papa refused their marriage because he was Chinese.

She didn't think Papa could feel that way. His vision for Northfield Hall had been inspired when Mr. and Mrs. Chow had been turned out of service and couldn't find help because they were Chinese. She knew Papa did not believe any of the terrible things people said about *Chinamen*—like that they were dishonest, untrustworthy, or barbaric.

But neither did it make sense to her that Papa would refuse this marriage solely because Eddie was a tradesman. Not when they could live comfortably at Northfield Hall at Papa's direction.

None of Papa's objections made sense, and so when Eddie asked that question, Caroline couldn't help but wonder if there was truth to it.

And if there was, how could she ever love her father again?

Eventually, she stole an hour or two of sleep. When she woke up again, Eddie was sliding out of his hammock, illuminated by a few shafts of sunlight leaking in from the deck above. His black hair stood at all ends, and his eyes were swollen from sleep.

"Are you going up?" Caroline asked, throwing out a hand to catch him while he stood so close.

Eddie clasped her palm. A smile jumped to his lips. "I didn't know you were awake."

"Yes." Relief flooded her that he was no longer sulking. Suddenly, she was self-conscious about how raspy her voice sounded—and her own hair must look frightful. "I'll come up with you."

"Let me have a minute or two in advance. I've got to...how would a gentleman put it? I have some private business to attend to."

"Ah. Please see to it, then." Caroline couldn't help giggling. It was so strange and wonderful to be sharing such an intimate conversation.

Eddie, still playing the gentleman, pressed an overly polite kiss to the top of her hand. Then, Linnie at his heels, he bounded up to the deck.

Caroline saw to her own business with a bucket, which she then carried up and emptied over the side of the boat herself, like a proper tradesman's wife. She made a point of making eye contact with the skipper as she wished him good morning; he tugged at his hat, as if he hadn't all but called her a whore the night before.

"How is the wind?" she asked.

"Should get to Scotland midday," the skipper replied.

"Excellent."

Caroline joined Eddie at the prow. The morning was shrouded by clouds low and heavy in the sky; she drew the hood of her cloak over her head as a slight drizzle began, even though it meant she couldn't see Eddie's face. She focused on his legs, which stretched out in front of him. Linnie sat between his knees, her face turned up as she tried to drink rain straight from the air.

"I'll be glad to get off this boat," Caroline said cheerfully. "It may be faster than a carriage, but it is equally uncomfortable in different ways."

"Makes me yearn to walk on my own two feet," Eddie agreed. He shook his boots a little so his ankles clanged together.

"At least then we could choose our company." She tried very hard to keep the comment light, but Caroline wanted to know how Eddie was feeling after everything they had heard the night before.

He gave a noncommittal grunt in reply.

"This crew leaves something to be desired."

Eddie reached out to stroke Linnie's fur. "As long as they get us to Scotland safely, I won't complain."

And of course Caroline didn't want him to. They couldn't afford a fistfight on a boat, nor did she approve of settling matters in such a manner. Yet something in the way Eddie was trying so hard to be peaceful made Caroline say, "Perhaps you should. I can't forgive the skipper for what he said last night."

At last, some emotion entered Eddie's voice. "About your character?" His toes turned to tap against hers. "He is only saying that because he is jealous *he* isn't the one running off with you to Scotland."

"I was referring to how he talked about you." Caroline hadn't recognized the words as offensive until Eddie had asked her if Papa saw him the same way. "What he said upset you."

"No."

But it *had*. Caroline had felt his injury in the air last night as certainly as she would have seen blood gushing from a knife wound. "It made you worry that Papa thinks the same sort of thing."

Eddie said nothing.

"Him calling you a good-for-nothing made you feel like a good-for-nothing, and for that, I can't forgive him."

"I *am* a good-for-nothing Lascar, Caroline. That's what everyone is trying to tell you, and instead you keep running off with me."

"No, you are not." She could see him tensing and knew they were about to get locked in a battle of wills. She threw out: "For one thing, Lascars are sailors, and you are not a sailor."

"When an Englishman can't be bothered to learn his geography, a Lascar is anyone from Asia. I *am* a Lascar."

"*You* are from Northfield Hall, same as me. You are English."

Eddie drew his legs into his chest. Linnie scampered into Caroline's lap—a warm, damp mass that pinned her to the deck. "It turns out no one cares where you were born if you look like me. I can never be English because I look so Chinese. Never mind that if I were to speak to an actual Lascar sailor, they would laugh in my face and call me a barbarian because my Cantonese is so bad and my manners are so British. I am both and neither. And our children will be too, if we have any."

"Of course we will have children. Why wouldn't we?"

Eddie blew out a breath. Caroline could feel his exasperation. Was it with her? With the world? With the journey to get married that never seemed to end?

Caroline decided she had replied to the wrong sentiment in his speech. "It must be very frustrating to feel all of that. It would make me want to punch every single ignorant person in the world. But I hope you know that *I* know who you are and where you are from. And whether you are a good-for-nothing Lascar or Briton or sea kraken, you are the person I want to marry."

She placed her hand between them, palm up. To her relief, Eddie took it. He even brought it to his lips and placed a kiss along their intertwined knuckles. "Thank you."

"And me? Do you want to marry me even though I am a good-for-nothing daughter of a peer who doesn't know how to make a simple stew?"

"Even though you are no better than a common whore," Eddie said, a smile in his voice, and he held onto her hand until they reached Scotland.

THEY LANDED AT A small fishing village just north of the Scottish border. The skipper and mate didn't even tie up the boat: they handed Caroline to Eddie on the dock, then pushed back off to return to their regular mooring in England. Eddie saw the mate spit over the side of the boat as if to rid it of bad luck.

Ignorant men. Eddie wouldn't let them or anyone else like them rob him of his joy again.

He and Linnie stayed a step behind Caroline as they walked into the village. It comprised a few brick buildings, a few more huts, and a stone church at the top of a hill. There was hardly anyone around; an old woman stared at them from behind a barrel of herring, and a few men watched them from a bench outside what Eddie presumed was a tavern.

No one made any gesture of welcome.

"Let's try the church, shall we?" Caroline said, and Eddie heard in her voice the same cheer he was forcing upon himself.

The hill was steep enough that the two bags he carried grew heavy, and he was huffing and puffing by the time they reached the church. It was beautiful, classic gray stone with a steeple rising far above their heads. Its double doors were painted a deep red; Eddie stepped ahead of Caroline to push them open.

Inside smelled of good wood and musty bibles. The weak sunlight filtered in through plain windows; Eddie remembered the Scots were Presbyterians and didn't go for adornments like stained glass. Still, even with the simple glass, the church was dark—and there was no sign of a living soul.

Caroline repeated what she had been saying all morning: "All we need is a minister and a witness."

"And a shilling or two, perhaps," Eddie added. He knew in Gretna Green, a wedding cost a pretty penny. The longer they remained in this fishing village, the more he suspected they would need to pay a higher bribe for cooperation.

Luckily, money was no longer an issue.

They walked the aisle together, then found a door behind the pulpit. It led through a short corridor to another set of rooms: one full of robes, one full of books, and—at last—a small kitchen and scullery in which an old woman stood at a sink, scrubbing dishes.

"Please do excuse us—" Caroline began, and the woman let out a shriek.

She was very tall and very old; when she turned towards them, Eddie saw her eyes were milky with cataracts.

"I didn't mean to frighten you," Caroline said.

"Well, you did." Her brogue was harsh and not as easy to understand as that of the Scots Eddie had encountered in London. "What is an Englishwoman doing in my church?"

"My name is Caroline Preston, and I am here with my fiancé, Mr. Edward Chow. We are hoping to be married. Do you know where we can find the minister?"

The woman wiped her hands on her apron. "Runaways, are you?"

Caroline replied, "We are eager to marry and have just sailed here from England so we can be man and wife."

"Anticipated the event, did you? Got yourself into trouble?" The woman's voice was still full of scorn. "Well, you won't be marrying here, not today anyhow. Reverend Fraser is off in Chirnside saying the last rites for Old Man Lindsay."

Of course he was. Each time they got close to marrying, some new obstacle announced itself. Eddie set down the bags to give his arms a rest. "How far is the next church?"

"Ten miles or so, and farther if you're looking for one in Scotland."

Too far to travel in an afternoon. Besides, Eddie didn't have high hopes for hiring a coach and horses from this little village. "Is there anywhere that takes boarders, then, so we can wait for Reverend Fraser to return?"

"No, sir."

She said it so baldly that for a moment, Eddie couldn't process it. He kept waiting for her to modify her statement, at the very least to suggest a coaching inn that would take hours to walk to.

Apparently, the Scotswoman was happy to let Caroline and Eddie become vagabonds.

"Is there no family nearby who could do with an extra shilling or two in exchange for shelter and a meal?"

The woman turned back to her dishes.

Eddie prodded: "We don't need a bed, even. We can stay in a barn."

"The MacPhersons down in the valley might take you in. If you don't mind staying with a witch, that is."

Eddie looked to Caroline. She raised her eyebrows, which he took to be agreement that they didn't have much of an option.

Besides, neither of them put much stock in witchcraft.

Eddie picked up the bags again. "We'll do that, then. Can you tell us how to get down to the valley?"

"Follow the road away from the sea, of course. Now leave me be."

Caroline hesitated before leaving a few pennies on the counter. "For your trouble."

The old woman spat at the ground, as if to rid herself of such gratitude, but she pocketed the money all the same.

Outside the church, Caroline took one of the bags from Eddie. "I can carry that as well as you can, and we haven't any idea how long this will be." Her forced cheer was diminishing, the high pitch of her voice replaced by steely determination.

Eddie didn't want her to feel that she needed to marshal him into agreement. "It can't be that long if they live in the parish. A skip and a hop on the witch's broomstick, anyhow."

That earned him a laugh, the sweetest sound in the world. Caroline's eyes glimmered at him from beneath her bonnet. "If only I had become a witch instead of a lady, we'd have flown ourselves to Gretna Green and back by now."

They returned to the dirt road. This time, they went down the opposite side of the hill, so that soon the North Sea was but a memory behind them. For as far as Eddie could see, there was nothing but heather and grass. But then, they couldn't quite see the bottom of the valley, only a slow, hilly, deserted descent.

"Imagine she made this witch up," Caroline said as they passed their first stone mile marker. "Imagine she heard my English accent and decided to send us into the wilderness to be eaten by bears."

"I don't think there are bears in Scotland, but I am worried about that wildcat over there in the heather."

Caroline whipped around, her mouth hanging open in fear, before she realized he was jesting. "How dare you tease me, Eddie Chow!" She swung her bag at him; Eddie defended himself with the bag in his arm. The impact shuddered through his shoulder. He whirled towards her to avoid her next parry. He clamped an arm around her waist and lifted her off the ground to destabilize her entirely; laughing again, she kicked her feet uselessly through the air. "Mercy! Mercy!"

Pretending he was the worst kind of villain, Eddie growled into her ear, "If I put you down, do you promise to behave?"

Caroline's lefthand fingers tightened around his forearm. "I make no promises. I am a very wicked woman."

He set her feet on the ground but didn't let go. Her body was so soft and perfect. The feel of her waist inside his elbow and her bum hugging into his groin erased all good sense from his mind. Eddie dug his lips into her from behind, claiming a twisted kiss that went directly to his cock. His prick, as she had murmured on the boat the previous afternoon.

"Are you going to have your way with me right here, Mr. Highwayman?" Caroline rasped.

The fantasy washed over him. There wasn't a soul around. Their bed would be the heather. Their witnesses would be the birds. Their heat and shelter and safety would be their love.

Something sharp grazed his ankle: Linnie, nipping at him in her interpretation of play.

That was enough to bring Eddie back to reality. They still had to find the witch's house—and if that didn't exist, they had to find *somewhere* to shelter for the night.

It was up to Eddie to make sure that Caroline was safe and warm.

He let her go. "You're spared for the moment," he replied, still in his highwayman voice. Then, taking her free hand, he tugged her down the road. "Come along, let's see about this witch."

CHAPTER FIFTEEN

S ECRETLY, CAROLINE WAS GLAD that Eddie didn't take their game too far. She didn't want him to know it, but her nerves were on high alert after being turned away from the church. Things weren't supposed to be complicated in Scotland. They were supposed to be married by now.

Caroline wasn't sure how many more obstacles she could bear to face.

She played with Eddie because she didn't want him to know how she felt. And for a moment, when Eddie lifted her from the ground, Caroline had been able to let those worries fly. But even with him growling deliciously in her ear, she had wondered: was there really a witch somewhere in the valley? Would the witch allow them to stay the night? And once they made it through the night, would they find a minister to marry them?

They walked hand in hand further into the valley. The air grew cooler as they lost the direct sunlight, and Caroline hugged closer to Eddie's body for heat. She tried to brighten up the journey by pointing out a strange cloud here, an interesting plant there—and accidentally, by shrieking at the slither of a snake across the path. They tossed sticks for Linnie and made bets about how far she would go before turning back to make sure Eddie still followed. Time passed; a mile or two passed; and it was wonderful because she and Eddie could talk about anything and everything, and it was terrible because they couldn't say any of the things that were really hammering behind their heartbeats.

And then, just as darkness began to fall, they reached a cow path that led across a brook, into a copse of trees, and up to a stone barn beside a stone house.

Eddie let go of Caroline's hand to stride ahead of her. Playing the servant again—Caroline hated it when he did that. She didn't object, however, just as she hadn't objected in the village. She was trying to learn to trust Eddie's instincts—and change her own.

It took forever for anyone to answer the knock on the door. Waiting behind Eddie by the vegetable garden, Caroline worried no one would. The witch might not be home, or she might not be at home to strangers.

She might even be casting an evil spell to expel Eddie and Caroline from her property.

But then the door creaked open.

"You'll be looking for somewhere warm to stay," a kind voice said.

Caroline had expected a short, haggard woman with white skin and warts on her nose.

This witch was as tall as Caroline and carried herself erect, with strong shoulders and brown skin free of any blemish. The only indication of her age was the gray hair springing in all directions from her head.

"Come in, come in," the woman urged. "Your dog will have to stay in the barn, though."

As Eddie settled Linnie outside, Caroline stepped into the witch's house. It was not large; in fact, it was only one room. A great hearth took up most of the back wall, with a cabinet on the right, a bed on the left, and a table in the center of the room. Later, she noticed a spinning wheel in the corner—half a skein of yarn completed—and a string of fish drying against the wall.

For the moment, Caroline was distracted by the man sitting at the table: *he* was white and wart-covered and looked far more like a witch than the woman. Yet he, too, welcomed them: "Lost on your way somewhere, are you? Come in, come in, sit by the fire. The chill is setting in for the evening."

Caroline opened her mouth to offer some explanation, but she could find no words. She was overwhelmed by embarrassment that she and Eddie were going to beg charity from these people who had so little to offer.

Entering, Eddie said: "We are looking for somewhere to stay the night. The woman at the church said you might have room for us. We've money and would be happy to pay you for your hospitality."

"We insist on paying you," Caroline corrected.

Eddie cast her a look that seemed to tell her to hush.

"You'll stay here, but you won't be paying us," the witch said. "I don't take money for doing the right thing. That Hattie MacPherson should have put you up in the church for no money, but she isn't a Christian woman no matter how many of the minister's dishes she cleans. Did she say I was a witch?"

Caroline's cheeks heated.

Eddie answered, "She said a great many things we don't put much stock in."

The woman evaluated this with a sucking sound of her tongue against her front teeth. "Then you have good sense. I'm no more a witch than Mr. MacPherson here is the King of England. They only say that in the village because they're scared of anyone who doesn't look like them."

She hesitated, her eyes resting on Eddie, and Caroline felt the two of them exchange unspoken words.

Caroline couldn't find anything to say. Was everyone in Scotland named MacPherson?

"We don't begrudge them their ignorance, even if Hattie MacPherson is my own sister." With this startling disclosure, Mr. MacPherson rose from the table and started collecting battered tin plates from the cabinet. "I got on a sailing ship as a boy and have visited all seven corners of the world. I've seen people of all kinds. I knew a prize when I saw one, and didn't think for a second before bringing Annie home with me. But these people haven't left Scotland. They think an Englishman is a stranger. They don't know any better, but it is harmless."

He set the plates around the table. Annie went to the iron pot hanging over the hearth and removed from it a whole roasted bird, which she placed in the center of the table. "In any case," she said, "we welcome your company. Sit down and tell us your story."

But Caroline had more questions about *their* story—and, for reasons she couldn't define, she was reluctant to tell them too much about herself. She had met people from all over the world at Northfield Hall; she had witnessed poverty in London on a tour with her father; she knew intimately the two- and three-room cottages of Northfield Hall that families called their home. Yet there was something jarring about happening upon the MacPhersons here in the emptiness of the valley, where they insisted they were perfectly happy with no allies except their cows.

She sat silently as Eddie explained they had come to Scotland to get married and were waiting for the minister to return. He was, Caroline noticed, careful not to mention that she was a Preston. When Mr. MacPherson asked where they were from, Eddie said only, "Berkshire," and then explained he had finished his apprenticeship in London.

"And you are from Cathay?" MacPherson asked, using the old word to refer to China as if it were still the sixteenth century.

"My family is."

Caroline interrupted: "Mr. Chow was born in Berkshire, same as me. He is British."

Annie quirked her lips knowingly and lifted meat to her lips.

"Our children were all born here," MacPherson agreed. "Right in this very room. Still, the village acted as if they didn't speak a lick of English."

Startled, Caroline searched the room for evidence of children. There was only one bed: where had everyone slept? "How many children do you have?"

"Eight living, two dead, God have mercy," Annie replied. "All gone off in search of work."

This launched Mr. MacPherson into a monologue on the sorry state of cities, of the impossibility of honest work when one had to enter into a factory life, of the general dissolution of society. It was nothing Caroline hadn't heard before, and he said it all so congenially that she understood he was merely filling the air—he might recite the same gripes with or without an audience—yet with each word, she grew a little more uncomfortable. It was the knowledge that there had been a whole family here once, yet not a single child could afford to remain behind to look after their parents. It was realizing that Annie had spent a lifetime in this valley, yet still the woman at the church called her a witch. It was hearing, for the first time, the gripes of a good-hearted family trying to make an honest living and realizing she herself would have to somehow survive like this.

It was discovering that this lonely, one-room house might be her own future.

If she married Eddie.

"In any case," Annie said eventually to cut off her husband's lecture, "you'll be wanting your rest after all that traveling. Let's finish the chores so we can go to bed."

Standing, MacPherson slapped Eddie on the shoulder as if they were old friends. "Will you help me with the cows, Chow?"

"Certainly." Eddie looked at Caroline, a question in his eyes. "You'll be all right in here?"

Caroline put on a smile. "Why shouldn't I be?"

The answer arrived on its own when Annie handed her the stack of dirty plates and a bar of soap. "You can wash these in the brook. You remember where that is?"

Caroline remembered. What she didn't dare admit was that she didn't know how to wash a dish.

It couldn't be that difficult. She knew how to wash her hands; this was the same concept, applied to plates. Caroline carried her burden carefully, not wanting to drop anything in the darkness. Crouching beside the brook, she dipped the first plate in the water—and almost lost it to the surprising force of the current. When she added the soap, the bar slipped from her grip and she had to splash into the brook to catch it before it disappeared out of sight.

Her feet protested the icy cold. Her wet boots sank into the mud as she retreated, and she could feel it dirtying her skirt. The night air was chilly, too, and Caroline's fingers were quickly going numb from the cold water.

She still had three more plates and the serving platter to go.

"Good thing you have a change of clothes," she told herself. "There's a fire inside. The sooner you finish, the sooner you can warm up."

In spite of her words, tears burned her eyes.

"You're exhausted," she scolded herself. "You are overwrought. You are not actually crying. And you are certainly not..."

She didn't know the word for it, or if she did, she couldn't even say it in her mind, much less out loud for her own ears to hear.

She loved Eddie. She would wash all the dishes in the world in the coldest stream for the longest night, if it meant she could be with him.

She would suffer the censure of all the strangers in the world and of her aunt and siblings and father and everyone who had ever mattered to her, if it meant she could always love Eddie.

She believed that. She really did. She would get used to this, and soon, she would even learn to like it.

But—as she lost the soap a second time and ended up knee deep in the water to catch it again—she allowed herself a little crying fit, just so long as she was alone in the darkness and failing so terribly.

It couldn't hurt to sob.

Not if she was the only person to hear.

A T FIRST, EDDIE THOUGHT the sound was an owl hooting in the night. Hooting, however, was usually uniform, whereas the noise coming from beyond the barn was unsteady and scaling up and down.

He wondered next if it was some poor cow lost in the dark.

It wasn't until he followed MacPherson out of the barn that he realized the sound was human.

That it was Caroline.

"A bride gets nervous," MacPherson said kindly. "You'd best go see if you can't cheer her up."

It took Eddie a few minutes to find her. She had wandered beyond the path to a shallow curve of the brook. She knelt in the mud, tin plates catching the moonlight as she hung her head over her legs. Her whole body shuddered with sobs.

Eddie hadn't seen her cry since her mother died.

"Caroline, what's wrong?" He asked it softly so she wouldn't jump. Even so, she jerked backward in surprise. Eddie crouched beside her and flattened his palm on her back. "You're crying."

"No, I'm not." She wiped her face as if to erase all evidence.

Eddie could allow her some pride. "You *were* crying, then."

"I was washing the plates. The brook is noisy." When her voice broke, betraying her emotions, Caroline glared at him, as if it were his fault. "I'm happy. We are going to be married soon. Why would I cry when I am happy?"

Eddie brought his other hand to her knee and discovered her skirt was practically soaked through with ice-cold water. "I would cry if I were as wet as you."

"That's foolish. Crying is a waste of time. You should just finish washing the dishes so you can go inside and warm up by the fire. Crying only makes you remain wet for longer." She started off her rant bolstered by anger, but her last few words came as choked-off sobs.

Eddie gathered her in his arms. Her head tucked into his chest; her tears landed on the harsh wool of his coat. He didn't have any words to say, so he held her and hoped he was stalwart enough for comfort.

His heart ached because he loved her so much. The idea of being apart from her—well, their parents had forced them to test it already, and Eddie knew what it brought him.

Misery.

Loneliness.

The constant, burning feeling that he was missing all that was good in the world.

Yet, as everyone kept reminding them, he didn't have much of a life to offer her. He believed Caroline when she insisted she didn't care.

But maybe his mother was right: maybe even love wasn't enough to keep a baron's daughter happy when she had to wash dishes in a cold, dark stream.

"I'm being silly." Caroline's hands rose to cup his biceps, but she didn't try to push out of his arms. "I'm not crying because I'm unhappy, Eddie, I swear. I'm embarrassed. What kind of stupid girl am I that I don't even know how to wash a plate? I thought I could figure it out, but—look at me!"

They were holding too tightly to each other for him to actually see much of her. "Do you think I knew how to fit a window on my first try? This is all new for you. Give yourself time."

"Washing a dish is hardly as complex as installing windows." Sniffling, Caroline groped his chest until she found a handkerchief in his coat pocket. Then, withdrawing from him a little, she wiped her cheeks and blew her nose like a trumpet. "I'm fine. I'm glad to learn how to do this. It has been a long day, that's all."

Eddie didn't miss how the explanation for her emotions shifted each time she offered one. "Let's go inside and warm you by the fire, shall we?"

"I haven't finished the plates."

In fact, they were now muddy from sitting wet on the ground. Eddie washed them quickly, shook them dry, and drew Caroline to her feet.

"You made that look so easy," she protested.

"I've been washing dishes since I could walk. I've got more practice than you." He saw a storm cross her brow again, so he dotted a kiss on her forehead. "There's plenty you can do that I can't. Name every capital city in Europe. Explain the legislative processes of Britain, the United States, France, *and* Spain. Draw comparisons between Christianity, Judaism, and Hinduism."

"Yes, that will help me keep house and cook your meals." At least Caroline allowed him to lead her along the path back towards the stone house.

"It might. You can tutor well-to-do children and earn money for a maid."

"Governesses generally aren't married. I could teach music, except I never could do more than memorize a few songs on the harpsichord."

"We will sort it out. We've come this far, haven't we?" Eddie wasn't sure, as he said it, if he was lying or not.

The MacPhersons were generous and kind when they discovered Caroline so very wet. Annie took the plates from Eddie without comment, while Mr. MacPherson said, "You must get dry, of course, or else catch cold. Annie and I like a walk in the moonlight, anyhow. Take off those wet things and dry out."

Caroline objected that she had fresh clothes in her bag and needed only long enough to change outfits, but the couple still disappeared out the front door, insisting they wouldn't be back for at least an hour.

"They must think me a complete fool." Caroline's voice was rough in texture and soft in volume.

"They think you a nervous bride." By the light of the fire, she glowed: her hair was like a gold halo, her eyes gleaming jewels, her skin iridescently pink like an ember that refused to go out. If she were really his bride…if they really could make this work…he would go to her now and never let her go.

Instead, he asked: "Would you like me to give you privacy, too?"

She turned sharply towards him. The light that had been illuminating her face fell to her back, casting her now in a black shadow. "Never."

It was as if their hearts beat to power the blood in *each other's* veins. Eddie would cease to exist if he wasn't beside her. He shoved aside the hovering doubt and went to her. One hand at a time, he took her cheeks in his palms. He kissed her lips with all the love he had been bottling up. With each taste of her, he reminded himself: she was his destiny, she was his desire, she was his.

Whether he deserved her or not.

Button by button, he undid the layers of her outfit. Together, they pulled her wet gown up over her hips and shoulders; Eddie draped it carefully over a chair beside the fire while Caroline removed her stays, petticoats, and stockings. As she handed Eddie each item to hang, he fought harder and harder to focus on the task at hand. He stole her in glimpses. Small, tight breasts. A navel puckering the center of her soft, curved stomach. Thighs defined by the ridge of her stockings—and then, as she unrolled them, by the globes of her knees. He managed to hang every piece of clothing without dropping it to the floor. He managed not to drool as he ogled her.

But once that last stocking hung from the spokes of the chair, Eddie stopped resisting any urge except his instincts. Closing the gap between them, he took her hips in his hands and let his body take over.

The dance they choreographed was similar to the one they had shared at the inn: endless, desperate kissing; hands trailing through new and exciting territory; breaths growing shorter and shorter as Eddie's body grew harder and harder.

Except it was entirely different, too. This time, they stood, even though Eddie soon lost his grip on physics and worried vaguely he might drop Caroline on the ground. This time, Linnie was outside and there was no innkeeper coming to catch them in a lie and there was no family on the other end of their journey about to cast judgment.

This time, it wasn't about proving that they loved each other more than they needed their parents' approval. This wasn't a question of courage or daring or even exploration.

This was love stripped bare to its physical definition.

"Your clothes are too rough," Caroline murmured into Eddie's ear, and so together they pulled those off, too; since his suit had hardly gotten wet at all, he let it pool on the ground where it landed.

Now they were skin to skin. His cock was painfully hard. Eddie knew there was more to the act than plunging inside the woman, and yet that was all his body wanted to do. Their legs interlocked, he walked her back towards the bed.

When she fell onto the mattress, Caroline objected. "We can't be rude. It's *their* bed."

"They meant for us to do this," Eddie said, surprising himself with how confident he was that the MacPhersons knew exactly what he and Caroline were up to.

"It's *their* bed," she repeated. "And I don't think there are any clean sheets for us to put on afterward."

Which reminded Eddie that she lived in a world of endlessly fresh linens and property and private rooms.

He wanted to comfort her. He also wanted to shake her. The MacPhersons were rich compared to what he could offer Caroline. That they *had* a bed with a real mattress was a stroke of luck. That they owned this house and didn't share quarters with some other family—or a dozen siblings, children, and grandparents—was as luxurious as the private bath he had taken at Hope Hall.

He knew this was all as foreign to Caroline as Reading had been to him when he arrived for his first apprenticeship. He remembered his own shock at being told to sleep in the kitchen cabinet; he remembered the injury of being fed only bread and butter after growing up with generous meals at Northfield Hall; he remembered how suddenly, he had realized he was poor—and stupid, for not having known it before.

But hadn't Caroline realized all of that already?

"We don't need a bed." He dipped his lips to hers again, reviving the certainty that pounded through his veins when they were touching. "As long as you want to do this, we don't need anything except each other."

As if he had offered her water in a desert, Caroline surged closer to Eddie. He had known she would. This was the refrain they kept promising each other. It was a vow—or a myth—and by now, it was as heady as a glass of whiskey. Caroline dug her fingers into Eddie's hair to demand an even deeper kiss. Her breasts smashed into his chest. His cock throbbed against the soft skin of her upper thigh. It brushed some of the hair protecting her—Eddie didn't know what word to think, had barely any thoughts in his head left anyhow, and so he could only visualize it—and he knew they were entering the realm of torture.

Either he needed to take her now, or he needed to run out in the cold and find release alone like a wild animal.

"Are you ready?" he asked, though his lips barely left hers to form the words.

Caroline nodded against his mouth.

Eddie didn't need any further encouragement. Gripping the underside of those soft thighs, he lifted her in the air and backed her against the nearest wall. Their height difference was such that with her pinned against the wooden siding, her weight in his hands, Eddie's cock was in the exact right position to plunge inside her.

He didn't have much rational thought left, but some emotion compelled him to say before he did anything else: "I'm going to make you mine."

"I've always been yours," Caroline replied, and she squeezed her ankles against his buttocks.

Eddie thrust inside her, the way his body told him to do, and when she gasped, he assumed it was because it was as breathtakingly sensational for her as it was for him. His whole essence was distilled into her hot, wet body, which was so tight around his cock that he was quite sure he would remain inside her until he died. His hips moved by instinct until he caught on to what felt good; then he got into such a rhythm that he realized he was properly fucking her.

It felt like it would last forever, yet it was over sooner than Eddie knew. He came in a great, sudden jerk inside Caroline. His mind shattered with ecstasy. He was molten glass in a fire, red hot and formless.

He was joy.

Kissing Caroline again on the lips, Eddie withdrew his cock. He landed her feet on the ground and turned away to find a handkerchief from his discarded suit. It was only when he brought the handkerchief to his still-hard cock that he saw the blood.

It was all over him, as if he had dipped his prick into a butcher's bucket. Turning to Caroline, he saw it on her legs, too, smeared like a murderer's fingerprints across the tops of her thighs.

"I hurt you."

"It is supposed to hurt." Her voice was small and unsteady. He saw now that her legs were trembling; she braced her hands against the wall to keep herself up.

"You're bleeding."

"I'm supposed to bleed." But as brave as she was trying to be, her eyes were red with tears.

Eddie had known he was destroying Caroline's life in so many ways by marrying her. He had been so close to accepting that she wanted it and that he didn't need to feel guilt for stealing away her fortune and status and comfort.

Never had he thought he could be a brute.

Yet here she was, shaking.

Eddie didn't dare touch her again. "Did you enjoy it?"

A tear slid down her cheek. Caroline slapped it as if it were a mosquito. "I don't think I am supposed to the first time."

She was fierce. Lifting her chin high, denying her own experience, all in service of making *him* feel comfort. All in service of this myth they were trying to build that, despite all odds, they were meant to be together.

If they were living in a myth, it was a different one: Eddie was a vampire, and Caroline his victim whose lifeblood he slowly but surely sucked away.

He retrieved her fresh clothes from her luggage. He handed her the handkerchief, too. Turning his back, he dressed himself without looking at her.

He couldn't believe what he had done to her.

When they were both dressed, Eddie spread out the straw-stuffed pallet Mrs. MacPherson had left for them. "You can have it to yourself, if you want. I'll sleep on the floor."

"Don't be ridiculous." Taking his hand, Caroline guided him beside her. They had to lie on their sides to fit. She was the one to curl around him. She was the one to say, "It will get better. It is like the dishes. I will learn how to be your wife, Eddie. By the time we land in Lower Canada, no one will know I was ever anything *but* your wife."

Eddie's breath escaped him. "Lower Canada?"

"Yes." Her voice too high and reedy, she said, "Before then, even. By the time we board the ship, I'll be very accustomed to being your wife. You needn't worry."

He had decided so quickly not to follow Lord Preston's plan. Had he really never told Caroline? All this time, had she expected they would return Aunt Charlotte's horse and get on a ship as if nothing had happened? "Monkey, we are not going to Lower Canada."

Her arm trembled where it sat on his torso. "Of course we are. As long as we get married in the next day or so, we will be back by January eighth."

"You misunderstand." Eddie shimmied out of her grasp. "I'm not taking the position with the regiment."

She looked so fragile in the firelight. "What do you mean?"

"I am not taking that position. I don't want to be a part of the army, and I certainly don't want to go live in the wilds somewhere." Eddie paused to breathe, trying to find the best next words.

Caroline interrupted him. "But what are you going to do instead? Do you have a position lined up in London?"

"No." It was as if the air between them were hardening into hot glass, growing thicker with each revelation. Eddie couldn't tell who was more shocked: she by his news or he by her ignorance. "Monkey, that's what I've been trying to say all this time. I have to find work.

Somewhere in the countryside, I hope. Somewhere we can have a cottage like this eventually."

"Have you any connections? Any idea where they need a glazier?"

"No." It was, he knew, a flawed plan. But he had thought Caroline understood it from the start.

She blinked at him, her hands clasping her heart as if to slow it down.

"We have the money from Max." Eddie felt desperate to erase the panic from her face. "That will tide us over long enough to rent a room wherever we decide to go."

Woodenly, she said, "A room. Not a cottage."

"Not at first."

"And when the money runs out, if you haven't found steady work, we shall have to apply to Ellen and Max for more."

"I thought you understood this." He thought it was what they had been discussing ad nauseum the duration of their elopement. Yet apparently, Caroline had been saying yes to marrying an employed man—even if he was employed by the King to spread colonial ideas in some wild frontier where life would be even rougher than this.

"I didn't understand it." Swallowing visibly, Caroline ran her fingers across her braid, her gaze somewhere far away from him. "Is it too late for you to join? Have you given the position away?"

It was the one thing that had been clear to Eddie in all the confusion of London. Despite his instinct to please her, he clung to it now: "I don't want to do it."

Caroline stared at him. "Then, hadn't we—perhaps you were right—I could stay with Ellen until you sort out a job and accommodations..."

Eddie's heart disappeared from his body. He had been the one to suggest a delay back at Hope Hall, but only because it seemed prudent to consider.

She had been the one to refuse.

She had been the one to say she would marry him no matter what.

And here they were at the no matter what. "I thought you wanted to marry me."

"I do." Yet her hands remained on her body, not even attempting to break through the air between them. "Only, if we waited, we might be able to set ourselves up better."

He knew all the arguments for waiting. If they waited, he could get hired without employers worrying about the burden of his wife. If they waited, he could save enough to lease appropriate rooms. His plan from the start had been to wait so that he could come to Caroline with enough money.

But if they had waited then, she would still be locked up at Aunt Charlotte's. If they waited now, Eddie would have to return her to Ellen's care and hope that she wouldn't change her mind.

Who wouldn't change their mind, when they returned to sleeping on a feather mattress after nights on nothing better than a straw pallet?

Who wouldn't change their mind, after being so brutally disappointed by a terrible lover?

"I don't want to wait. I *won't* wait. If you want to marry me," he heard himself say, "then you'll marry me now, as soon as we find a minister."

If he waited, he would lose her.

Caroline held out her hand. "I want to marry you."

He took her fingers. They still trembled. His shook now, too.

"We'll talk more tomorrow," Caroline said, pulling him back towards her. "We'll make a plan tomorrow."

They didn't need to make a plan. They already had a plan. They would marry, and then they would start their life together.

Eddie didn't argue with her. He had already put her through enough that night: she had cried, she had bled, and now she stared at him as if she had seen a ghost.

Eddie circled her in his arms. He made sure the blanket covered her from toe to chin. He pressed a gentle kiss just behind her ear. "We'll get married tomorrow," he promised, and when she didn't reply, he told himself it was because she had already fallen asleep.

Chapter Sixteen

T HE MORNING AIR WAS so heavy it felt hard to get it into her lungs. Caroline knew it wasn't the cold—though the ground had frosted overnight—nor the uphill climb as she and Eddie headed back out of the valley. It was all the words she needed to say, and all the muscles in her body trying to stop her from saying them.

They had left the MacPhersons about an hour ago. Eddie insisted on carrying both their bags: "You didn't sleep well," he said, as if he had been snoring away while she lay awake worrying.

Caroline knew exactly how tense his body had been, too, and how his breath had never quite deepened into a relaxed sleep.

That was two nights in a row without proper rest. Caroline was beginning to wonder if she would ever sleep well again in her life.

In any case, she let him carry the bags. An hour in, he was beginning to switch them in his hands every few minutes or so, but when she offered to take one, he batted her away again. "I'm used to labor like this."

Which only underscored the fact that she was not. Nor was she accustomed to walking this far, this often. Nor did her body know what to do with its bruises from sleeping on the floor.

All of this was Eddie's life, and none of it was Caroline's. Unless, when they got to the top of the hill, the minister married them.

Then Caroline would be Eddie's wife, and they would have nothing concrete left in their plan.

She wasn't sure if it was the absence of the plan that frightened her, or the fact that she and Eddie had managed to get so close to marrying while completely misunderstanding each other's expectations for the future. If not for the comment she had thrown out last night, when would Eddie have admitted to Caroline that he didn't have a position lined up? Would she have made it all the way to the transport ship before finding out that Eddie had changed his mind about the regiments?

"Let's say our favorite things about each other," she said, suddenly desperate to divert her thoughts.

"The list is too long." For the first time that morning, Eddie looked like he might smile.

"Try anyhow. I'll go first." She took advantage of the moment to look him over: those sweet eyes, devastating cheekbones, and kissable lips; the broad, strong shoulders that she knew now could carry her across a room and back; the legs that were long and muscled and so very beautiful when bare.

She could dissolve like honey into tisane just by looking at Eddie, yet the way he looked didn't nearly top the list of things she loved about him.

"You always know exactly how to deal with me. You don't let me be *too* silly or *too* stubborn or *too* anything, yet you also don't stop me from being any of those things. You let me be me, but keep me from being too much of me."

Eddie raised his eyebrows. "I'll remind you that you like this about me the next time I'm trying to get in the way of one of your wild schemes."

"I like that you are so steady," Caroline continued. "I know that I can count on you to be you, and that you will be where you say you will be at the time you promise. You are entirely dependable."

"Ah, dependability. Famously a trait that makes women swoon."

"It makes *me* swoon." Caroline was glad she had started this game; teasing each other now felt like a match lit in the dead of night. "How many other women do you care to have swooning over you?"

Eddie, looking at the road ahead of them, shook his head. "None."

"I don't want any other men swooning over me, either. It is you or no one." She threaded her fingers together, wishing she could hold his hand instead. "Anyhow, I also like that you are conscientious. If you are going to do something, you do it well. You don't grow impatient or frustrated and leave it half done." Which was what she herself was known to do.

"If you don't stop, my head might grow so big that I shall float away." Eddie's cheeks were pink, and his shoulders hunched up to his ears; despite all that, there was a little smile on his lips.

"Good thing our bags are heavy enough to weigh you down."

"I think it is my turn to pay *you* a compliment."

"Well, I shall not stand in your way. Except to say one more of my favorite things about you: you are so abominably silly, but only with me." She had meant to say it to torture him, a verbal tickle that would make him writhe and reply with something incredibly ridiculous, all to prove her point. Yet she did love that so much about him that her voice broke as she said it, and unexpected tears assaulted her eyes. And as much as she adored that there was this secret Eddie no one knew except her, she realized how sad it was that Eddie couldn't be himself with anyone else. "I wish everyone knew you the way I know you."

The air felt too thick to breathe again. Caroline turned to look at the heather to her right and forced a deep inhale.

It was pretty here, if bleak.

Eddie said, "Everyone thinks you are stubborn and single-minded and..."

"Impossible?" Caroline volunteered.

"That too. But the secret *I* know about you is that you are optimistic. When you have an idea, you believe it will come true. Even if it is a dream of a sailing ship that flies through the clouds. That's what I love most about you." Eddie's voice softened. "That is what I rely on you for the most, too."

Even though she had suggested the game, Caroline didn't know how to absorb the compliment. She hugged her arms around herself. "I don't know how I could live any other way. There is so much future ahead of us. What am I supposed to do except dream about what might come to be?" There were those damned tears again, choking her words.

She hadn't had any dreams last night. She had lain still with only straw between her body and the wood floor and had been unable to picture a single moment of her future. All this time, she hadn't known what to expect from Lower Canada, but at least she had been able to conjure up stories of raccoon hats and trees as tall as giants. She had imagined sharing a hammock with Eddie on the crossing; she had even pictured herself nursing him with water and hardtack should he succumb to seasickness.

Knowing now they would remain in England, she should still be able to picture Eddie wrapping his arms around her, even if she didn't know what the room would look like or whether it would be in a city or a village. Yet even lying beside him with his arms already wrapped around her, Caroline's imagination had been blank.

She didn't want to say what she had to say next. "I thought all this time I was dreaming about a life in the colonies. A life neither of us particularly wanted, to be sure, yet one that guaranteed a roof over our heads and money in our pockets. I have been imagining how I shall learn to sew furs onto our clothes to keep us warm."

"I will keep a roof over your head."

His promise was gruff, the tone Eddie so rarely used to warn her away from a topic. Yet they had come so close to getting married without understanding each other at all. Caroline couldn't let the topic disappear on the wind like the *Jolly Molly*. As kindly as she could, she rebutted: "We've had some close calls in that regard already."

Suddenly, Eddie wasn't walking anymore. "What are you trying to say, Caroline?"

Now there was an edge to his voice she had never heard before. Not in all their life. She hugged herself more tightly. "I want to have a plan. One that is more specific than 'we shall go somewhere in the countryside and find a way to live.'" Hearing her own voice waver, she tried to rein it back under control, adding: "I thought we had a specific plan."

"And if not for that specific plan, you wouldn't have eloped with me? If not for thinking of a cozy future in the hold of a transatlantic sailing ship, you would have decided you were better off at Aunt Charlotte's?"

"No." She looked up at the sky helplessly. "But I think it would be prudent to at least have *some* idea of where we are going to begin our life before we..." She was running out of words as panic—at life, at their argument—set in. "...begin it."

"I'm not going to Lower Canada." He glared at her as if she had demanded it of him.

Had she the night before? She couldn't remember. She defended herself now. "I am not asking you to. Although, I rather think that if I *were* asking it of you, and you loved me as a husband should love his wife, you would at least consider it, in the absence of any better plan."

"If you loved me the way you claim to, you wouldn't need to have a plan at all. You would just want to marry me and see what happens next." His words were loud. Energetic. They lived a life of their own, breaking through the air and stinging her skin like shards of glass.

That was what she had been promising him all this time, after all. They had gotten this far without much of a plan. Except Caroline had thought it was them together who didn't know how they were going to get married. She didn't realize that she had one idea of their future and Eddie had a completely different one—nor that they were so unable to communicate with each other.

Did he want her to follow him so blindly that he never shared his ideas for the future?

"How is it, do you think, that we managed to spend all this time together trying to get married, yet we never had an honest conversation about what we were going to do after the wedding? Is it another case of me being 'Determined Caroline'? Or were you never going to tell me about the regiment?"

"I wasn't keeping it a secret. I thought you knew. I was *never* going to accept that position, not even before we decided to elope."

Caroline's fear tightened every muscle of her body. "I know we love each other, Eddie, but we don't seem to be very good at planning together. Not plans that hold up in the real world."

For a moment, Eddie only stared at her, his nostrils flaring with his breath. Then, softly, he asked, "So you think it's a lie, what we've been telling ourselves? That nothing matters except that we love each other?"

Caroline couldn't believe she was standing in the heather saying what she was saying. Her heart was so large and tender and needy. But her stomach was growling and her body was aching and her spirit didn't have the energy to summon optimism. "I think marriage is love meeting reality. We have the love, but we seem to struggle with the reality part."

Eddie stared at the ground, his face red, especially around his eyes.

As if it were all her fault. "I want a plan, that's all. I want to wait until we know where we are going to live and how we are going to do it."

"Life has no guarantees. Even if we waited six months and came up with a plan, the next day, I could crush my hand in an accident and be unable to provide for you. Would you turn away from me then?"

"No—"

But before she could argue further, Eddie stepped back from her. "I'm not willing to wait, Monkey. Either you marry me today, as soon as we find that minister, or we don't marry at all."

Caroline paused, willing optimism to sweep her off her feet again. All she felt was cold and sore and tired. And she knew what her answer had to be, even though she didn't want it to be: "I can't marry you today, Eddie."

She waited for Eddie to take back his ultimatum. She waited for him to argue with her, to insist that she was being stubborn, to come up with a plan that would solve everything.

He lifted their luggage once more and said only, "Then I shall see you safely back to Hope Hall."

T HERE WAS A CERTAIN peace in accepting the inevitable. Eddie felt suspended in air, gliding through the day, now that Caroline had finally spoken the truth. No, they wouldn't marry—and that broke his heart. No, he couldn't provide enough for her as a husband—and that crushed his soul.

Still, trudging up the heather-covered hill to the seaside village, Eddie was mostly aware of relief. At last, they could let all pretenses fall. They didn't have to lie to each other anymore to convince themselves that their love would conquer all.

If anyone could have proven that fairy tale true, it was Caroline. But now even she had surrendered to reality, and in a way, Eddie felt lighter for it.

They didn't talk much now that the decision was made. Eddie focused on the arrangements: booking passage on a sailing boat headed south, haggling for some bread and cheese from the public house, planning with Caroline how far they would travel together. Perhaps it was because he knew he had a few more days with her to see her safely to Hope Hall that he didn't feel his heartbreak yet.

Or perhaps it was because he no longer felt guilty about every little moment of the journey. When all he could procure was stale, two-day-old bread for their supper, it didn't feel like an omen from some higher power to indict their future marriage. When the fishermen cursed in front of Caroline, Eddie didn't feel that demonstrated how he would always fail in protecting Caroline from vulgarity.

He was no longer trying to prove to himself that she could accept this life, which made it easier for him to live it again.

"This won't be the last time we see each other," Caroline assured him as they watched the eastern coast sail by. They sat side by side, but this time, Linnie occupied the space between them. No matter that they knew each other carnally; by unspoken agreement, they were avoiding touching each other now that they had decided they had no future. "We can be friends, can't we?"

Eddie was too exhausted to try to nicen his answer. "I don't know. I want you to be happy, but I don't know if I want to see you happy with someone other than me."

"I'm not going to marry anyone else."

Such a big sweeping statement was what had gotten them into this mess. It provoked Eddie now. "Oh, so you'll live your life all alone without those dozen children you want?"

She frowned at him. "A dozen of *your* children. Besides, that was an exaggeration. A half dozen would be sufficient."

"Do you really think your longing to be a mother will disappear? What about everything else? Where will you live? How will you spend your days? You can't believe you will be happy living in Ellen's shadow at Hope Hall for the rest of your life." Eddie could hear the anger bleeding into his words, but for the life of him, he couldn't stanch it.

Caroline drew her knees into her arms, moving infinitesimally away from him. "I need not be in her shadow. There are my nieces and nephews, and I am sure there are useful things I can do from Hope Hall. Perhaps I shall travel with Sophia."

"You shall be the spinster sister who lives at the mercy of her siblings' generosity."

Her frown sharpened into a classic Caroline glare. "It is *my* future. I may do with it what I want."

"Yes." And what she *didn't* want was to live it with him. For a moment, the relief insulating his heart disappeared, and Eddie couldn't breathe for the pain of it all. He focused on the shoreline, on the cold air, on the fact that her misery, at least, had an end point.

Angry Caroline went on: "One day, once I have sorted Papa, I shall return to Northfield Hall. If you don't live there, then at least you shall visit, and we may count on seeing each other again."

"I'm not going to visit," Eddie found himself saying. "I'm going there to speak to my parents, and then I'm never going back. I think I will go to China after all."

"Go to China?" Caroline hissed.

"Yes, China."

The anger sharpened between them. At his side, Linnie growled, and the vibrations rumbled through Eddie's body. He waited for Caroline to reach her breaking point. He welcomed the curse words and yelling that might come next.

He baited her: "Did you think I would wait around at Northfield Hall for you? Have you been imagining you could have me as your lover and make the best of both worlds, as lady of the manor with her faithful manservant waiting to be called upon for her every need?"

He didn't mean for his words to be sharp or dangerous, but at his tone, Linnie lunged forward. With a growl, she plunged her teeth into Caroline's skirt.

Caroline jerked away, shrieking, and her ankle caught Linnie. The dog went sliding towards the edge of the boat. Eddie caught her by the collar just before she fell into the North Sea.

He couldn't stop himself from shouting at Caroline. "You nearly killed her!"

"*She* nearly bit *me*! I was only reacting like anyone would." Caroline curled away as if Eddie and Linnie might both do her bodily harm. "You love that dog more than you love me, and that's the truth of it."

"She is a dog. She needs my protection."

"She can protect herself just fine. It is embarrassing how much you dote on her."

"I don't dote on her."

"And what kind of name is Linnie anyhow? Why couldn't you name her Andromeda or Cassiopeia like any other dog?"

"It's a nickname for Caroline." He was so angry that his voice broke. He repeated more softly, "It's a nickname for Caroline."

Her hand still clutching her heart, she turned to stare at the sea. She was trembling like she had the night before. Eddie hugged Linnie to his chest.

In a whisper, Caroline asked, "Am I being cruel to you, or are you being cruel to me?"

That was enough to erase all the unreasonable fury that had possessed Eddie. "The world is being cruel to us, and we are taking it out on each other."

Linnie whimpered. Tentatively, Caroline reached out to pet her head. "I can't bear it if we never see each other again," she said. "Do you really want to go to China?"

He didn't. "I don't know if I can stand to see you after all of this."

"Then I shall stay away from Northfield Hall for a while. Come up with a plan for what will make you happy. Stay as long as you need. The next time I return, I'll send word far in advance so that you can take a trip somewhere and not see me."

Eddie put his hand over hers. "I don't know if I can stand *not* to see you, either."

"Oh." Biting her lip, Caroline turned her fingers to intertwine with his. Linnie wiggled out from beneath them so they held hands without any pretense.

Eddie had been fooling himself thinking they could break away like two friends at the end of a misadventure.

They were lovers torn asunder. Not even poetry could capture this agony.

Caroline released his hand. "I want you to be happy, Eddie, even if it means you marry someone else and have a dozen children with *her*."

"And I want you to be happy, and I think that will require you to marry someone else and have a dozen children with *him*."

"I can't imagine that."

"I can." He imagined it too vividly—Caroline with her carefree smile and adorable little ones crowding around her skirts—and hurt his heart all over again.

"Go to Northfield Hall, then," Caroline said, saving him from the vision. "Make things right with your parents. When you think you can bear for me to return, write to me. Perhaps, by then, something will have changed..."

"Nothing will change." He couldn't allow himself to even wish for it. No matter if he inherited a hundred thousand pounds; no matter if he discovered he was descended from King George himself; nothing would make him worthy of Caroline, and so he didn't dare think about it. "But I will write to you, when I am ready to see you happy without me."

Chapter Seventeen

CAROLINE DID NOT BID Eddie an emotional goodbye. She did not want to torture their hearts any further. As she stepped out of their hired carriage in front of Hope Hall, she handed Eddie what remained of the five pounds lent them by Ellen. "For your travels back to Northfield Hall." She took her bag from the coachman and allowed herself to look at Eddie one last time. "I'll see you there someday soon."

Then she turned away, the carriage went back down the drive, and Caroline faced Hope Hall alone.

It wasn't the same as when she had left it. The sun no longer gleamed off its marble pillars; the excitement that had pervaded the house at its new name had died down; and Caroline was alone.

She was greeted first by a butler, then a maid, and finally, by Ellen.

"Where is Eddie?" her sister asked as she entered the room. "They didn't get snobby with him and send him to the servants' entrance, did they?"

"No. He is not here. He is on his way to Northfield Hall." Caroline opened her mouth to confess the rest of it, but instead, dishonesty rushed out: "We decided we had better sort a few things out before living together."

It was what she wished were true. Perhaps some part of her that she couldn't control believed if she said it aloud, she could make it true.

"Ah, well, that's wise of you." Ellen squeezed her fingers.

Caroline returned to the truth. "I am hoping to beg your generosity again and stay here for a little while until I can...sort things out with Papa."

Which was when true anxiety creased Ellen's face. "Papa is here. He came looking for you and Eddie."

Only a few weeks ago, Ellen and Caroline would both have celebrated Papa's surprise arrival.

Caroline hated how it now stabbed panic through her stomach.

"Nate and Amy are here, too," Ellen continued. "I hope you don't mind, but I wrote everyone after you and Eddie set off for Scotland. I didn't expect them to come running, but..." She touched Caroline's shoulder lovingly. "At least we'll have some of the family together for Christmas this way."

And so, a few hours later, after a change of clothes and a snack of bread and cheese, Caroline found herself in another sitting room—this one a little smaller, with furniture slightly more comfortable—alone with her family.

Max opened the conversation. "As an honorary member of the Preston family, I should like to point out something that may not be obvious to you. You all love each other very much. No matter what has happened up to this point, I hope you will remember how much you respect and cherish each other. Let us assume the best intentions of every word said."

On an inhale—far too shallow to sustain her—Caroline took stock of the room. After his speech, Max retreated to Ellen, who was nervously whittling a block of wood on a small sofa. In a wing settee on the other side of the hearth sat Amy, Nate's wife of four months, while Nate paced between her and the window.

And then there was Papa. He sat in his own throne-like chair at the apex of their misshapen circle. He had dressed formally, his gray hair pulled back in an old-fashioned queue, and his demeanor did not spare so much as a sliver of warmth for any of them.

Caroline had never seen him so severe. She had never felt so little love from him. And as much as she knew she owed him a few apologies, neither had she ever felt such fury at him.

It was time to be brave.

"I must begin—" she tried to say.

But Papa cut her off. "I am owed an apology, Caroline, as is your Aunt Charlotte, whose vehicle and horse you recklessly stole, and if you are not going to issue one, then I suggest you do not speak at all."

Around her, the siblings stiffened. This was not how Papa spoke to them. This was not how Papa handled conflict—in the family or out of it.

Caroline wondered how they interpreted it. Would they take it as evidence that Caroline had crossed a line so terrible that she did not deserve forgiveness? Or would they, like her, view this new Papa in dismay?

She swallowed down her knee-jerk anger. "I apologize, Papa. I knew when I ran away that it was against your wishes and that it would upset you. I also knew that borrowing Aunt Charlotte's carriage and horse was illegal. Please believe me when I say it was all my idea and Eddie was acting under my instruction. If anyone is to face consequences for that act, it should be me."

"They would never hang a peer's daughter while letting the glazier who drove the cabriolet live free. You would both be arrested—if your Aunt Charlotte were insulted enough to prosecute."

All Caroline could hear in Papa's words was the hypothetical. Despite his fury, even he didn't think Aunt Charlotte would call for Eddie's arrest. In a world of agony, it was her only relief.

She bowed her head. "I put my trust in Aunt Charlotte's family feeling, and I am grateful to both her and you that it has remained a private matter."

"You abuse that family feeling. What you did—committing a felony, running off in the dead of night, marrying *against* my express wishes—in most families, Caroline, you would be turned out penniless on the street. I do not know how to forgive you when you have wronged me in so many ways."

Caroline wished she were strong enough that the threat did not strike her mute. Yet—the memory of washing dishes in a cold brook still fresh in her mind—she could not find any words through the despair that gripped her.

"Papa, surely you are being too harsh," Nate interjected. "Caroline loves Eddie and she was determined to marry him. Can you not accept her apology and let us welcome her home?"

Papa didn't even look at Caroline as he replied, "Eddie asked for my permission, and I denied it. Caroline asked for my permission, and I denied it. They expressly disobeyed me—and put their own lives as well as our family's reputation at risk to do so. How am I to forgive this?"

Fingers pausing at her knife for a moment, Ellen asked, "Are you angry because Caroline was disobedient or because she put herself at such risk?"

"Of all my children, I should think *you* would not have to ask the question. Which would upset you if Rosalind were to steal a horse to run off to Gretna Green? If she were so stupid, reckless, and terrible as to throw your guidance in your face and become a common criminal? I need not differentiate between the two because they *both* upset me, and they are both unforgivable!"

By this time, Papa had leapt out of his chair. His face, red as a tomato, contorted into a mask that Caroline couldn't recognize.

Ellen replied gently: "Rosalind is eight years old. Caroline is twenty, and she has loved Eddie for years. We all knew they would want to marry."

"We all knew they could *not* marry." Papa stalked to the window and glared beyond it.

"*I* did not know that." Caroline's body felt as heavy as a lead weight. Was she so stupid? Was she so naïve that all these years, she was the only one in her family that did not understand whatever rule divided her from Eddie? If someone had only told her when she was twelve or sixteen that she couldn't marry him, would she have let her heart roam free to someone else?

Then Nate spoke: "Nor I." Moving from behind Amy, he came to stand behind Caroline, his fingers braced against the back of her chair. "Why shouldn't they?"

"Why shouldn't they? Nate, be serious." Papa gaped at him. "Eddie is a *glazier*. Caroline is a peer's daughter."

"I'm a disgraced naval captain, and Amy is a *viscount*'s daughter, yet still, you did not fight our marriage."

"You are of the same class. You understand each other's worlds. Not to mention, you can keep Amy in the comfort she is accustomed to."

From her seat on the sofa, Amy refuted this: "I am very happy with my life, but we live in only three rooms at the moment, when I am *accustomed* to a house of twenty."

"That is a far cry from being the wife of a tradesman who cannot even afford to ride the stagecoach to Gretna Green," Papa replied.

Caroline wished he wasn't so right about that.

"You were happy to see Sophia married to John Anderson, who is gauche enough to earn money," Ellen said. "So your objection cannot be that Eddie is a tradesman, only that he is not a wealthy enough one. That is a problem you can solve. Give Eddie a workshop at Northfield Hall. They can live in their own cottage, and Caroline can dine with you every evening."

"I can see the headlines now: *Lord Preston's Experiment Forces His Daughter to Marry a Commoner*." Papa's bitter words had already filled the room when he edited them, "*A Chinese Commoner*, at that!"

The emotions of the conversation were beginning to make Caroline tremble. She didn't try to mask it as she asked, "Is that it, Papa? If he were a white-skinned glazier, would you be able to overlook it?"

"How can you ask me such a thing? After everything I have done for the Chows? After everything I have done for Eddie?" Papa's hands slashed violently through the air. "You do not marry a man so different from you in every way, Caroline. It is not done, and it is not done for a reason."

Now Ellen came to stand behind Caroline. "Peers do not share their wealth with their tenants, and yet we do. Britons do not eschew imports from distant lands, and yet we do. Good households do not hire felons or runaways or servants without character references, and yet we do. You have raised us to do the things that are not done, Papa, so you must not be shocked that Caroline is doing exactly that."

Papa opened his mouth to reply.

This time, Caroline cut *him* off. "I owed you an apology, Papa, and I have given it sincerely. Now, you owe *me* an apology. You are my father, and I thought you would love me no matter what. Yet you have put a condition on your love. You will love me only if I do exactly as you say. You will support me only if I obey commands that deny me what would bring the greatest happiness of my life. You will let me starve in the street if I do not make you a proper apology." Tears stung her eyes, and Caroline could do nothing but let them fall. "If you knew all along that Eddie and I wanted to marry, as you say you did, then you could have supported it, Papa. You could have sent him to become a barrister or a clerk instead of a glazier. You could have made sure someone taught me how to cook and clean so that I would be prepared to run a smaller household. You could have done any number of things differently, Papa, but instead you listened to your prejudice—yes, Papa, your *prejudice*—and you made it impossible. For that, you owe both me and Eddie an apology."

Pale and gray, Papa stared at her.

She brushed the tears from her cheek. "In any case, Eddie and I decided not to marry. If my family does not turn me out, I shall stay here at Hope Hall until I sort out what I shall do next."

From where he stood behind her, Nate gripped Caroline's shoulder. "Papa doesn't speak for me. I am by your side, Caro, no matter what."

"As am I," pledged Amy.

Ellen cupped the top of Caroline's head the way Mama always used to do. "You are welcome here for as long as you desire."

They all looked at Papa. Caroline dared to hope: he was a reasonable man who loved his family. Surely now, he would say the right thing.

But he only stared at them as if they had all, suddenly, transformed into snakes.

She prompted him, "If you haven't anything new to say, Papa, then we must not say anything else to each other."

Papa shook his head. The bluster seemed to have left him, leaving an unreadable emotion seeping like sweat through his skin. Caroline waited for him to shift the conversation with an admission of wrongdoing or regret or, even, a glimmer of hope that he *might* be able to see how he had hurt her and Eddie so terribly.

He didn't say anything at all to her. Not then, nor as he retreated from the room, nor even when, a few hours later, he departed for Northfield Hall. Then, his words were for Max and Max alone: "No one can break your heart like your children can."

Which only proved to Caroline that he underestimated love of every kind. For, after all, by leaving, her father broke her heart all over again.

NORTHFIELD HALL LOOKED EXACTLY the same and entirely different. Eddie had never approached it so wearily; he had been walking for days now, and he wasn't sure his feet would sustain another step. Yet even as the mansion house rose as a crown to the yawning fields, Eddie knew he had much farther to go. A mile or so to get to the house, and from there, a quarter mile to his family's cottage.

Eddie had never come back to a Northfield Hall bereft of Caroline. Always, he had looked at the house and let himself imagine her in a window, waiting impatiently for him. He was accustomed to his heart quickening at the sight of the house simply in anticipation of being reunited with Caroline again.

It looked gray and small and disheveled without her.

He went to the family cottage first. It was the middle of the afternoon, which meant Father was at the carpentry workshop and Mother was at the main house. Eddie took advantage of the solitude to wash his face, hands, and armpits; he brushed Linnie's fur to make her a little more presentable; he drank a whole pitcher of water from the well. There were pork chops in the cold pantry, but Eddie didn't dare touch them.

He didn't want his parents to consider him a thief as well as a rogue.

Refreshed, Eddie flagged down one of the children running around the cottage yards and charged him with telling Eddie's mother he had arrived. He tried to offer the boy a penny for his trouble, but the boy waved him off. "This is Northfield Hall, sir. We don't need money."

Eddie couldn't believe he had forgotten.

He didn't use the wait to practice what he would say. There was too much on his heart and too few words to capture it—in any language. He sat on the porch in the old rocking chair that Father had built Mother ahead of Eddie's birth and watched the world around him. The small, simple world of Northfield Hall: the cottages that housed happy families, some of them boasting neat vegetable gardens and some of them decorated with curtains or colorful paint; the children inventing a game, in ecstasy from being released from school for the day; the goats wandering lazily in search of weeds to eat.

Eddie missed feeling as if he had a right to be there.

Mother and Father came together. Eddie spotted them holding hands as they turned into the cottage yard; by the time they were fully visible, they had let each other go. Mother looked thin and pale, while Father was murmuring to her, his face as cloudy as a thunderstorm.

Eddie missed Caroline with a physical pang through his chest. What he would give to be able to cling to her hand before facing this difficult conversation. Yet she was out of his future—and it was as much because he had forced her hand as it was her decision not to marry him.

"Jules told us you were here, but I didn't know whether to believe it," Mother said in Cantonese by way of greeting.

By now, Eddie was standing, of course. He moved down the steps so he didn't tower over his parents. Still, even though he was close, they did not reach out to hug him. Mother did touch his elbow; then, pulling away, she rubbed her fingers together and peered at them in disgust.

"You need to clean your clothes."

"I've been traveling."

Father *hmmed* at this. He stood with his hands behind his back, his feet braced, his strong torso on display as if he were preparing for Eddie to take a swing at him.

Eddie knew that wasn't personal. This was Father's stance whenever facing conflict.

If only Eddie's homecoming weren't a conflict.

"Lord Preston wrote us from London," Father said. "You stole a horse and carriage."

What was there to say to that? "Yes."

"You kidnapped Miss Caroline to marry her."

Eddie was prepared to take responsibility for the whole affair. He was ready to apologize—to grovel—to beg for forgiveness he knew his parents could not give him. But *kidnap*?

Did Lord Preston really mean to lay that all on Eddie's head? Did his parents really believe it?

A flame of anger, one that had first appeared in London, flickered in Eddie's breast. "I did not *kidnap* her. She wanted to come."

Father did not flinch. "If you were arrested, that isn't what the officials would say. She is not of age, and you are. She is a helpless woman, and you are a Chinese man. In the eyes of the world, you kidnapped her."

"Do I care what the eyes of the world see? You are my parents. You must know I did not kidnap her."

Mother surprised him with tears in her eyes. "You had such a good future ahead of you. Lord Preston got you a good position. You would have had money and respect. Why did you throw it all away?"

Her implications rang clear: Eddie *wouldn't* find a job now. Eddie would never have money and respect now. Eddie had been a hero, and now he was a villain.

Her words only flamed his fury. Eddie switched into English because his Cantonese couldn't contain it. "Why did you send me away from Northfield Hall? Why couldn't I stay here like Spencer and Oliver did, to learn to be a carpenter? You are my parents. You are supposed to love me, not expel me from your sight."

"We are supposed to give you *life*." Mother stuck to Cantonese. "A life that will sustain you. A life that will have as little suffering and hardship as possible."

Eddie knew his parents had suffered far more than he ever had. When Mother had been pregnant with Martin, they hadn't even had anywhere to live. Yet not having the unconditional love of one's parents felt worse than any night spent shivering outside.

Eddie didn't know how to say that to them.

Father touched Mother's arm. "Do you think it was easy to send you away? We had already lost Martin. Each Sunday that you lived in Reading, I came home to find your mother crying in bed because she had to say goodbye to you again."

She objected now, as if her sorrow needed defending: "They didn't feed him enough. He was too small and skinny."

"And me, I had to shake hands with your master each week and thank him for taking good care of you, even when you *were* too small and skinny." Father's voice didn't quite fill with emotion, but it was there in the air, like rain about to come.

"It was a good workshop," Mother said, "and a good opportunity. It opened up the world for you."

All his life, his parents had been as wooden as idols. Even when Eddie got ill, he didn't remember Mother batting an eye or expressing a whisper of fear. And Father had always been fair but unyielding, careful in how many smiles he doled out so that if Eddie ever received one, he felt he had really earned it.

He didn't know what to do now that they had burst free of their wooden casings. "But why send me away? Why not let me stay home like Spencer and Oliver?"

Father shook his head—almost as if to deny the question. "You loved Miss Caroline from too young. We wanted you to see something beyond Northfield Hall and meet other people. We thought you could find happiness elsewhere, if we only gave you a chance."

"Because you never thought I was worthy of being her husband."

"Because we knew Lord Preston would never allow it," Mother corrected. "As soon as he sensed what we sensed, I saw that he disapproved of it."

Disapproval—something so small and yet so consequential. Eddie didn't have the stomach for it anymore. "Why not try to change his mind? Why not at least hope that he might?"

Father flexed his shoulders. "This is our home, Eddie, at the generosity and mercy of Lord Preston."

That was not the way it was supposed to be. That was not the glorious experiment Lord Preston extolled to his peers, nor was it the ideals Caroline and her siblings carried into the world. Northfield Hall was supposed to give commoners the power they could not find beyond the estate's borders.

Yet not even the Chow family, the very first beneficiaries of Lord Preston's model, dared challenge Lord Preston on such a matter of the heart.

Eddie's anger disappeared, and he was overcome with a tender protectiveness towards his parents.

When he was rejected by Lord Preston, so too were they. When he was deemed unworthy, then they too were not good enough.

They had sent him away. They had not invited him home. They had not told him they loved him nearly as much as he needed to hear it.

Yet it was not because they did not love him, as Eddie had always thought. It was because they loved him so much that they did not want his heart to break.

A memory washed over him suddenly of Mother happening upon him and Caroline in the middle of a game, around the time of Ellen's wedding. They were gathering flowers, nuts, and sticks to stock their new "home," a hollowed-out tree with just enough space to fit the two of them. Caroline had explained the game to Mother; Eddie, expecting censure, had promised, "We'll be back in time to wash for supper."

But Mother hadn't scolded them at all. Smiling, she had handed them each two blossoming wildflowers and said, "In a few months, you'll be too old for this. Enjoy it while you still can."

He had thought she meant they would outgrow it—and vowed to himself he never would.

He realized now that she had been bracing herself for the hard work of separating Eddie from Caroline. Hard work that included sending her own son away, just to protect him from the very heartbreak he had now brought upon himself.

Love, perhaps, did not always look like the kisses Lady Preston had pressed upon her children, nor the compliments and encouragement Lord Preston offered.

Love could be as silent as all the words his parents didn't say.

He cast his gaze to the ground instead of hugging them. "I did not marry Caroline. She is with Lord and Lady Meretta at Hope Hall. If you would allow it, I mean to stay here while I look for glazing work in the neighborhood." Glancing up—too anxious to see their reactions to keep his humility for long—Eddie searched his parents' faces for signs of relief. "The one thing I am certain of right now is that I would like to be close to home."

There were no longer tears in Mother's eyes. She smiled, a broad, toothy grin he hadn't seen in so many years.

Father put his hand on Eddie's shoulder, and it was as warm as a heated brick on a winter's night. "Welcome home."

Chapter Eighteen

For the first time in her life, Caroline didn't have any kind of plan at all.

She woke each morning at Hope Hall without a clear ambition. She wandered through the days at her siblings' whims—breakfasting with Ellen, walking with Nate, sitting in the drawing room with Amy—or entertained her nieces and nephews. She ended the evenings alone in bed, without any motivation for what the next day might bring.

She did her best not to think of Eddie.

She spent most of her days thinking of Eddie.

She knew she had done right to listen to her instinct and refuse him that morning in the heather. Yet she had betrayed him by following her instinct. And for that, she could never forgive herself.

In the same moment, though, he had betrayed *her* by demanding they marry that day or never at all. If only he had been willing to wait, she could be spending her days at Hope Hall planning their life together. It wasn't what they had set out to do by eloping, but waiting for a few months—just long enough for Eddie to sort out a job and a place to live—would have allowed them to begin their marriage on good footing. Footing that was more than borrowed money. Footing that didn't leave them searching the countryside for strangers who would offer them somewhere safe to stay.

The fact that Eddie had suddenly become so stubborn and insisted she choose now or never only proved to Caroline that there was something wrong in their relationship that would not be solved by marriage. They didn't need to make any more daring, impetuous moves.

They needed to focus on practicalities.

Sometimes, she grew angry with Eddie for issuing his ultimatum. It was because he had in that moment suddenly grown inflexible that she was now facing a future as empty as a winter field.

Yet being so stubborn a person herself, Caroline understood what Eddie had done. When one became so determined, it was usually because one absolutely needed to be in order to protect oneself—and often, in Caroline's experience, without quite knowing what one was protecting oneself from.

If Eddie had really wanted to marry Caroline, he wouldn't have issued the ultimatum at all. He had done it to protect himself from the truth that he didn't want to marry her.

He had done it to make *her* the one rejecting *him*, instead of the other way around.

Some days, that made Caroline furious, because she didn't want to walk around with all the blame on her shoulders.

Mostly, it filled her with a sadness as heavy as all the books in Max's library. Everyone had harped about how Eddie wasn't worthy of marrying her, when all along, it was Caroline who fell short. She could bear to be a bad niece, disappointing daughter, or embarrassing sister, but to feel that even Eddie found her wanting—it was enough to knock her heart right out of her body.

On Christmas morning, after everyone had exchanged presents and Max had read a prayer to the servants, they all walked out as a family across the frozen park. The older children raced around the group while Max and Ellen pushed the little boys in matching prams. Nate and Amy walked arm in arm, laughing about something.

Caroline wondered if Eddie was celebrating. She hoped he was with family, even if it was just Oliver and Samantha in London. She hoped that if he thought of her, it wasn't with anger.

But she expected he was angry with her, just a little. He deserved to be angry with her, if only to even out the furious thoughts she harbored occasionally towards him.

"Have your thoughts taken you somewhere wonderful and exciting?" asked Nate, suddenly at her side.

Perhaps not so suddenly. Caroline discovered the path was already leading them into the woods, when she had last noticed the woods from at least two hundred yards away.

"Oh. I was thinking of..." She tried to think of some sort of lie that Nate would believe.

But Nate had always been the sibling who knew her best, even if he was four years older than she. "I imagine Eddie is thinking of you, too. Do you know where he is?"

"No." That felt like a cardinal sin. How could she claim to love Eddie if she didn't even know where he was? "He wanted to visit his parents at Northfield Hall, but I don't know if they received him."

Especially not if Papa had returned.

Nate was kind enough not to voice that. "Perhaps you would like me to get a letter to him."

How Caroline *would* like to write Eddie a letter. Except—besides the fact that she had promised she would leave him alone—she hadn't anything to say. *I still love you, but I know I have proven too spoiled to be your wife.*

Too spoiled. Too impatient. Too impetuous. Everything everyone had always told her were her worst faults had come to bear, at the cost of Eddie's heart.

Caroline couldn't forgive herself, and neither should Eddie.

"He asked me not to write to him," Caroline answered Nate.

"Ah." Her brother walked a few paces in silence. Then he asked, "And Papa? Have you heard anything from him?"

She hadn't. She wasn't even sure she would open a letter from him if she received one. Except, of course, that each day when the butler set out everyone's mail at the breakfast table, Caroline kept expecting to receive *something* from her father. "Unless he is going to admit he is behaving like any other prejudiced old man, I would not like to hear from him." She peered at Nate. "I still don't understand how Papa can be the lord and master of Northfield Hall and yet believe such closed-minded things about the laboring classes."

"It's right there in the phrase 'lord and master.'" Nate walked a few paces before elaborating. "For all that Papa has done at Northfield Hall, there is also much he has *not* done. Who lives in the manor house, and who lives in the cottages? Who cooks and cleans, and who spends their days at leisure?"

Caroline had never questioned it, not even on her journey with Eddie. She didn't know how to wash a dish because she was a Preston, and Prestons were served by a household of servants.

But why should being a Preston—a position she was born into, same as Eddie was born a Chow—entitle her to any such assumption?

"Someone must do the cooking and cleaning, I suppose," she countered Nate as she turned the new idea over in her head. "Besides, Ellen took up carpentry, and Papa didn't object."

"He still encouraged her to marry a viscount."

Memories were realigning in Caroline's mind as they spoke: Mrs. Chow always insisting on serving Caroline first at family meals; her friend Renee leaving the schoolroom to take on more work as a housemaid; and all the summer festivals, when Caroline directed which tablecloths to lay out and where to hang the garlands of flowers while everyone else lugged tables, spent days cooking, and built stages.

"He told me our family was meant to use our minds and that I would be unhappy if I spent my life as a tradesman's wife." Papa's words felt even more sinister as Caroline repeated them. Did he really believe that Caroline was born with the right to a different life than Eddie? "Good riddance to him, then, if that's what he thinks."

"Perhaps we may not be so quick to declare him a villain. I mean only to say that for all the good Papa has done, and for all the ways he has seen clearly where others do not that there are unnecessary divisions between people, he has always been unable to see the harm in our hierarchy of stations."

"Now I have shown it to him, and he has chosen to defend his prejudice rather than reform. Is that not villainous?"

Nate suggested, "He may be reforming as we speak."

"It is too late." The harm had already been done. Even if Papa apologized that very moment and gave her his blessing to marry Eddie and live at Northfield Hall as she had always dreamed, Caroline had been forced to do without—and had hurt Eddie as a result. "I shall never forgive him."

Nate fell silent again. Caroline almost didn't notice because her thoughts had reverted to Eddie and all the times she had assumed *he* would do the hard labor in one of their schemes. Was it because he was a boy, or because she was a Preston? And in either case, how could he forgive her for wronging him so?

Approaching Ellen's storehouse, where they would spend the morning taking inventory, Nate said, "Everyone deserves a chance at redemption, don't you think?"

Caroline didn't see how that could possibly be true.

IN THE COURSE OF its life, a sheet of glass had to suffer several breaks. It had to be severed from its rod as it emerged from the kiln, and though that left a scar, the glass could not be a sheet without that first break.

From there, the great vast circle was cut into sheets. It happened so neatly that Eddie could forget that his cuts were forever separating the glass from itself. Yet that was precisely what he did in the glazier's workshop: break glass so that it could fit into its final hanging place.

He thought about himself as window glass as he built a life in Thatcham. Like glass, he did not begin in his final form: he began by hiring himself out as a man-of-all-work to the public house in exchange for room and board. Then, as the weather improved, he started a business washing windows for all the local shops—followed by a commission to clean all one hundred windows of Folkestone House, the very estate that had once turned his mother out for being pregnant with his eldest brother Martin.

It was far from enough money to lease his own workshop or invest in the necessary tools to begin a proper glazing business.

Yet with each step he made, Eddie felt a little less like shattered glass. The diamond-tipped knife that had separated him from Caroline had been a little jagged, the glazier's hand unsteady, but they were cut apart, and with a little more time, it might no longer hurt at all.

He didn't hear from her. He tried not to think about her. He focused on building his own life, one that was completely on his terms, and didn't let wishes or regrets turn him away from his tasks. When he had been an apprentice in London, anticipating a future that always felt so distant and dear, life had never felt like Eddie's. He had watched himself as if through a window—a poorly made one, at that—living one day after another that didn't make sense.

His week with Caroline had shattered the window. Now, even though Eddie wasn't with her, he was at least himself. Each decision he made, each opportunity he chose to follow, each mistake he fumbled through was his and his alone. As much as Eddie thought of Caroline with almost every breath, he felt more grounded in his makeshift life in Thatcham than he had since he was a child.

After all, this was his dream, enacted from his own plan: to build himself a business in the countryside, in a village where no one looked twice at him, and close enough to his parents that he could visit them as often as he liked. He didn't have Caroline, but he had his power of choice. He missed her, he longed for her—but never did he wish himself on that ship to Lower Canada in exchange for being beside her.

He caught the first piece of gossip about Caroline in early January: "A falling out between Lord Preston and all the children," someone told the publican knowingly. "Miss Caroline is refusing to come home, that's what I heard."

His parents—who had more access to Lord Preston than most people—said little on the matter, save Mother's reassurance that "Miss Caroline is staying with Lady Meretta for now, and I know she will be well cared for there."

In February, when Lord Preston departed for London earlier than usual, the Thatcham saddle maker wondered aloud to Eddie, "Do you think his lordship is lonely without any of his family? I heard they quarreled fearsomely about a marriage match for Miss Caroline."

The townspeople knew that Eddie had grown up at Northfield Hall, and those who had been in town a long time even knew that he and Caroline were bosom friends. Sometimes—as with the saddle maker—he sensed they were passing on the information knowing Eddie thirsted for it.

He didn't answer questions like the saddle maker's, nor did he encourage the talk. When Caroline existed only in the spaces between the beats of his heart, he could believe his metaphor that they were two sheets of glass that were always meant to be severed.

As soon as he heard her name, however, the cut felt fresh, deep, and impossible to recover from.

He wanted desperately to see her again, yet Eddie couldn't bear to see her if it was from a distance. Vividly, he envisioned her arriving in the Preston family carriage, waving regally at the Thatcham villagers as they caught flashes of her blond hair through the window. Or, as he visited his parents at Northfield Hall, he imagined a polite conversation in the cottage yards, in which Caroline asked after his family and he asked after hers and the air filled with all the things they couldn't say to each other.

Eddie didn't want that. Yet as the weeks wore on, he lost sleep over *not* seeing her. He wondered if it was true she had quarreled with Lord Preston after returning to Hope Hall. He worried that she was unhappy in Norfolk—or worse, preparing for a London Season, putting Eddie out of her heart with her typical efficiency.

As much as he didn't want to hear about Caroline, he couldn't stand that he didn't hear from her. And so, in March, he found himself awake at night, writing her a letter.

After all, two sheets of glass, once separated, could still exist in the same window. He and Caroline had not married, but that did not mean they could not be friends.

He went through three drafts—almost all of the paper he had on hand—before finishing it.

Dear Miss Preston,

Please forgive my forwardness in addressing myself to you directly. I did not want you to have to rely on others for news of me. I am living at the White Hart in Thatcham. Currently, I am making a living washing windows as well as doing a few odd jobs here and there. I hope to one day be Thatcham's own glazier.

I hear from friends that you are installed at Hope Hall. I am glad to know that Lady Meretta remains your ally. Please give my best wishes to all your family, if they will accept them.

Yours always,
Eddie Chow

He walked around with the letter in his pocket for three days before he forced himself to send it. Then, he waited in agony to find out if she would reply. Eddie imagined the letter on its route to Hope Hall, the same roads he had taken in reverse after parting from Caroline. By now, the sheep would be in their pastures ready for lambing, and the trees along the turnpike would be growing green buds. His little piece of paper might catch raindrops as it transferred from one bag to another in London, and then as it headed into the marshy lands of Norfolk, it would stiffen again, braced by the salty air. At last, it would end up on a silver salver, presented to Caroline at breakfast by a stuffy butler.

One week passed into another, and Eddie had convinced himself she would ignore him, when the publican handed him a letter.

Dear Eddie,

I am delighted to hear from you. I have been imagining you all sorts of places—even on a sailing ship!—and I am so very glad to hear that you are in Thatcham.

May I take this to mean that your parents have welcomed you home?

As for me, I am indeed still at Hope Hall. My siblings have all been so very kind to me, and I know they would like me to pass along their good wishes to you as well. I am to stay here as long as I want, though I do not yet know what it is that I want. I have been thinking of the past much more than I ever have before, which leaves me little capacity to sort out the future.

I am struggling to reconcile my convictions with reality, you see. Nate made me realize that even at Northfield Hall, where we pro-

claim so much about the equality of humankind, we Prestons remain the lords and ladies while everyone else labors.

Of course, I always understood we were divided by station. The trouble is I never questioned it. I thought that these social classes were like walls and that at Northfield Hall, we had opened the windows for anyone to climb through whenever they liked. Now, I see that you were never offered a tutor as I was offered a governess. When we both came down with that terrible fever, your mother saw to me before going home to care for you, not because of a sense of duty but because she lives in service to my family. I am thinking of all the men and women who have arrived at Northfield Hall and who have remained in exactly the same station. Perhaps they are a little richer or better fed or safer. Still, no one is climbing through my metaphorical windows because those windows never even existed.

I am so ashamed, Eddie, that I never saw it before, and I am so ashamed that I have lived with such freedom, assuming that everyone else was as carefree as me.

Most of all, I am ashamed that I ignored you all the times you tried to show it to me. I understand now why you did not want to walk beside me at the Tower and why you tried to stop me from arguing with our parents oh so many times. I thought you were afraid, yet really, you could see I was about to slam my head into a brick wall that I thought was an open window.

The worst part of it all is that as ludicrous as these divisions between us are, they are material, which I had to learn by dragging you to Scotland and breaking your heart. That morning when we did not get married, it was not so much because we did not have a good plan, but because even with five pounds in our purse, we were not guaranteed a warm place to sleep at night. Even with the welcome of Mr. and Mrs. MacPherson, we could not count on an income, a meal, or a safe place to live.

Like you said, there are no guarantees in life. But it turns out that I do not have the courage to live outside the safety of a community that will support us in good and bad.

I am so very sorry that I was so ignorant of your experience, so stubborn when you tried to explain it to me, and so careless as to put your life at risk because I thought I knew better than everyone else.

This letter is growing long, and I have already rewritten it five times, so I had better finish if I want it to make today's post. Please give my love to your parents and an extra biscuit to Linnie on my behalf.

Yours always,

Caroline

Eddie first read it right there in the pub, surrounded by Thatcham villagers and some errant Northfield Hall laborers singing bawdy drinking songs. He took it upstairs to his private room and read it again. Then, instead of sleeping that night, he read it five more times.

He hadn't expected this kind of response. He had only wanted to know that she was safe and, if not happy, then not miserable. At the height of the workday, when his spirits were buoyed by honest work, Eddie had imagined she might reply with a limerick about Hope

Hall. In his weaker moments, he had hoped for her to pour her heart onto the page about how much she loved him and missed him.

This letter was something else entirely. Parts of it made Eddie feel like a weary traveler who had finally happened upon an inn, for he *had* been trying to make her understand their fundamental differences for so long. Yet something about her approach infuriated him, too, the way she wrote as if she alone bore the burden for how people sorted themselves into groups.

And most of all, he was bewildered because, while he and Caroline could talk about almost anything, these words she wrote were so frank that Eddie knew she would never have been able to say them aloud to him. Whenever this topic had come up between them before, Caroline had dissolved it immediately, either by insisting that the idea of such a division was wrong and therefore not worth entertaining, or by making little jokes until Eddie joined in her charade.

Eddie wasn't sure how to feel now that she was taking it seriously.

It took him a week—two days to wait for more paper to come in at the store, and another five to find the right words—to make his reply. By the time he posted it, the early spring tulips and irises were blooming around Thatcham.

Dear Monkey,

You owe me no apology—except for assuming that I followed you to Scotland with no will of my own. I have never been your servant. If you will recall, I am the one who invited you to Scotland in the first place.

I do not think there is anyone living at Northfield Hall, besides you, who supposes that class divisions have been eradicated—and fewer still who desire them to be. Your father offers a share of his wealth, which means that we are all the richer and that we have the economic power to walk away at any time.

(You see my use of the word 'economic'? That is vocabulary for which I give your mother's school credit. Never say your family has not tried to level the differences between class stations.)

For me, I never supposed your father considered me an equal with your family. I did hope that he would consider my heart worthy of yours. I suppose we proved him right that, ultimately, love is not enough to overcome our differences.

Please, do not waste your time on guilt. I should prefer you to make a decision about your future soon. What schemes have you been planning of late?

I am still at the White Hart, and I am kept busy by all sorts of jobs that fill my coffer.

Yours truly,

Eddie

Almost as soon as he parted with the letter, Eddie wished he could yank it back and rewrite it. He was sure he had come off sounding like a pompous fool. He wished he had written a letter that didn't reply to her last one at all but instead shared all the hundreds of thoughts that had crossed his mind in the last week that made him think of her. The strange cloud that had looked like a baby's rattle. The rumor going around Thatcham that ghosts were haunting old man Griswick. His disastrous attempt at eating honey straight from the jar.

Or perhaps he would tell her about how the saddle maker and baker had offered him one pound each as an investment in his business, to be redeemed when he found a building to lease for his own workshop. How they had told him they knew a good worker when they saw one and that they longed for Thatcham to have a glazier of its own.

If Eddie was going to correspond with Caroline—and he thought he did want to correspond with her—he wanted it to be about his life, not intangible concepts over which he had no power.

Which made her next letter a little easier to bear.

Dear Eddie,

I have only three schemes these days: teach my niece Rosalind how to steal biscuits from the tea table, ignore my father's letters, and decide how I shall spend my birthday this year.

Rosalind is far too well-behaved, you see, and so I have decided I must foment some form of rebellion in her. She reminds me a great deal of you: stalwart, well-mannered, and deeply loving.

My father writes me every week. He was terribly angry with me, but now he seems like he is back to the Papa to whom I am accustomed. He writes with great reason about fatherly duty and how love is not always easy and how he sees that he hurt me. He has apologized but still will not—or cannot—admit that he is wrong. He only says that even though we disagree, he should not have been so harsh, and that perhaps we could have found a different solution if he had only been willing to entertain the idea.

I am doing a terrible job of ignoring his letters, if you can tell. I only succeed in not replying to them.

As for my third scheme—it is very hard to think of my birthday with any joy. I expected to celebrate it at Northfield Hall as a newlywed. Then I thought I might celebrate it in the woods of Lower Canada. Now, I'm not sure what would make it feel like a celebration. I shall be twenty-one at last, the mistress of my own destiny, but I do not have much imagination for that destiny these days.

What schemes have you been planning of late?

My love to Linnie,

Caroline

He did not like that she was so preoccupied with a grudge against her father. He hated to think she was so discouraged about her birthday. And worst of all was the fact that her schemes were so small.

Of the two of them, Caroline had always been the one with the wildest dreams. Yet now she was stranded at Hope Hall without any energy to make a plan for herself—not even a hopeless one. Meanwhile, Eddie was not only dreaming, he was building his new life one day at a time.

Eddie couldn't help but feel he had stolen that skill from her when he forced her to choose between him and her future.

He hastened to reply, to try to give some of that magic back to her.

Dear Monkey,

I cannot condone the corruption of your niece, who sounds like a delightful young person far too smart to fall under your influence.

As to ignoring your father's letters, I hope you are not so severe with him on my behalf. I have never hoped for an apology from him. If your father ever sees fit to offer one, then I shall decide for myself whether to forgive or not.

All these years, I thought my parents had sent me away for apprenticeships because they did not love me enough to keep me around. When I returned to Northfield Hall to admit what had happened between you and me, they corrected me: they could see your father was against the match even back when we were children—before you and I were even thinking of it!—and they wanted to protect me by sending me away so you and I might not fall in love after all.

I think it would break your father's heart as much as it breaks mine to know that my parents do not trust he would not turn them out if they dared suggest to him that I am, in fact, worthy of being your husband.

In truth, I do not want an apology. Words do not change the future. What I should like from your father is honest, rigorous thought about whether his view of the classes keeping us apart is worth protecting. If anyone can offer me that, it is Lord Preston.

As to your third scheme, I am informed that Northfield Hall already plans to celebrate your birthday in its usual fashion, and they are expecting the guest of honor to be there. Again, I hope you have not ruled out that option on my account. It is your home as much as it is mine—and I have no qualms about crossing paths with you, if that should happen.

I have only one scheme at the moment, which is to build my reputation as a glazier. Since there is none in the neighborhood, I have been able to pick up a fair amount of work, but without a workshop of my own, I cannot offer a full complement of services. I am close to purchasing cutting diamonds so that I may begin installing windows, but until then, I am limited to washing windows and maintaining their casements. My scheme is to work hard and spend little so I may establish a full shop within the year.

Eddie

He resisted the urge to add that this dream would have been sweeter with her beside him.

They had tried to marry, and it had failed, and now Eddie was resolved to focus on the future.

In truth, he wasn't sure how he felt about Caroline returning to Northfield Hall. He yearned to see her again—so much that almost every day, his imagination conjured her on the streets of Thatcham or in the fields near his odd jobs—yet he couldn't fathom what would happen if they met again.

Would they be able to stay out of each other's arms?

Would they be able to find words that didn't hurt?

Two weeks later—after six days away assisting a glazier in Reading—Eddie received Caroline's reply. Carrying her letter out to a private spot between two meadows, Eddie opened it carefully.

Dear Eddie,

Your last letter has given me great cheer, and I have decided to return to Northfield Hall for my birthday. I am even going to try to find it in my heart to forgive Papa. I should be arriving around June 6, if the travel goes according to plan.

May I count on seeing you at the festival?

If I see you, may I greet you?

If I greet you, may I steal you away for some private conversation? I only want to catch up properly without everyone overhearing us.

Please send your reply, if any, to the London townhouse, as that will be where I am able to next collect my mail.

My love to Linnie,

Caroline

Her questions crowded Eddie's vision, and he had to put the letter down in the meadow grass to anchor himself back in reality.

They had chosen not to get married. The two of them together, in their own painful way, had come to that decision: Eddie by declaring it was that morning or never, and Caroline by choosing never.

If they actually saw each other again—if they stole away for private conversation—if they were close enough to kiss—Eddie didn't know what would happen to that decision. He didn't know what he *wanted* to happen to that decision.

There were so many things that were different now that it was spring and he had a home in Thatcham and almost two honest pounds to his name. Eddie was no longer running from a destiny someone else had chosen for him, and he did not feel the need to marry Caroline just to prove that they could and should be together. As much as he had hated parting from her, Eddie had chosen this life on his own terms, and he was proud of it.

If he saw Caroline again, would he lose the peace he had worked so hard to earn in a desperate urge to capture her forever?

But if she was at Northfield Hall and he didn't see her, could he even take a breath?

Eddie turned the question over and over in his mind and his heart and his hands until her letter tore at its crease for being folded and unfolded so many times. Until the spring flowers gave way to the year's first crops. Until it was far too late to write her a reply.

Until a job came up with a fat paycheck, and he had to choose: return to his past with Caroline or bet on a future of his own.

CHAPTER NINETEEN

Caroline arrived at Northfield Hall with two plans in mind. One was to be clear with Papa, whether that led to a reconciliation or not.

The other was to not worry about hearing from Eddie. By the time her carriage drove through Thatcham, she had gone nearly three weeks without a reply from him. She didn't know if it was because his letter had missed her on the road or because she had pressed too many questions to him or because his answer to all of them was no and he was afraid to write that in ink.

She told herself that, either way, she would have a good birthday. In the past six months, she had learned to stop waiting for some future far away. She took the good with the bad of whatever was happening, and on her birthday at Northfield Hall, she would find only the good.

That was what she told herself, anyhow. She kept it in mind as she sat through a painfully polite supper with Papa, Ellen, and Sophia. The next morning, when still she had not received any message from

Eddie, Caroline told herself she had not expected one and that it was not at all a knife twisted in her heart.

She lasted all three days until her birthday celebration. Then, as the maid Leyla twisted Caroline's hair into a crown of braids, she couldn't help asking: "Do you think Eddie Chow will come from the village today?"

Leyla, who had been Ellen's maid for a decade and knew the family as well as anyone, asked, "It's true, then, that you two had a falling out?"

Caroline hoped no one had said anything too unkind about Eddie in the whorls of Northfield Hall gossip. "We didn't have a falling out."

"Then why shouldn't he come?" Leyla tried to look cheerful now as she finished Caroline's hair. "There, you look as beautiful as any princess on her twenty-first birthday."

Words Leyla had offered every year. For the first time, Caroline wondered why she should want to look like a princess—and whether the other young women of Northfield Hall were given the same compliment.

"Did you ever think Eddie and I were going to get married?"

Leyla busied herself with putting away the hairpins. "I always thought you were sweet on each other, but I am careful not to assume that might lead to marriage."

"Especially in the case of a baron's daughter and a glazier?" Caroline didn't know why she had asked. She wanted to enjoy the day, not rehash all her heavy feelings from the past six months.

"Eddie would make a fine gentleman," Leyla surprised her by saying. "At Northfield Hall, anyhow. I don't like to assume because you are so young and have spent so much time apart, that's all." She put a firm hand on Caroline's shoulder. "Now, down to the festival with you, or you'll miss the party altogether."

The celebration was like any other Northfield Hall festival. Near the pond, where there weren't any crops growing, they set up tables and heaped them with food: roasted meats, steamed buns, fresh fruit, cold salads, and honeyed cakes. By the kitchen gardens, they had built a stage for the children to put on a pageant. Later, some of the residents would pull out their fiddles or drums or sing all the folk songs everyone loved to hear. Girls were braiding flowers into their hair, and more than a few of the young men were setting up competitions to see who could race the fastest or throw axes with the greatest precision.

For as long as Caroline could remember, this was how she had celebrated her birthday. An exhibition of joy everywhere she looked.

Always before, Eddie had been at her side. Caroline told herself she could still enjoy the festival. She could still eat the honey cakes, still sing along, still crown the winners of the various competitions. Yet each moment felt empty—and the afternoon never seemed to end, as she kept looking backward to see if Eddie had arrived from Thatcham yet.

"I suppose you'll be marrying soon, now that you're twenty-one," Renee, Caroline's friend and housemaid, said as they watched the maypole dancers. "I hope you'll do it this summer so we can have another festival. Will you be taking over Lady Meretta's suite after your marriage?"

Caroline's heart thumped sorely. "Whom do you suppose I'll be marrying?"

"Why, Eddie Chow, of course." Renee grew a little paler with each word. "Isn't—am I—oh, Miss, I hope I haven't offended you."

The fuss of everyone else using formal titles for the family while she used only first names chafed Caroline. She had never liked it; now, more aware of it than ever, it burned her like a flame leaping from the fire. She reassured Renee, "Not at all. I never considered taking Ellen's apartment as a married lady. I always supposed we would take one of the cottages."

"One of the cottages? Why, they're not nearly fine enough for you. You'd have to fetch your own water from the well. We'd much rather keep you in the manor house."

"You would be happy for us, then, if Eddie and I married? Even though we are from different classes?"

Renee beamed at her. "It would be like a fairy tale, Miss Caroline, only much more real because it would be happening to two such worthy people."

A fairy tale—in other words, an impossibility. Yet Renee's vision for Caroline and Eddie felt practical, more practical than any plan Caroline herself had concocted. Renee made it simple: Caroline and Eddie would marry, move into a suite of rooms suitable for a young family, and live at Northfield Hall like always.

She tapped her fingers three times against her skirt to keep from being overcome by emotion.

If only Eddie would arrive.

Finally, she sought out Mr. Chow and Spencer, who stood together by the footraces, minding Spencer's toddler. They each bowed at the neck to greet her. "Hard to believe you're twenty-one now," Spencer said. He wasn't one to smile, but the volume of words alone indicated friendliness. Spencer wasn't one to make conversation.

"I feel as if I've been waiting for this day for a century." Caroline couldn't help the anxiety that flooded her words.

"Now that it has come, is it everything you hoped it would be?" Mr. Chow asked.

The question was unfair, considering he knew what Caroline had dreamed of all this time. She looked down at the ground because she could not look either of them in the eye. "Do you know if Eddie plans to come today?"

Neither spoke for a moment, which was enough to tell Caroline the answer was no. Spencer said, "He wanted to, but he got hired by a coaching inn in Theale to wash their windows."

"Of course, he must take work when he can get it." Caroline wished she hadn't asked. Now she knew for certain that she wouldn't see him. A birthday without Eddie!

She had never borne it before, but she would have to now.

It was, apparently, what he had chosen. Just like that morning in the heather, when he decided their love had an expiration date. She had lost faith in him, and her punishment was to not see him again.

"Miss Caroline," Mr. Chow said, catching her attention as she turned away, "I never believed our family worthy of being attached to yours through marriage, but it would have been an honor to welcome you into ours."

His words evoked Eddie's letter, and Caroline's body began to tremble. "The fact that we have made you feel unworthy makes us the undeserving ones." She summoned a deep, calming breath. "I thank you all the same. It would have been an honor for me to join your family."

She hurried away before the words could embarrass any of them too badly.

The majority of the party was drifting towards the makeshift stage in anticipation of the pageant. Caroline remembered the excitement of performing—and how, when she inevitably had such stage fright that she didn't believe she could possibly go on, Eddie had always been there with the right words. For years now, she had been too old to perform, but she always looked forward to the creativity of the plays.

This year, she wished she could go seclude herself in her room rather than sit among all the people who knew her best and pretend she was happy.

Before the pageant began, however, she had one more person she needed to address. Caroline had been putting off her conversation with Papa, but in the mail that morning had arrived her birthday present to herself, and she wanted to show it to him before he heard about it from anyone else.

Caroline headed for where Papa was likely to be, sitting on a bench in the shade, when she saw him by the back door, one hand raised to beckon her over to the garden drawing room.

At least she wouldn't have to pull him away from some deep conversation in order to speak to him. Squaring her shoulders, she joined him at the door. "I'd like to have a word with you, Papa, if I may."

"I welcome it. I'm sure we all would."

It was only once she stepped inside that she discovered her siblings were all assembled. Nate and Benjamin stood on either side of the sofa, with Ellen and Sophia on the furniture between them. Most surprising of all was Aunt Charlotte, who sat on the settee, immaculate as always in a silk gown with her chin held in perfect posture.

"Your aunt has arrived in time for your birthday," Papa said, "and I wanted to take a private moment as a family to address you."

Caroline had written an apology to Aunt Charlotte, to which she had received no reply. She cut a curtsy. "Thank you for coming, Aunt Charlotte. I hope you will allow me to express how deeply sorry I am. You were very generous to me, and I paid you back atrociously."

Aunt Charlotte regarded her without an ounce of humor—but her signature kindness remained. "It was in this house over thirty years ago that my parents disowned my sister for even less of a transgression. They intended to punish *her*, yet it punished me, as well. I am resolved not to allow such an amputation to occur again in this family. Therefore, I forgive you. I trust you have learned your lesson."

"Thank you." From above the mantelpiece, a portrait of Mama observed the room. Caroline didn't know if she had learned the lesson Aunt Charlotte wanted from her. She had learned not to be so rash. She had learned that she knew nothing of the practicalities of the world.

She had learned that love was not as strong as she thought it should be.

"In honor of your majority, we will put it all behind us as youthful indiscretion," Papa said. For the first time since Caroline had absconded from London, he smiled at her. "Would you like a birthday present now?"

"Thank you." In years past, Caroline would have jumped onto her toes at the mere mention of a present. No matter what a person got her, she loved to be bestowed with the attention and love that a gift represented.

She couldn't help but feel curiously removed this year as Papa revealed a wrapped parcel. "I had this commissioned for you in hopes of our happy reunion."

Carefully, Caroline removed the paper to discover a beautiful wooden writing box decorated with her monogram. Inside was a collection of beautiful pens, bottles of ink, sand, creamy paper, wax, and a marble-handled seal carved again with her monogram.

"A proper kit of your own so that you can begin directing a worthy organization without always going in search of writing paper." Papa watched her for a reaction.

Caroline forced herself to find some kind of emotion beneath the numbness from all the disappointment of the day. She smiled into Papa's familiar eyes. Yet seeing his gladness—his relief!—made her feel worse. If he had only lent his support—if he had seen fit to offer Eddie a position that would allow him to take a wife—Caroline might have had the courage to marry Eddie.

But she also knew she could not blame Papa entirely. In Scotland, it had been *she* who had insisted on waiting, at the cost of not marrying Eddie, and so she must now be happy with what life could offer her. How could she be so ungrateful as to find Papa and his writing desk wanting?

"Thank you," she said, trying hard to sound as if she meant it. "I look forward to using it."

Papa embraced her, a small and awkward hug that made Caroline feel more desolate than ever. "You'll find your way to the other side of this storm," he said softly, "just you wait and see."

She freed herself from his arms and cleared her throat of emotion. "This will be very useful, actually. I just had my first article published in a newspaper."

Her siblings reacted, but Caroline was too focused on Papa to notice. She withdrew from her pocket the folded paper boasting her article. "It was in the *Moral Philosopher* this past Monday. Not as large a readership as the *Times*, perhaps, but I am proud to be published anyhow."

Papa took the article, his expression inscrutable. He read aloud: "*A Treatise On Unnecessary Social Classes by a Lady of Quality.*"

Aunt Charlotte let out a sigh. "At least you had the good sense to leave your name out of it."

"I wanted to include my name, but they required that it be published anonymously." A fact that would have rankled Caroline if she hadn't been so relieved to have her thoughts taken seriously by a paper at all. "I hope to one day be able to share my opinions publicly. As you do, Papa."

She didn't mean the comparison as praise. Watching him for a reaction as he skimmed the article—which said what she had discovered these past few months, that too much of society was dictated by the status one was born with—she held her breath, wondering what she wanted most. Would she be happiest if he threw it away and denounced it as trash, since she espoused views so different from his own? Or would it really be better if he clutched the article to his heart and confessed she had changed his mind?

He delivered neither reaction. Lifting his eyes to meet hers, he smiled—a genuine, loving smile, the kind he had offered most of her life. "You are an excellent writer, Caroline."

"I believe every word I said, Papa."

"I hope you wouldn't write anything you don't believe."

She didn't want his praise. "Doesn't it make you think any differently at all?"

"It gives me plenty to consider." Papa folded the article along its original creases. "You have given me plenty to consider this whole year, Caroline. I'm sorry you feel our different views so deeply. I hope you know I have only tried to protect you as I believe I, your father, must."

She knew it. He acted only out of love, even though it wasn't the kind of love she wanted. She reached out to take the article back. She thought she might throw it in the fire, for all it was worth.

Papa held it back. "Do you mind if I keep this? I should like to read it more closely. Perhaps, after a second or third time, my old brain will understand what it is you've been trying to tell me."

It wasn't a change of heart, but it was a start. Caroline felt a little hope steal into her body as she nodded her assent.

Nate cleared his throat. "We have a gift for you, too, Caroline."

At first, Caroline thought he meant him and Amy. Yet her siblings all stirred as one at the announcement, and then Ellen handed Caroline a folded piece of thick, creamy paper. "The worst feeling in the world is to be beholden to someone else because they have money and you do not. We decided to pool together to establish a trust in your name."

Benjamin explained, "It is yours to spend whenever and however you see fit. My solicitor is overseeing all the legal matters, and his information is in that packet so that you may contact him yourself if you need to."

"You can use it to travel the world," Sophia suggested, "or purchase yourself a home somewhere that will make you happy."

"Or to establish a glazier's workshop," said Nate, a soft smile on his lips, "with a home attached."

Even though Caroline opened the paper, she could not take in any of the words.

Aunt Charlotte objected: "Surely she cannot access it until she is married, Benjamin."

"Why should she need money?" Papa asked. "Have I not always provided what each of you needs?"

Ellen rose, crossed the room, and wrapped an arm around their father. "Caroline has the right to make her own decisions, even when they aren't what you wish her to do."

"No one wishes for a further rift in the family," Benjamin added.

"I was denied the right to marry the woman I loved because her family didn't deem me worthy," Nate said, "and I do not wish that fate on either Caroline or Eddie. If this money helps her make a life with him, then I celebrate it."

"And if she squanders it at gaming hells, I celebrate that, too," Sophia chimed in. "Except I do recommend you make sure you can always pay for your own carriage home."

Benjamin promised, "No matter what, Caroline, you will never be alone in the wilderness. You will have the four of us, whether you want us or not."

Caroline had felt so alone with Eddie in Scotland, yet holding that paper, she realized how wrong she was.

She might lose Papa—and even after all that had happened, that would break her heart. She might not ever be invited back to a

London drawing room. Yet she had her four siblings, who would embrace her even if she decided to become a witch in a distant valley. She could count on Leyla, Renee, and the Chows, and the rest of Northfield Hall.

And now she had eight hundred pounds to her name. A fortune. A gift.

A path to Eddie.

"Papa." She broke through whatever the family was saying. "Aunt Charlotte. I love and respect you both very much. All my life, I have heard how hurtful it was that my grandfather disowned Mama when she decided to marry Papa, and I do not want to be in such a position. However, as dearly as I crave your approval, and as much as I want to maintain your good will, I cannot ignore my heart. I know you want to protect me, but two of the things standing between me and Eddie are the lack of money and the opinion of others. For a time, it was too much for me to bear. But these past few months, I have learned that so many people who matter to me would not desert me, even though you would. And now thanks to my wonderful, generous siblings, I need not worry about being so impoverished as to find happiness impossible."

Raising her head, she took a survey of the room: Nate beaming at her, Sophia at the edge of her seat, Benjamin and Ellen looking equal parts worried and happy. Aunt Charlotte had not moved a muscle, but her eyes shone red with unshed tears.

And Papa. This time, there was no anger contorting him into a stranger that Caroline could easily flee. This time, he looked gray, ashen, and heartbroken.

"I hope you won't disown me, Papa," Caroline said, "but I have to go find Eddie now to see if he can forgive me."

It felt like forever, but eventually, Papa replied: "Come home once you have found him."

CHAPTER TWENTY

EDDIE HAD BEEN RAISED to welcome the sweat that accompanied hard work. It dripped down his forehead and obscured his eyes; it pooled in his armpits and groin and feet and made his clothes drag across his skin; it matted his hair and tickled down his neck. Still, it was all evidence of a job well done and a day honestly spent.

He was finding it difficult to welcome the heat on Caroline's birthday. He could have been in the cool breezes of Northfield Hall, but instead he hung from the side of the Fox and Hound, baking in the sun. And it was hot, even for June: his water for washing windows was warmer in its bucket every time he plunged his hand in. The sweat didn't feel like a prize won from hard work. It felt more like punishment—for which crime, Eddie couldn't decide.

From where he perched now, Eddie wished he had chosen to go to Caroline's festival. He could have seen her without losing his heart. They could have shared a smile, exchanged a few words, and moved towards some kind of friendship.

But he intended to build a life on his own terms. Which meant when the job at the Fox and Hound came up, with enough pay that Eddie could order a whole box of cutting diamonds, Eddie had to accept it, even if he missed Caroline's birthday for the first time in both their lives.

The inn boasted twelve bedrooms, each of which had its own sash window, plus large windows along two sides of its public room and another, finer plate glass window in the private dining room. This part of being a glazier did not require expertise so much as it did courage. To wash a window on the upper floors, he screwed a board into the windowsill, then perched on that board. Eddie had started doing this kind of work when he was a lightweight, lanky boy; as a full-grown adult, he sometimes felt the sway of the board beneath him and worried he was about to plunge to the flagstone yard below.

Easing himself out a third-story window, Eddie minded his hands rather than look down. He scrubbed the rag clean in his bucket of water, then brought it to the window raised in its sash. He used wide, broad strokes to begin, before going back to catch any spots. For the most part, his eyes remained on the glass. Transparent though it was, there was plenty to see: its original scar, warps where it magnified vision to the other side, the weaknesses where it sat within its sash. Eddie scrubbed it three times before he was satisfied it was clean enough.

Finally, depositing the rag in the bucket, he reached for the dry cloth tucked in his pocket.

When he looked back up, a person waited for him on the other side of the frame—and he nearly fell off his board in shock.

She reached through the open window and grabbed his wrists with strong hands, pulling Eddie's center of gravity back against the inn wall. Slowly, Eddie's mind caught up with reality: he was safe, his water was sloshing out of its bucket, and the person holding him was Caroline.

She looked stunning. Her hair shone brassy gold in its braids, her cheeks were as pink as her lips, and she wore a blue linen gown fit for a fairy. Even now that he was balanced again on his board, they held fast to each other's wrists—and Eddie was quite sure he couldn't let go of her even if he tried.

"What are you doing here?"

"Sailing the *Jolly Molly*," Caroline replied. "I'm looking for you, what else?"

With only the window frame between them, Eddie could have kissed her. He resisted. "You nearly scared me to my death."

"I'm sorry. I tried calling to you from below, but you didn't hear. The landlady let me come up here for a penny."

Eddie was greedily trying to notice everything about her. She smelled like horses and dust. She looked thinner. Her voice was exactly hers: a little low, a little fast, a little breathless. "You're supposed to be at your party."

"Spencer told me where you were. I drove the gig here." Which wasn't an answer at all, but then Eddie realized he hadn't asked a question.

"I couldn't turn down the work. There aren't many places left in the neighborhood that need their windows washed, and the Fox and Hound is paying me a premium to complete it before the Duke of Somerset's family travels home from London."

Almost before he finished speaking, Caroline said, "I wanted to come see you as soon as I returned to Northfield Hall. I didn't know if you wanted me to."

He hadn't wanted her to, yet what came out of his mouth was the more honest truth: "I'm glad to see you."

Caroline beamed. She was like a lantern glowing on a dark night. Eddie didn't need to think about the past or the future; he could bask in her and this moment and her fingers holding him fast.

She tugged him closer. "Can you come inside? I have to tell you something."

"Let me dry this window first." It was already streaking from his neglect. Eddie couldn't see a job badly done, so after Caroline released him, he washed it once more with his cleaning rag, then dried it off with the same careful movements he would apply to any window, regardless of the beautiful woman waiting inside the bedroom for him.

When he finally climbed through the window, Caroline reached for him again, and their hands clung to each other before Eddie could even think about it. He knew there was a reason why they shouldn't be touching, but he didn't remember it.

"The window looks very clean," Caroline said. "You are an excellent glazier."

"There's a lot more to it than washing windows, but this will do for now. Did you really drive the gig all the way here by yourself? Where does your family think you are?"

"Benjamin put me in the gig himself. He did offer to come with me, but I didn't know how long you and I would need to speak alone, and after all, no one should have to miss a Northfield Hall festival." Caroline was grinning, her teeth shining in the low evening sun. "Eddie, there is so much I have to say, but all I want to do is look at you."

Without quite meaning to, Eddie tugged her closer. "Let me begin, then. I'm sorry for how I twisted things in Scotland. I listened to fear that morning. I felt poor and like a brute and..." These thoughts that had been swelling in him for the last few months were almost impossible to put in the correct words. "I didn't think I deserved you, and I couldn't bear that, so I forced you to reject me."

"*I* listened to fear that morning. It was too much for me that we couldn't have a proper conversation about the future. I lost my faith. Not in you, Eddie, but in *us*. I'm the one who is sorry."

Eddie hated the self-censure dimming her light. "All you wanted was some time to recover. I should have given you that time."

"I should have married you first. We could have married and then taken the time to sort out our plans."

"We were both wrong in some ways, and we were both right in some ways."

Caroline smiled again—but there was something holding her back, that made her fingers tremble as she pulled them away from him. "I have received the most wonderful birthday present. My siblings pooled together to gift me funds that are entirely in my name. It is a sum that could sustain a family of a modest household for...well, at least long enough for a tradesman to establish himself and earn his own income." She handed him an envelope from her reticule. "I do understand if your feelings have changed, Eddie. I am spoiled and stubborn and perhaps not as constant as I once thought. Even so, I would like to marry you, and I wonder if you would do me the honor of being my husband?"

Eddie took the paper because she handed it to him. His eyes skimmed over its fine, spidery script. All he comprehended was the number. Eight hundred pounds—far more than he had ever dreamed he would see in his lifetime.

Caroline added, "I know the aphorism says that money does not solve all problems. We shall have plenty of others to face, but I do think this will make us happy."

Eight hundred pounds didn't erase the hurt they had caused each other. Nor did it solve the way they talked about everything except what was necessary to say. But eight hundred pounds would make so many of their worries disappear.

"Don't say yes if you don't agree. This isn't a caper or adventure or plan. I only want to marry you if you, too, wholly and entirely, want to marry me. And I am willing to wait, as many years as necessary, if you need time to consider it."

Eddie handed her back the piece of paper. "I don't need your money, Monkey."

Caroline's fingers fumbled against his.

"I've been working hard and saving on my own. I'm planning to open my own workshop in a year."

"I know—"

She was interrupting him, her voice trembling, and Eddie interrupted her right back. "It is important to me that you know that. Money is not what stands between us, and it isn't what is going to join us, either."

"It isn't?" She stared at him without breathing, her eyes wide and bright in the fading light.

"You're not here because you have eight hundred pounds. You're here because you love me." He swallowed. "You're here because I am worthy of being your husband."

"Yes." Caroline took an inhale at last. "Yes, you are. But that was true in Scotland, too. It was always true."

"I wasn't worthy that morning when I put my own fears above your needs. If I had listened to you, then today would probably be our wedding day."

"I wasn't worthy of *you* when I let my fears dictate my needs. If I had just had a little more faith, we would already have been married for six months."

"So." Eddie had to swallow again. His heartbeat was pounding in his ears, but it wasn't from fear this time. "I didn't come to your birthday celebration because I was afraid if I saw you again, I would lose all the confidence I have earned these past six months and give up everything to fit into your life again. But actually, I feel more confident than ever. I'm a glazier, Monkey, and I think I can earn a good living at it. A living worthy of you, even."

"So you'll marry me, then?"

"Hadn't we better discuss the specifics of the plan? Where we are going to live and whether we can afford a maid and all that?"

"I don't need a specific plan, Eddie. I only need you. If you'll accept me in spite of my newfound wealth."

They grabbed each other's hands again, the letter about the eight hundred pounds drifting down to the floor, and Eddie had the distinct impression the rest of the world had disappeared, leaving them alone in the clouds.

"Then." Eddie reeled her into his arms. "The only question remaining is if we can do what a husband and wife do without me hurting you."

Caroline's grin returned. "Is that a rhetorical question?"

C AROLINE HAD THOUGHT SHE loved Eddie before, but now she realized what she felt had been minuscule com-pared to the deep, tender joy sweeping over her now that she had him in her arms after six months of believing she never again would.

She didn't wait for any more clever banter before kissing him straight on the mouth. She had sworn to never forget his kiss, yet now, there were a hundred details that came flooding back to her. The softness of his lips. The rasp of his close-shaven chin. The way his fingers curled around the back of her head as if to fasten her in place.

Reality was better than any memory she had stored so carefully in her heart.

"Tell me if you don't like something," Eddie murmured, moving his lips to her ear. She was so distracted by his breath flooding her senses, his mouth brushing that tender skin, that she forgot to respond. He prodded, "Will you?"

"I will if you will." Caroline tilted back her head so that his lips fell naturally down her neck. Her whole body quivered in response. "I like that."

"You do?" Eddie did it again. Caroline began to feel there was liquid gold coursing through her veins. Hovering just above her skin, Eddie murmured into the curve of her neck, "I didn't know one could be so sensitive just here."

She nearly lost her footing at the caress of his breath. She clung to his elbows for support. "I'll faint if you keep doing that."

"Faint?" Eddie raised his head, an eyebrow quirked. "Or are you thinking of some other, more exciting reaction?"

She pulled him into another proper kiss. She had the strange sensation that she would not be fulfilled until they were fused together like glass melted in a kiln. She needed his mouth on hers and his hands on her body and their hearts beating in the same rhythm or else she would die.

This was so different from that night in the MacPhersons'. Then, too, Caroline had craved Eddie—she had craved Eddie since that searing kiss under the night sky as sixteen-year-olds—but she had needed his touch to prove to herself that she could face the future.

Now, she needed his touch because without it, her heart would break and her body would wither and she would hang like unpicked fruit on the vine, sad and alone and wasted.

They walked as one across the room—tongues and arms still entangled—to the bed. When Eddie hesitated ever so slightly, Caroline pushed him onto the mattress. Their mouths separated, and she climbed on top of him to correct that. His hips were padded with rags and tools for window washing. She undid his toolbelt, knuckles skimming the hard bulge in his trousers. Eddie hissed. His expression had gone slack, his eyes unfocused, in a way that Caroline had hardly witnessed before.

In a way that she wanted to make last forever.

"Do you like that?" She ran her palm over the bulge.

Eddie groaned: "Yes." On her next stroke, he corrected, "Not so hard."

She pretended her fingers were feathers trailing over his trousers. Now Eddie's eyes shut and his head tipped back, and Caroline felt like the most powerful woman in the world.

Stretching out beside him, she kept one hand playing at his hips. The other braced her weight as she leaned to kiss his neck. She imitated what he had done to her: first, soft kisses along its stretch; then little huffs of breath as she whispered nonsense; then sturdier kisses, ones that matched the pressure of his cock straining into her palm.

Suddenly, Eddie captured both her wrists, flipped her over, and pinned her to the mattress. "No more, or I won't have anything to pleasure you with."

The surprise maneuver stole Caroline's breath and replaced it with desperate, wicked desire. She bucked her hips upward against his. "But did you like it?"

"I did. Too much." Eddie kissed her, distracting her with that tongue of his and those naughty lips. He still trapped her against the mattress, so she had to press her weight into the backs of her arms to meet his mouth halfway. Her hips remained in the air, grinding against his, acting purely out of instinct. Soon, her skirts fell backward, baring her skin from the tops of her stockings to the bottom edge of her stays.

She didn't know how, but suddenly she knew that the one thing she wanted in all the world was for Eddie to take her bare bottom in his hands. "Grab me," she urged when his mouth moved away to steal a breath. "Grab my bottom."

"Your arse," he corrected. "You won't be a lady once we're married, Monkey. You must get used to common language."

"Grab my arse." The word thrilled her almost as much as did Eddie bossing her around. Then, when he obeyed and clapped her arse in his rough, steady hands, she nearly lost all rational thought.

Squeezing her cheeks in his palms, Eddie eased her spine onto the mattress and backed away until he knelt on the floor before her. He locked those hazy eyes with hers. Then, he touched his mouth to her quim.

This was an act a woman was supposed to enjoy. Yet for a few moments, all Caroline could register was the scrape of his cheek against her inner thigh and the strange circumference of his lips around her folds. She opened her mouth to say something—a correction, an objection, something.

Then Eddie's tongue slicked against the hard, eager spot at the top of her quim. Her hips jerked in delight, and all thought melted away. What came out of her mouth was not an objection at all, but a rude and delicious "Fuck my cunny!"

Eddie paused. "Say please."

And that sent Caroline to another plane. "Please," she begged, her last rational act. She didn't exist except as pleasure personified. Eddie's tongue remained on that spot, exploring it, teasing it, flicking it, until it became the entire center of the world and Caroline dissolved in a spiral of ecstasy.

She was aware that between her legs was gushing wet desire. That Eddie had climbed onto the mattress again to torture her neck deliciously. That somehow, somewhere, sometime, he had stripped his clothes and his cock gleamed purple. And that she desperately needed him inside her.

"Please," she said again, since it had worked so well for her before. "Please fuck me, Eddie."

He didn't oblige. Caroline's quim got wetter and wetter as he remained still as stone beside her. She twisted towards him, wondering what he might demand of her now—and whether it was possible to get even more liquid than she already was.

"Please, Eddie."

"Will you tell me if it hurts?"

Their past pierced through the magic of the moment, and Caroline saw Eddie was not playing a game. His hand circled the base of his cock, his eyes were heavy, and his lips were swollen from all the kisses they had shared, yet he could not move forward because of what had happened before.

Caroline took his free hand, fingers intertwining, just like she had been doing her whole life. "I promise."

Together, they moved into a suitable position: lying on their sides, Caroline's leg hiked over Eddie's hip. Gently, Eddie nudged his cock between her legs. Her hips bucked in delight again. She nuzzled lower until he was at her entrance and then, without meaning to, they both moved at the same time and Eddie was inside her.

At first, Caroline felt pressure more than pleasure. Again, she opened her mouth, about to say something. But then their hips started moving, and his cock slid against a vein of pleasure somewhere deep inside her, and Caroline didn't feel an ounce of pain.

"I like this," she said instead. "I love this. I love you. Fuck me, Eddie."

They moved in tandem, his cock sliding up as Caroline ground down, and though the rhythm was uneven, it was perfect. She looked directly into his black irises, and he watched her back, except for the moments when he dipped forward and stole a kiss. At some point, he palmed her breast, his thumb pressing into her nipple. That unlocked a squeal of pleasure from Caroline, and the noise heightened her own sense of the moment. She started panting louder, searching for more of that feeling, and Eddie matched her, so that soon they were a cacophony of moans and pleas and the mattress rattling in its ropes.

And somewhere in that mess, Caroline came again, her rapture defined by Eddie's skin and sweat and hard, fast grip.

Not long after, Eddie erupted too, announcing his pleasure: "Oh, Monkey, here I come!"

Even that didn't end the moment. Eddie withdrew from her and cleaned himself with a rag, but then he nestled against her again, and Caroline hooked her ankles around his, and they existed as one in their cocoon of happiness.

Later, Caroline said, "I think we have answered your remaining question."

Eddie kissed her on the mouth. "*I* think we had better call the banns sooner than later."

Chapter Twenty-One

One month later, Northfield Hall hosted another festival. This time, the hydrangeas bloomed instead of the lilacs, the path from the house to the pond was strewn with white rose petals, and the portable stage was erected not for a pageant but for a wedding ceremony. When Hamlyn struck his bow to his fiddle, it wasn't a folk song he began, but a hymn blessing the upcoming union.

Eddie had expected that finally reaching their wedding day would feel like a dream to him. He had prepared himself to doubt every detail, for surely even now, he and Caroline *wouldn't* actually marry. This was a fever dream from which he had not yet awoken.

In the end, it didn't feel like that at all. He woke in his parents' cottage to the same ceiling that had greeted him every morning in the first twelve years of his life. He ate his mother's steamed buns, helped his father fetch water from the well, and tied a ribbon around Linnie's neck. Even as he dressed in his new wedding suit, Eddie felt each moment of the day was more real than any other moment before in his life.

And now he stood on the stage waiting for Caroline. Behind him were his brothers Spencer and Oliver. In front of him, in the shadow of the manor house, sat the two hundred or so people who lived at Northfield Hall. His parents watched from the front of the crowd, little sparkles of happiness sneaking into their expressions. Caroline's siblings gathered by the stage, too, chatting happily as they waited for the ceremony to begin. And at his feet, Linnie sat patiently, her nose twitching in the direction of the manor house.

Above, rain clouds threatened from the south, and a surprisingly cool breeze cut through the July heat. Eddie resisted the urge to stand on his toes for a view over the walls of the kitchen garden into the drawing room where he knew Caroline waited. He told himself not to doubt that she was there. He told himself not to worry that at that very moment, Lord Preston was talking her out of the wedding.

They had spent too little of the last four weeks together. Eddie had been busy arranging a household for them in Thatcham, while Caroline had remained at Northfield Hall organizing their wedding. Eddie had seen her on Sundays, on the afternoon he came to Northfield Hall to sign the marriage contract written by Lord Preston's solicitor, and two days before the wedding when he showed her the old farmhouse he had arranged to lease.

On each visit, Caroline had still been excited to marry Eddie. Yet now, waiting for her to emerge from the hall, Eddie couldn't help worrying: had she decided that even with money for a proper household, she didn't want the life he could offer?

Just when his stomach was beginning to drop, Caroline appeared around the garden hedge. She wore a yellow gown, a wreath of daisies in her hair, and a smile as big as a sunbeam. With her arm looped through Lord Preston's, she advanced through the parted crowd with the same fast stride that had always carried her towards Eddie across the Northfield Hall grounds. Lord Preston walked her up the stairs onto the stage, then placed her hand in Eddie's.

"Make her happy," he said solemnly.

"I will," Eddie promised, and he swallowed back any bitterness towards Lord Preston. Caroline had reported that her father was making an effort to wish them well, and they agreed that was all they could ask for, knowing as they did all his misgivings.

"We'll prove him wrong, just as he has proved all of Britain wrong about his own ideals," Caroline had promised Eddie as she walked him out after their marriage contract was signed. "And when we do, things between me and Papa—and between *you* and Papa—shall return to the way they were before all of this."

For now, Eddie didn't have room in his heart to worry about Lord Preston. He held Caroline's hand, warm underneath her lace gloves, and tugged her closer to him.

It was their wedding day, and she had joined him on the stage just as she promised to do.

As the rector began the liturgy, Eddie whispered to Caroline: "Are you sure?"

Caroline grinned at him from the depths of her steady brown eyes. "If the *Jolly Molly* can fly, why can't we?"

Yet this time, it didn't feel like they were jumping on an imaginary ship to soar through the sky. This time, with Caroline's hand in his and all their tribulations layered beneath them, Eddie felt as if they were taking a step onto ground as firm as the soil of Northfield Hall.

When the rector asked them to make their vows, saying "I do" to Caroline was nothing but a formality.

And when the rector introduced them as man and wife, Eddie knew Lord Preston was right: a man was born into a specific role, one he could do nothing about changing. But Lord Preston was wrong: Eddie was not born to be the son of Yin and Jian Chow, nor was he born to be a glazier, nor even to be a Briton without a place in society.

Eddie was born to be Caroline Preston's husband, and at last, he was.

EPILOGUE

1844

Twenty-Four Years Later

From the landing in Dover, Caroline took a stagecoach to Thatcham and then old Farmer Phillips's gig the rest of the way. She hadn't sent word ahead to say she was arriving that day. Surprises, after all, were the spice of life.

Their house rose from the middle of its little pasture like a hug. Ten years ago, they had purchased its lifetime leasehold along with ten acres surrounding it. That was enough space for a dairy cow, some pigs, and a chicken coop, as well as a vegetable garden, all of which were tended by Caroline's dear housekeeper, daily maid, and man-of-all-work. They had expanded the house, too, from its original four-room footprint to six rooms on the ground floor and another story with three more bedrooms.

As a girl, Caroline hadn't known to dream about a home of her own, but seeing the house now after three months away, she felt as if it was exactly what she had wanted all her life.

She descended from the gig with far more creaks and groans than a younger version of herself, but she waved away the farmer's offer to carry her little luggage case to the front door. She was forty-four, not seventy-four, and a proud tradesman's wife who could do for herself.

Besides, she didn't want to have to invite in Farmer Phillips. She hadn't seen Eddie for over three months, and she intended her first sighting of him to be alone.

Pushing open the door, she called out, "I'm home!"

Silence answered her.

Caroline took stock of the house as she stepped in, set down her luggage, and removed her outer garments. The parlor with its cast-off furniture from Northfield Hall was tidy but empty; the dining room beyond it boasted the tablecloth her daughters had embroidered for her last birthday but otherwise looked unused; the snug with its bookshelves and armchairs was dark; the second parlor that caught afternoon sunlight didn't even have ashes in its fireplace. Caroline was about to check the bedrooms when she thought to stop in the kitchen.

And that was where she found her husband. Her sweet, thick-shouldered Eddie stood at the kitchen counter, slurping soup straight from the bowl.

"Have you lost your manners so completely in my absence?" Caroline asked.

Startling, Eddie clattered the bowl to the counter and turned, wiping his mouth with the back of his hand. "You didn't say you were coming home today!"

"Surprise!" Caroline indulged in a dramatic twirl. Then she rushed across the room to leap into his arms.

He was the same as always: steady, strong, and soft.

"You're very wicked to keep such good news to yourself," Eddie murmured into her hair. "I'd have met you at the stagecoach if I had known."

"But I couldn't do this to you at the stagecoach." Caroline captured the curve of his bum in her palm as she raked her lips across his.

"A respectable lady such as yourself couldn't, perhaps," Eddie agreed, taking her rear into his own hands, "but a common man such as myself might be excused for greeting his long-lost wife with enthusiasm."

Caroline couldn't decide which she had missed more: the press of his lips against hers, his scent rushing her senses, being handled so expertly by his palms and fingers, or just the feeling of being held—of disappearing from the world into his arms.

"It has been far too long," he murmured to her.

"It has only been one hundred eighteen days." Then, resting her cheek against his, she asked, "Did you miss me?"

"I missed you every second of every day, Monkey. Did you miss me?"

"With every beat of my heart. Did you get my letters?"

She had written every morning, though she couldn't always post the letters directly. She and her sisters had taken a trip to Egypt, which had involved several ships, overnight rail journeys, and one harrowing carriage ride through a mountain pass.

"I received them. It sounded like a marvelous experience. I began to worry you might decide to keep traveling rather than come home."

"If Ellen didn't make such a fuss about calculating whether people were fairly paid for the production of every piece of food that passed our lips, I might have." That was a joke; as wonderful as it had been to see parts of the world so different than hers, Caroline had yearned to return to Thatcham and Eddie almost as soon as she had left. "Besides, I have too much to do here."

She had learned so much on the trip that she wanted to apply to her organizations at home. As a leader of the Berkshire Women's Commerce Committee, she had new connections to women across Continental Europe who ran their own business-es that she wanted to foster. And for the Reading Orphanage, where she served as adviser, she had purchased maps and history books in each country to show what children learned depending on where they lived.

Eddie pulled her closer against his chest. "Ah, so your return has little to do with me."

"Nothing at all." Grinning, Caroline basked in his arms. She had been afraid that three months would age Eddie with new wrinkles, a bald head, or lost teeth. Instead, she thought he almost looked younger than when she had departed. Or perhaps it was just that when she looked into his dark eyes, she was looking at him aged five, sixteen, twenty-five, and forty-four all at the same time. "Have you kept yourself amused in my absence?"

"I installed enough windows to pay for my supper."

As the primary glazier in Thatcham, Eddie had plenty of business to keep their coffers full. She almost asked about the hobbies that brought him more joy, but she held back. They had time to catch up on the moments she had missed. "And the children? Are they doing all right without us?"

They had two daughters and a son, the youngest of whom had finally left home that summer to take a position as a secretary to a ladies' aid society in London.

"They have made no complaints to me, other than to ask for money to come visit for the Christmas holiday." Eddie investigated her neck with soft kisses. "Their letters await you on the bedside table."

"Then, as a dutiful mother, I should hasten to the bedroom."

"And as a dutiful husband, I should see you there safely."

Not quite letting go of each other, they hastened upstairs to the bedroom overlooking the back garden. Caroline climbed onto the bed, unbuttoning her gown, not even glancing at the promised stack of correspondence.

But Eddie hesitated. From the foot of the bed, he asked, "Did you see your gift?"

Caroline followed his gaze to the bedside table. There, beside the letters, was a ship in a bottle.

Her gown flapping open, Caroline lifted the bottle in her hands. It was almost as large as a two-gallon jar, and its glass was scratched in a few places, aging it. Yet it was clear enough to display the ship in all its glory: a sailing ship with a white deck, white masts, and a bright red rose on its foresail for good luck. It floated on a cloud made of dandelion fluff. And on its prow, Caroline read its name in fine, spidery paint: *Jolly Molly*.

"You made this for me?"

Joining her on the mattress, Eddie wrapped an arm around her waist from behind. "Even when we're apart, we fly through the clouds together."

She had brought him a dozen gifts, at least one from each city they had visited, but none as special as this. Setting it carefully on the table, Caroline twisted around, wrapped her arms around his neck, and claimed him in another kiss.

The *Jolly Molly* could take her nowhere more beautiful or wonderful than here, her magical life with Eddie.

HISTORICAL NOTE

My descriptions of the Tower of London are largely pulled from an 1817 guidebook, *An Improved History and Description of the Tower of London*, which uses different terminology for some of the rooms than we use today. Also, the crown the Caroline calls the Imperial Crown is now referred to as the St. Edward's Crown. (The current Imperial Crown wasn't constructed until 1937.)

Apprentices were not legally allowed to marry, and elopements to Scotland were indeed a way for people to marry without a license. Traveling was expensive, and the trip to Gretna Green took several days. That said, I pulled a sailing trip to coastal Scotland from my own imagination.

If you would like to learn more about marriage laws and customs, what it was like to take a road trip in Regency England, or what a glazier did, please head on over to my research deep dives, available to my newsletter subscribers!

https://bit.ly/katherinegrantresearch

ACKNOWLEDGMENTS

Thank you to everyone who helped make *The Miss Without a Mister* possible! I've known Caroline and Eddie's story for so long that it was intimidating to write and even scarier to revise, so I am grateful for everyone who has helped me trust my instincts.

My professional team includes Crystal Shelley of Rabbit with a Red Pen, who served as authenticity reader and helped make sure Eddie and his parents finally found a way to hear each other. Abby from Victory Editing lent her excellent developmental editor eye once more. Sara Israel from Thimble Editorial helps me keep track of everything from series timelines to naming flowers correctly. Julia Gerbach continues to design gorgeous covers for the Preston family.

I would also like to thank my sister, Sarah, and my husband, Michael, for reading in-between drafts of this book and giving me crucial pep talks.

And finally, thank you to my readers! I cannot tell you how meaningful it is to hear directly from you that you enjoyed my work. I received several messages like that in the long process of drafting *The Miss Without a Mister*, and I return to them whenever I need a reminder that someone out there wants to read this book. Thank you for reading!

About the Author

Katherine Grant writes award-winning Regency Romance novels for the modern reader. Her writing has been recognized by Foreword INDIES Book of the Year Awards, the Next Generation Indie Book Awards, the National Indie Excellence Awards, the Romance Slam Jam Emma Awards, and the Shelf Unbound Indie Book Awards. If you love ballgowns, secret kisses, and social commentary, a book hangover is coming your way.

Katherine also hosts the Historical Romance Sampler podcast! Find out more at www.katherinegrantromance.com

THANKS FOR READING!

I AM SO GRATEFUL you joined me on this journey back in time. If you enjoyed it, please consider leaving a rating or review on your ebook retailer, Goodreads, Storygraph, or wherever else you talk about books!

Until next time...

www.ingramcontent.com/pod-product-compliance
Lightning Source LLC
Chambersburg PA
CBHW011412310726
48972CB00011B/2938